THE
DEATH
OF
REX
NHONGO

THE
DEATH
OF
REX
NHONGO

C. B. George

Quercus

First published in Great Britain in 2015 by

Quercus Publishing Ltd
Carmelite House
50 Victoria Embankment
London EC4Y ODZ

An Hachette UK company

A CIP catalogue record for this book is available
from the British Library

HB ISBN 978 1 78429 232 4
TPB ISBN 978 1 78429 234 8
EBOOK ISBN 978 1 78429 231 7

10 9 8 7 6 5 4 3 2 1

Typeset by CC Book Production

Printed and bound by Clays Ltd, St Ives plc

'All that is very well,' answered Candide. 'But let us cultivate our garden.'

Candide, Voltaire

PREFACE

On 15 August 2011, fire engulfed Alamein, a farmhouse in Beatrice, about forty minutes out of Harare, Zimbabwe. Inside was the body of General Solomon Mujuru, also known by his 'Chimurenga name' or *nom de guerre*, Rex Nhongo. The general was a hero of the Zimbabwean War of Independence, former chief of the army, then MP, businessman, husband of Vice President Joice Mujuru and one of the most powerful men in the country. In 2002, he had seized Alamein from a white farmer, Guy Watson-Smith, at the height of the government's Fast-track Land Reform Programme. Almost a decade later, this was where he died, his body burned to a state in which his remains could be identified only through dental records. He was sixty-two.

On 15 March 2012, following an eight-week inquest, the coroner's court in Harare ruled that the general had died of smoke inhalation. However, many people, not least members of his family, believe he was murdered, whether as a result of his business dealings or a plot within the political establishment. Certainly, the Zimbabwean rumour mill, a productive operation at the best of times, has been working at full capacity ever since.

Whatever the truth, the inquest revealed remarkable, and

inconsistent, testimonies. A maid and private security guards reported hearing gunshots two hours before the fire was discovered. Police on the VIP security detail just metres from the farmhouse denied hearing anything, though they admitted they might have been asleep. The same police claimed they'd been unable to raise the alarm because their radio was broken and they had no airtime (pre-paid credit) on their mobile phones. There was uncertainty as to whether the general had arrived alone or with another man because it was dark and there was a power cut. The fire engines dispatched from Harare were forced to turn back because of their leaking water tanks. The broken radio, the power cut and the faulty fire engines give the death of one of Zimbabwe's most influential figures an ironic twist.

Several of those who were first on the scene reported that, while the general's body was burned to a cinder, the surrounding carpet remained largely undamaged. Speaking in South Africa, Alamein's former owner, Watson-Smith, said: 'Our house was a sprawling single-storey building, roofed entirely with asbestos sheeting. That makes it absolutely fire-proof ... Our main bedroom alone had three doors out of it and four double windows. How do you get trapped inside that?'

What follows happened in Harare in the months after Rex Nhongo's death. The story begins on 19 August 2011.

PART ONE

I

The guy in the back of the cab was an Indian: Salim. He was one of Patson's regulars, a gambler who played the blackjack tables at the Showgrounds casino. Generally, he called at two or three in the morning and Patson had to judge from his tone of voice how the night had gone – how many times had he picked him up only to discover the guy had no money? Salim would say, 'Next time, my friend,' and laugh in a way that showed he understood it was no laughing matter. He always did pay next time, but that wasn't much use if Patson was stuck in Belvedere without enough fuel to get home. Then he had to ease into town and hope that one of the other fellows on the rank would lend him a buck or two. Or else he spent another night in the car, knowing that when he finally got back to Sunningdale, Fadzai would be bursting with unspoken accusations and for a couple of days they'd skirt each other like unfamiliar dogs. Patson often thought how remarkable it was that he and his wife could spend so little time in the same room when they had only a three-room house.

But tonight, Friday night, it was still early, so the taxi driver had no such worries. He collected Salim from the Queens where the Indian liked to drink and flirt with the bar girls. He was maybe

two whiskies down and his mood was good – nothing could go wrong at seven o'clock on the weekend when you had money in your pocket and Harare at your mercy.

The guy was talking non-stop. He said, 'You saw that girl I was with the other night? You took us to Beer Engine. She had a blue dress. You remember?'

Patson grunted. He was only half listening. The downtown traffic required concentration.

'Beauty. Her name was Beauty. I could lose my heart to a girl like that. And she was beautiful, isn't it? I said, isn't it, Patson?'

'Yes, Uncle,' Patson replied, as he wrestled the wheel left and swerved wildly across the road to avoid an oncoming ET. As the minibus passed, the conductor swung out and slapped the taxi's roof, whooping. Salim was thrown sideways by the sudden manoeuvre and cursed in his own language. He dropped his mobile phone and scrabbled on the floor beneath the passenger seat.

Patson checked the rear-view mirror. 'Sorry, Uncle.'

Salim sat back and straightened his jacket, parting his hair with one hand and putting his phone into his inside pocket with the other. 'Fucking driving,' he said. 'What's wrong with this place? People are not scared to die. People die for nothing.'

'Fucking driving,' Patson agreed, unwrapping a stick of gum with one hand. He put it into his mouth and began to chew vigorously. He wanted a cigarette but Dr Gapu, who owned the cab, had told him he couldn't smoke in the car.

'Beauty,' Salim said. 'You remember her?'

'I remember.'

'I really think she likes me, that one. The way we talked. We had such a good time. She could take my heart, a girl like that. I think she likes me. Do you think so?'

6

'Yes, Uncle,' Patson said.

He pulled a right onto Samora Machel Avenue, forcing an SUV with diplomatic plates to slow down, sounding its horn. As he turned, Patson got a glimpse of the driver, a white woman. Her expression shocked him: a rictus of fear and anger.

Patson dropped Salim outside Mokador on Nelson Mandela Avenue. It wasn't so long ago that this restaurant was a first-class place to pick up business – white kids out for a good time, looking for a ride back to the suburbs. But those good times were gone. Now it was just another city-centre joint, unloved and unloving; the same dozen waiters from that previous era, wearing the same waistcoats and black bow-ties, shuffling slowly from table to table as if they hoped nobody would notice their profligate under-employment.

Salim leaned in at the driver's side, his wallet in his hand. His breath was sour with the grain. He handed Patson a five. He said, 'Thanks, my friend.' Patson began to reach for change but thought better of it.

'Can you wait for me?' Salim asked.

'No problem, Uncle. Just ring when you want a pick-up.'

'But I don't want to be waiting half an hour because you've gone on a job. You wait for me.'

'How long?'

Salim shrugged. 'Half an hour? An hour? Just wait, OK? You know I always look after you, isn't it?'

'You look after me, Uncle,' Patson said. He glanced up and down the road. There was nowhere to park. 'I'll stay local,' he said. 'Don't worry. Just ring.'

2

Patson dawdled up Nelson Mandela. He tried double-parking outside Standard Chartered but was quickly moved on by a cop. He turned at Second Street, again at Samora Machel, and slowed to walking pace outside the looming block on the corner. There were spaces here – there were always spaces here, because every cab driver in the city had heard the rumours. Nobody knew the truth and nobody wanted to be the one to find out. Patson weighed his alternatives. He wasn't by nature a superstitious man. There were few lights on in the building, none on the ground floor, so he decided to take a chance and pulled in.

Patson flicked off his beam and reclined the seat. If anyone came they'd think he was sleeping. He told himself that no one would be so bored as to give him trouble on a Friday night. He sat back in his chair and pulled his cap low over his eyes – he could certainly use the rest. But maybe he was too cold to sleep or maybe, subconsciously, he knew he was making a mistake. Either way, he couldn't seem to get comfortable so he stepped out of the car to smoke.

He stood behind the taxi, lurking in the shadows. The cigarette brought back his cough. Perhaps it was a good thing Dr Gapu didn't let him smoke in the car – perhaps he was thinking as a doctor, not as a businessman. These days, everyone wore as many professional hats as they thought could turn a profit. Sometimes it was hard to work out to whom you were talking.

The glass double doors of the building were black mirrors, and when they swung open, Patson glimpsed the amber cherry of his cigarette in reflection. From the darkness a man emerged – a young man in a black suit with a white shirt and dark tie. Patson cupped the cigarette tip in his hand and walked a few steps away until he was hidden behind a Range Rover – he was just a passer-by, smoking. He heard the beep of an alarm and saw the lights flash on a BMW parked half a dozen spaces down. The man walked towards his car and Patson dropped his head. He heard the clunk of the BMW's door opening. It sounded weighty and expensive. The door shut again and Patson dared look up. But the man hadn't got in. Instead he was approaching. Patson dropped his cigarette and squashed it with his toe. He buried his hands deep in his pockets.

'Who are you?' the man said.

Patson kept his chin down as he raised his eyes cautiously. 'Me? I am just . . . Nobody.'

The man stood next to Patson's car, his hands behind his back. Up close, he was even younger than Patson had thought, maybe no more than twenty-five. His expression was contemptuous.

'Your name,' the man said.

'Chisinga,' Patson answered immediately, and immediately regretted telling the truth.

'Where do you stay?'

'Sunningdale.' Patson moved towards the driver's door and opened it casually, looking at the ground. 'Sorry, sorry. You know, I thought everyone was gone now. I will move my car. I have a customer to collect.'

9

'You can't stop here.'

'I know, Comrade. Sorry, sorry. I thought everyone was gone home.'

The man stepped around the car and took hold of the open door. Patson had no choice but to look at him. The man was smiling.

'Comrade?' the man mused. 'Are we comrades?' Patson shook his head quickly. His heart was beginning to race. 'You know you can't stop here, *Comrade*, but you stop here. I don't understand that. Perhaps you can explain it to me inside.'

'No. I cannot explain it, Boss. I was not thinking clearly.'

'Boss? I am your boss now? Do you know what this building is?'

'No.'

'You don't know what this building is?'

'No.'

'You just know you cannot stop here?'

'Yes.'

The man touched Patson on the shoulder. 'You should look me in the eye when you talk to me, Chisinga. Men look each other in the eye when they talk. Otherwise how can they know what the other is thinking?'

Patson cautiously raised himself upright and looked squarely at the man. He was surprised to find they were exactly the same height. The man was still smiling. But some men – such men – have learned to make this the very cruellest expression available to the human face. 'What am I thinking, Chisinga?' the man asked.

Patson felt compelled to look away. As he did so, he saw another man approaching from the doorway of the dark building. His mind began to kaleidoscope scenarios. None looked anything short of desperate. Despite the cold, Patson noticed he was beginning to sweat. He knew he had to stay calm. Either he would talk his way out of this in the next two minutes or everything was going to go very badly wrong. He turned back to the first man and affected confidence. 'You are wondering if I am one of us,' he said and he thought he saw something else flicker behind that smile.

The man nodded abruptly. 'You are right, Chisinga. That is exactly what I am thinking.'

'What is happening here?' This was the second man speaking. He was now just five metres away; older, heavy-set, carrying a briefcase, out of breath, like he'd been running.

Patson's mobile rang in his pocket. The jollity of the ringtone and its insistence seemed like an insult to all present. The first man said, 'Answer your phone.'

Patson took out the phone. The display said, 'Salim'. He made excuses. Salim was angry. Patson had bigger problems.

The two men were talking. Occasionally they glanced in his direction. He returned the phone to his pocket. He didn't know what to do. Should he just stand there and wait? Did he dare get into the cab and turn on the ignition? He remembered something Salim had once said to him about gambling: 'Every time you make a bad bet, it is easy to start chasing it with worse.' He had never fully understood this before. He chose to stand and wait.

The two men finished their conversation. The first walked away towards his BMW and didn't look back. The second now approached the cab and, without a glance towards the driver, got into the back seat. He then leaned through and slapped the horn at the centre of the steering-wheel. 'So,' he said. 'Let's go.'

3

Patson drove small circles around the Avenues. It was a familiar routine. The man in the back didn't say much, just 'Left . . . Left here . . . Left . . .' But the driver quickly realised the reason for his passenger's breathlessness: he was almost stupefied with alcohol. Eventually the man said, 'This one,' and Patson pulled up to one of the street walkers.

The man got out of the car. The negotiations were fast. Patson flexed his fingers. He'd been gripping the steering-wheel as if he thought it might save him.

The man returned with the girl. Patson looked at her in the mirror. He'd seen many prostitutes in his cab, but it was always hard to estimate their age: there were too many things you had to see past to hazard a guess – material things, like make-up, but intangible things, too, like all that anger and experience. Patson had one client – a white – who was a regular on these streets. He'd once checked out a prostitute in the headlights and commented, 'Young girl, old pussy.' Patson, who was not shocked by much, had been shocked by the grim satisfaction in the *murungu's* voice. Nonetheless, the girl now in his back seat, even in her bravado, looked particularly young: maybe no more than seventeen, the same age as his daughter. Patson thought about Anashe. He thought about her in her school uniform. He thought about the way men looked at her and how she giggled at the stringy boys on TV during *StarBrite* on a Saturday. He caught the man's eye, challenging him in the mirror. 'The Belle View,' the man said.

The negotiations continued in the back of the cab. The man was forcing the girl's head into his lap. She was feebly trying to negotiate an extra fee. The man said, 'Don't be a fool.' Then there was silence. Patson kept his eyes on the road.

He pulled in outside the Belle View, a lodge that rented by the hour. There was no movement behind him. He sat still with his hands on the wheel. He bit down on his lower lip. He turned off the engine. He could hear the man's breathing. He wished he hadn't turned off the engine. Eventually the man said, 'All right!'

The girl got out of the cab first. She took a bottle of water from her handbag, rinsed her mouth and spat. Then she applied lipstick in the side mirror, pulling it outwards for her convenience. She was bending over right next to Patson. She didn't look at him and he didn't look at her.

Patson heard the man buckle his belt. Then he got out, too, and leaned in at the passenger side. He said, 'Wait for me.'

Patson nodded without turning his head. He'd already figured out his course of action – play it cool and get away from here as soon as the man was gone. Surely the man was too blazed to remember his face or the name of his cab. He just had to play it cool.

The man slammed the rear door. Patson watched the girl tottering towards the Belle View. There was nothing less glamorous than high heels in Harare dirt. He recalled a time in this very place when he'd seen a prostitute stop and peel a used condom from her stiletto.

Patson had his fingers on the key, but he resisted the temptation to turn it. Instead, he checked the back seat. The man had left his briefcase. He hooted the horn. The man turned and Patson buzzed down the passenger window a crack. He said, 'Your briefcase.'

What followed happened too fast for Patson to order it later in his mind. He remembered the girl disappearing into the shadows, the distress of the man's breathing as he reached across the back seat, the sudden awareness that they were not alone, the two men in military fatigues who emerged from the night.

He couldn't tell you who spoke first. Presumably it must have been one of the off-duty soldiers, who thought they'd found a way to a fast buck. He'd heard the rumours of this kind of shakedown from fellow drivers, but until tonight they had been just rumours. He heard, 'What do you think you're doing, fat man?' He heard, 'Who are you talking to?' He heard, 'You think we won't fuck you up?' He heard, 'Who do you think you are talking to?' He heard his passenger scrabble in his briefcase, then the gunshots stopped him hearing anything. He saw the two soldiers flee. He saw the man's face in his rear-view mirror. He saw the man mouth the word, 'Drive.' So he did.

He drove into town. He dropped the man at the Jameson Hotel. Before the man got out, he touched Patson's shoulder and said, 'What's your name?'

'Moyo,' Patson lied. 'James Moyo.'

'Let me take your number, Moyo,' the man said.

Patson gave him a fake number and watched him key it into his phone. 'I am Mr Mandiveyi,' the man said, and pressed 'call'.

Patson pretended to answer. 'I've got it,' he said. He hoped the man was too drunk to notice, and he was.

'You're a good man, Moyo,' Mandiveyi said. 'I will call you.'

Patson watched his passenger stumble into the Jameson public bar, his briefcase bouncing against his knee.

He went straight home. He'd had enough for the night. He was back in Sunningdale before ten. He told Fadzai what had happened. Her brother Gilbert was there too. Gilbert said, 'You're sure the guy was a Cee-ten? How do you know he was a Cee-ten?'

Patson considered his brother-in-law. Gilbert was lately arrived from the family home in Mubayira and he used the urban slang for secret police with affected ease. But his question was ridiculous: Patson had picked up a man from the offices of the Central Intelligence Organisation who'd shot at two off-duty soldiers – he wasn't a gardener.

As for Fadzai, she only seemed bothered that her husband had cut work so early – what money had he sacrificed, and could they afford it? Patson was startled both by his wife's lack of concern for his wellbeing and his own surprise at the same: there was surely no experience that would have led him to expect otherwise. But he was too tense to argue the toss and insisted on going to bed.

The next morning, their son Chabarwa cleaned the cab as usual. Patson, Fadzai, Gilbert and Anashe were eating their porridge when the twelve-year-old came in carrying the gun he'd found beneath the driver's seat. Fadzai stared at her husband, her eyes round with alarm. Patson said, 'Give that to me.'

He took the gun to the bedroom and stowed it in the chest of drawers. When he came back to the main room, he found Gilbert entertaining the two kids with an improbable story of the time he had killed a baboon with a stone. Generally, Patson disapproved of his brother-in-law's fantasies, but today he was grateful for the distraction.

Fadzai was washing the dishes outside. He approached her from behind and kissed her neck. This was typically his way of telling her that, whatever had happened, it would be all right. But she shook him off and plunged her hands into the soapy water. 'No, Patson,' she said. 'No.'

4

The clinic in Epworth was everything Jerry Jones had feared and, consequently, everything for which he'd hoped – a small brick-under-asbestos building with a tin sign that predated Independence and a queue of sick people waiting patiently at its locked door. It was due to open in five minutes, but there was no sign of his contact, Dr Tangwerai, so Jerry sat in his Land Cruiser listening to some alt country band from Swindon that his brother, Ant, had sent him on iTunes.

Jerry had been in Zimbabwe for three months as a diplomatic spouse. In that time, he'd played more squash, drunk more bad white wine and feigned interest in more despicable people than in the rest of his adult life put together. The plan had always been that he would work, but before they'd left London the conversations with his wife, April, about his status on her debut overseas posting had gone no further than the assumption that his experience would surely be valued in a place like this. He hadn't for a second anticipated that his professional skills might be positively unwelcome. And, if April had seen it coming, she certainly hadn't said so. Her lack of empathy with his frustration remained a bone of contention.

She was busy and he understood that. But he wasn't busy. And that was the point.

The first time he entered Likwanda House, the Immigration Office on Nelson Mandela, he'd breezed in full of bonhomie and absolutely confident of his position. His goodwill and his certainty had lasted less than a minute, when faced with a uniformed immigration officer who seemed to find his situation so tiresome that she might nod off at any moment. She sat behind the counter, one arm splayed out to the right, her head resting horizontally on her biceps. She considered his passport from this prone position, holding it up over her eyes with her left hand, like she was reading a paperback on the beach. She blinked so slowly that Jerry wasn't sure whether he should wake her. Eventually she said, 'You are on a spousal visa, Mr Jones.'

'Yes. That's what I said. I want to change it to a working visa.'

'Why?'

'Because I want to work.'

'So why did you not apply for a working visa?'

'Because my wife was transferred by the Foreign Office and we thought it would be easier to sort it out when we got here.'

'I see.' The immigration officer sniffed. 'That was a mistake, isn't it?'

'I guess so,' Jerry said.

The woman idly flicked through the pages of his passport. 'You have been to China?'

'Yes.'

'What's it like?'

'I don't know. It was a holiday. I was only there two weeks. It was great.' The woman raised her eyebrows. It seemed she wanted more. 'But very poor.'

'Poor? What do you mean, poor?' She perked up. She even lifted her head an inch or so off her arm.

'I mean the poverty. Where we went. It's very poor. Lots of people have no money.'

The woman made a small noise in the back of her throat, an exclamation of shock. 'I didn't know that,' she said. 'There are many Chinese things in Zimbabwe. I thought China is the richest country in the world.'

'It is,' Jerry said, then shook his head. 'It's complicated.'

The woman had allowed her head to fall again. 'You should have applied for a working visa from your country of origin,' she said.

'Can I do that now?'

'Of course.'

'Can you think of any reason why I wouldn't get it?'

The woman shrugged, in so far as it is possible to shrug with your head resting on your arm. 'The decisions are made on a case-by-case basis. What work do you do?'

'I'm a nurse.'

'A nurse?'

'Yes.'

'And you do not think we have nurses in Zimbabwe?'

Jerry had left the Immigration Office feeling discouraged but not defeated. The feelings of defeat came later, after meetings with Tapiwa, the HR fixer at the embassy, and two more visits to Likwanda House over the subsequent month.

At first Tapiwa had appeared almost beatific in her competence. 'Don't worry, Jerry,' she said, picking up the phone. 'I know a guy.' And Jerry returned to the Immigration Office with an appointment to see a senior official on the fourth floor. When he got there, it seemed that Tapiwa's 'guy' was not available after all and he was instead received by another official who, if somewhat less indolent, was no more helpful than the first.

'You see, Mr Jones,' he said, 'you are on a spousal visa that does not entitle you to work.'

'I know,' Jerry said. 'So how do I change it?'

'You should have applied for a working visa at the same time as your wife,' the man said.

Jerry reported this conversation back to Tapiwa and she was affronted. She vowed that she would accompany him herself and that would make all the difference. To arrange a suitable time for this took a further three weeks. When it finally happened, Tapiwa engaged in a heated conversation with an immigration officer that Jerry, despite not speaking a word of Shona, had no difficulty in understanding. Eventually, Tapiwa turned to him and said, 'He says you should have applied for a working visa at the same time as we processed April's diplomatic papers.'

As it stood now, Jerry's situation was in the hands of a high-ranking official at the embassy who would write a letter mixing indignation and contrition in equal measure to a similarly high-ranking official at Likwanda House. Jerry didn't know whether this letter had yet been written, but he was tired of waiting. Consequently, when Jerry met Godknows Mpofu, the director of a local orphanage, at some terrible embassy-sponsored poetry slam for former street kids, he was only too eager to volunteer his services to Mpofu's friend, Dr Tangwerai, at the Epworth clinic.

'I just want to do something useful,' Jerry told Mpofu. 'It's not about money.'

Mpofu smiled at him ruefully. 'Would that we could all say that. I will tell Tangwerai.'

There was a tap on the window of the Land Cruiser. Jerry buzzed it down and turned off the music. He would tell his brother he was unconvinced by the alt country band from Swindon, although perhaps their music wasn't flattered by context. He found himself looking down at a short man wearing spectacles, a suit at least two sizes too large, and carrying a small knapsack. He reached up his hand and Jerry took it. 'Tangwerai,' the man said. 'Nurse Jones, I presume.'

5

Jerry got home around seven. It would have been earlier, but he had stopped in Bolero at Newlands for a beer that turned into three. He sat alone. He actively didn't think about his day. In the decade between starting at Addenbrooke's and resigning his last position at St George's, one thing he'd learned was that a tough day needed to percolate for a few hours.

He fiddled with his phone. He downloaded his email. There was nothing of interest; mostly spam and mail-outs from music websites he subscribed to in the UK and US – Rough Trade and Vinyl Junkies, Seven Inch Special and Tru Folk. He perused these idly. They were somehow incomprehensible, laced with a kind of disingenuous irony that he vaguely recognised but to which, in his current state – of mind and place – he couldn't seem to assign meaning.

He gave up and watched the comings and goings in the bar instead. The clientele was local and male. They were all suited and booted, talking in loud voices and drinking Johnnie Walker Black. He had no idea what any of them might do for a living. This was the conundrum of Harare – all those 4x4s driven by well-to-do men like these with apparently limitless disposable income and yet, so far as Jerry could see, outside mining, government and the NGOs, there were no jobs. If you went over to Msasa, Graniteside or Coventry, the industrial areas were now wastelands of empty factories and warehouses, and the rusting signs of companies long since liquidated or departed. Jerry remembered a comment some guy had made at squash a couple of weeks ago: 'Zimbabwe used to manufacture cars. Now it imports paraffin stoves.'

At a nearby table, a handsome man in shirtsleeves pushed to the elbow raised a hand and began to snap his fingers at the waitress. His watch was heavy on his wrist. It could have been a Rolex or Breitling. It could have been a zhing-zhong knock-off. The man caught his eye. Jerry looked away. Surely all these guys couldn't be in mining, government or aid. Surely every one of them (including those with the last three great employers) was into something more or less illegal. They might not be thieves, but Jerry suspected they must be the greasers of the rampant klept-ocracy he'd heard so much about, neck-deep in bribes, kickbacks and God knew what. Belief in the kleptocracy seemed almost religious for white people here – they had rarely witnessed it but discussed it ad nauseam, and those who did have direct experi-ence acquired an almost prophetic reputation.

Jerry checked himself. He dreaded turning into one of the expats he met at embassy functions: sour people with big houses and staff, opulent lifestyles, and unattractive, self-righteous indig-nation about the injustices of their host country. Jerry had the house, staff and lifestyle – he couldn't afford the self-righteous-ness. He downed his third beer and stood up.

Subconsciously, Jerry was timing his arrival home to ensure that Theo was already asleep. At the moment, April was never home in time to put their two-year-old son down and Jerry was no good at it. Theo cried for his mother throughout the process and thrashed on his shoulder as Jerry rocked this way and that, singing 'Here We Go Round The Mulberry Bush'. Then Jerry would put him into his cot bed and listen to him scream for half an hour, feeling the destructive cocktail of impotence, pity and resentment. And when April finally got home, he was obliged to lie to her for fear of provoking endless questioning of his parenting skills.

Jerry pulled off Glenara Avenue into the back-streets of Greendale. Without street-lighting or signage, he found himself crawling myopically home, even after three months. He eventually located the house by the yellow bougainvillaea that climbed the garden wall, buzzed the electric gate and pulled in. The guard saluted as he drove by. The man was new, just sent on Monday from the security company. What was his name? Something curious and biblical: maybe Cephas, maybe not. He was an old man in a threadbare uniform. Jerry figured he'd be no use in the event of a robbery, but, on the upside, he seemed incapable of orchestrating one himself.

Jerry let himself in by the kitchen door. He found Bessie washing the dishes. Theo was flat to her back, wrapped in a *babu* cloth, just like a local child, his head lolling to the side, a picture of comfort.

'Good evening, sir,' Bessie said.

'Hey, Bessie.' He wondered, briefly, if he appeared drunk. 'He's asleep?'

Bessie smiled and looked over her shoulder. 'Good as gold,' she said.

Jerry enjoyed the girl copying his idiom and the erroneous lilt her accent lent it. He liked her smile too. There was something appealingly straightforward about it. It was a smile that conveyed nothing but a smile.

Bessie lived in the domestic housing at the back of the plot. She and Joseph, the gardener, each had a bedroom at either side of a small kitchen, with sink and two-plate stove, and a long-drop toilet. Jerry had been into the building just once and had sworn to himself that he'd make improvements. Such an oath, of course, ensured that he was the only one disappointed by his failure to live up to it.

He sometimes wondered what Bessie must make of his and April's complicated life of generators, boreholes, WiMax internet, gas cylinders and other lifestyle equipment that seemed to mal-function on a rotational basis; what, too, of the petty realities of their relationship, surely overheard, which malfunctioned like-wise. He didn't think about it too much, however, because it would make him feel both guilty and patronising. But he knew he never smiled like Bessie.

The girl stowed the last glass in the drainer. She said, 'Do you want to take him?'

Jerry was already in the fridge, cracking a beer. 'No,' he said. 'You take him. You've got the knack.'

He sat in the living room, feet on the coffee-table. Bessie reappeared five minutes later. 'I am finished, sir.'

'Did you make food?'

'Fish and potatoes in the warmer. Greens are on the stove.'

'Thank you, Bessie,' Jerry said. Then, 'I'm sorry I was late. Work ...'

'It was your first day at the clinic. How was it?'

'Fine,' he said. 'Yeah. You know. Fine.'

She hesitated in the doorway. 'My husband has come to Harare, sir,' she said. 'I want him to come on Saturday.'

Jerry looked at her. He hadn't known she was married. He didn't know what she was asking him. 'Good,' he said. 'No problem.'

Bessie smiled that smile. 'Thank you, sir. See you tomorrow.'

Jerry locked the kitchen door behind her. He drained his beer. He ate some tepid food because he couldn't be bothered to reheat it. By the time April got home at nearly nine o'clock, he was half asleep on the sofa. When he heard her key, he got up and carried his beer bottle and dirty plate into the kitchen.

April dumped her handbag and laptop on the dining-room table. She sighed. She said, 'Did he go down OK?'

'No problem.'

'Did he ask for me?'

'Not really.' Jerry gave his plate a cursory rinse in the sink. He felt his wife's eyes on him. 'You know. He misses you. But it was fine.'

'I'm busy at work.'

'I know that. How was your day?'

April sighed again. She did a lot of sighing, these days. She said that her day was fine until about five, when she got a call from a lawyer who claimed to represent a cleaner whom Jeff, her predecessor, had fired just before his departure. The lawyer was, April said, 'a war vet' (though whether he'd said as much or she'd simply assumed it, Jerry didn't know). He'd kept her on the phone for an hour of blather until she agreed to a meeting. She'd then spent a further two hours trying to track down Jeff at his new posting in Jakarta to find out exactly what had happened. 'It's just a fucking joke,' she concluded. 'I'm like some glorified HR manager.'

Jerry said nothing. He'd rather thought that 'glorified HR manager' was her job description, more or less, albeit couched in the peculiar ranking system of the Foreign Office.

'I'm going to take a bath,' April said.

'There's food. Do you want me to heat it up?'

'I'm too tired,' she said, and was gone to the bedroom.

Jerry locked the kitchen door again. He checked his email again. Nothing. He opened another beer. He looked in on his son. He couldn't see him in the darkness but he heard his even breathing. He went into the bathroom, which was hot and steamy. April was lying back in the water, eyes closed, her thick curls splayed out like a halo. Jerry loved her hair like that – she looked like Millais's *Ophelia*. He wondered how he would feel if she drowned. Without opening her eyes, April said, 'What are you doing?'

'Nothing. It was my first day at the clinic today.'

His wife murmured acknowledgement. Then, 'Are you drinking?'

Jerry twirled the bottle in his fingertips. 'Just a couple of beers.'

She sat up in the bath. She covered her breasts with her arms. She looked at him over her shoulder. 'Jesus, Jerry. If you snore tonight, I'll fucking kill you.'

6

Jerry didn't talk about his first time at the Epworth clinic until a few days later, at a small gathering they held at the house – beer in the fridge, meat on the *braai*, chatter on the veranda while the kids swam. Someone, a woman from the Alliance Française, asked him how it must be to work at such a place, and there was something in her tone and large inquisitive eyes that cast him as a hero and persuaded him likewise. He told her the story of his very first patient, Munya, an eight-year-old boy, and even as he hit his stride and began to embellish the facts for dramatic effect, he hated himself for doing so but was driven on by her murmurs of astonishment and approval. What was it about the white people in this country, foreign and local alike, that made them profess their love of the place, before complaining about its horrors and then, finally, sanctifying their various roles in its redemption? Jerry had noted the syndrome from his arrival and, now, here he was succumbing to its temptations.

That day, he had got out of the Land Cruiser and followed Dr Tangwerai into the clinic. There was a long queue waiting at the door. It was a week after the death (or murder) of that general on a farm in Beatrice and he'd read an editorial in *Newsday*, which claimed the Zimbabwean people might yet be pushed to uprising. April had even told him that embassy staff had been warned to be extra vigilant on any trip into a high-density area, and Jerry's stomach was fluttering with latent nerves. But the expressions on the faces of the silent line of people who watched his approach spoke of nothing more sinister than a kind of resigned suspicion. There was no sign of revolution here.

They were met at the door by the receptionist, a young man called Bongai, and the practice nurse, Sister Gertrude, a large woman in late middle age, wearing an NHS uniform from the early 1980s. The queue made an unthreatening but undeniable surge forwards and Tangwerai promptly locked the door behind him. He led them through the small reception area, past a desk, chair and two filing cabinets thick with dust. Bongai sat behind the desk and immediately began tapping at his mobile.

The back room was larger. There were two old steel beds, two chairs beside them, separated by a tattered partition. On one wall, bare shelves held a jumble of supplies and equipment – needles, rubber gloves, bandages and gauze. Next to the shelves, there was a brand new white porcelain sink with a sign above it, saying, 'Borehole Water', and then, beneath that in brackets, 'An Oasis Zimbabwe Initiative'. To the left, there was a door to a further room with a sign saying, 'Doctor'. The sign had a sliding panel next to it with the words 'In' and 'Out'. The 'In' was currently partially covered by half a beer mat advertising Castle lager.

'So this is where we work,' Tangwerai said. 'I'm sure it's not what you're used to.'

'No,' Jerry said. 'It isn't.'

'At least you don't try to bullshit me.'

'What do you mean?'

'Generally, when we have a white doctor come here, they

tell me they have "seen worse" in the DRC or Iraq or what-have-you. It is as if I should be grateful even to have paracetamol or a clean needle.'

'I'm not a doctor.' Jerry shrugged. 'And I've never been to the Congo or Iraq.'

'Neither have I. Perhaps they are still trepanning and blood-letting. Here we have only the problem of witchcraft.' Tangwerai looked up at Jerry seriously through his thick spectacles, then burst out laughing and clapped him on the shoulder. 'I will scare you away before you even start.'

The system was simple: Sister Gertrude and Jerry would take patients in turn and effectively triage them on the doctor's behalf. Most cases would, Tangwerai said, be pretty straightforward: HIV patients, who could come through to him directly for their ARVs, assuming they had the necessary paperwork, people suffering diarrhoea, undernourished kids, cuts needing stitching and so forth. Tangwerai showed Jerry the stocks of rehydration salts and Plumpy'Nut paste for treating malnutrition. He said, 'It is important you talk to them, OK? Say a kid is borderline: find out what is going on at home, if the father is working or drinking or what-have-you. Sometimes it is just best for the kid to go to the grandparents. We can't be giving out these sachets just because the father's a drunkard.'

Tangwerai retreated to his office. As he entered, he moved the beer mat to partially cover 'Out'. Bongai unlocked the door. Jerry washed his hands. Sister Gertrude took the first patient, a morose young man, who seemed a picture of health, but for his sadness. Sister Gertrude redirected him to the doctor's room so quickly that she was able to take the second patient too, a stooped elderly lady of about seventy carrying a baby. Jerry washed his hands again.

The little boy came in with his mother, a woman in her mid-twenties. He was completely calm, holding a wad of tissue over his left eye. Jerry smiled at them and held out his hand. The little boy smiled slowly back. The mother accepted Jerry's hand with just three fingers that were dry and cold. She looked up at him. She had been crying. Jerry gestured to the bed and chair. The mother sat in the chair. The boy perched on the bed.

'So,' Jerry said. His heart was quickening. 'How can I help you?'

'Doctor?' the woman said.

'Nurse. How can I help you?'

The woman reached into her handbag and produced a small piece of cellophane that she carefully unwrapped on her palm. 'He was playing,' she said.

Jerry looked at what she was holding and said, 'What is that?' in spite of himself, because really he knew what it was, but his mouth wasn't keeping up with his brain. He was looking at a small piece of metal wire, maybe from a coat-hanger, protruding from the soft sphere of a child's eyeball.

'I . . .' the woman stuttered, making a demonstrative movement with her other hand. 'I try to take it.'

Jerry looked at her. He blinked. 'Of course,' he said.

He turned to the boy. 'His name?'

'Munya.'

Jerry squatted in front of him. He took the boy's pulse. It was impossibly slow. No wonder he appeared calm. He was in severe shock. Jerry said, 'Can I have a look?' He peeled the tissue paper away from the eye. He had never seen an injury like this before. There was surprisingly little blood. He stood up. 'One moment,' he murmured. He called Tangwerai.

The doctor examined the wound. He spoke to the mother in Shona. He shook his head. He took the eyeball in its plastic from her and handed it to Jerry. 'Get rid of this,' he said. Jerry looked around. He wrapped it in tissue paper, but he somehow couldn't bring himself to toss it into the disposal bin next to the bed, so he went to the doctor's office and tossed it there instead – as if that were somehow more respectful of the boy's loss.

Tangwerai was bathing the socket with saline solution. He worked quickly and without fuss. He cut gauze and bandage and fashioned a patch. He administered an anti-tetanus shot. He spoke to Jerry over his shoulder: 'What have I just done that you could not do yourself?'

'Nothing,' Jerry said. Then, 'He needs to go to hospital. He needs antibiotics. We can't just patch him up and send him home.'

Tangwerai stood up. He turned to Jerry. He seemed about to say something, but thought better of it. He took a cloth from his pocket, removed his spectacles and began to clean them vigorously. He spoke to the mother in Shona. The woman dropped her chin and replied in a low voice. Tangwerai nodded. 'She doesn't have the money to go to hospital,' he said.

'How much is it?'

'Two dollars. Each way.'

Jerry took out his wallet. His smallest note was a twenty. He said, 'Can you ask her to wait?' He went outside to his car. The queue watched him go, but he didn't look at it. He beeped the alarm and opened the door. He peered into the ashtray where he and April stuffed the dirty and tattered dollar bills they received as change and used to buy water, pay for parking or hand out to particularly persistent street kids. He counted out four notes.

When Jerry returned, Munya and his mother were standing up, ready to leave. He handed the woman the money. She said nothing. He touched the boy lightly on the shoulder. He ushered them out. Tangwerai was watching from the door to his office. 'If you can do your job properly, you will be quite an asset, Jerry,' the doctor said. 'Not just a free nurse but a free ambulance too.'

7

At school, the white lady, Mrs Kloof, aks what difference I seen between here and there. I tell her kids here call their mom 'mummy'. If you done that at Pine Hill Elementary, you got trouble for sure from Donny Orsenbach or Shantay Bennet. They say, 'Mummy girl! Mummy girl!' Sumthin like that. Mrs Kloof don like my answer. She go, 'There must be something else, dear.'

Here sum things that different. 1. The food. 2. The weather. 3. The language.

Before we come, Mom say, 'Everybody in Zimbabwe speak English.' But that not true. When we visit Gogo and Kulu at the weekend an I sent to play with the kids ('Go play with your brothers and sisters,' Gogo say. But they not my brothers an sisters. How can they be like that when my mom an dad not they mom an dad?), they jus talk to each other in they own language an don answer no question I aks.

When I say this to Momma she look at me like I done sumthin bad. She say to Gogo, 'You see? That's why I had to come home.' Even though we not at home, we at Gogo and Kulu's house.

My dad say sumthin I don unnerstan in a jokin voice an he make Kulu laugh.

But Mom don laugh. She look at Dad like he done sumthin bad.

She look at him like that a lot, way more than me. Dad musta done a whole lotta sumthin bads.

Nutha thing that different: my name. In Amerika, my name Rosie McClaren. Now my name Rosie Appiah.

Before we come, Dad say he not goin back home with the name McClaren an he done research and our name now Appiah an he change it by law.

Mom say, 'Whatever, Shawn. So long as you know it's not your home, it's my home.'

Dad say, 'What, Kuda? Like you own the place? We called Appiah now and that's that.'

Mom say, 'You tell Rita? She can be Rita Appiah. Or Rita Perez-Appiah. That what you want?'

Dad say, 'Kuda! In front of Rosie? Jesus, you got some growing up to do, Ku!'

I got growin up to do too, cos I'm a little girl an I don unnerstan why Rita, who is Angel's mom, gonna have our name when she not our family.

Sundays we go to church: Momma, Gogo and me. Church nutha thing that different. In Amerika we go to Brooklyn Pentecostal Church of Our Saviour. Here we go to United Family International Church. They look the same, at least inside, but they different. In Amerika we fight the good fight against Satan and our triumph is certain. Here it sometime sound like we losin.

Dad come the first time, but not again. He go, 'I don't need to listen to that mumbo-jumbo. Come on, Kuda: spiritual warfare? You too smart for some bush pastor telling you what to think. You know what you believe.'

'I used to,' Mom say. 'But turned out I was wrong.'

'And Rosie?' Dad say. 'You think it's good for her to listen to all that? This some scary stuff.'

Mom turn to me. Her eyes got that look again, like she not quite there. 'You scared, Rosie?' she say.

35

An I don't know wotta say so I jus go, 'I dunno.'

An Mom say, 'You see?'

My mom say lotta things but summa them not true. Like, sumtime I seen her sittin at the table an she been cryin like a little baby. I say to her, 'You sad, Momma?'

An she say, 'No, little bird. I'm happy.' But that not true. Like when she say evryone here speak English.

When I say this to her she smile and touch my cheek. She go, 'You're too clever, my little bird. But most people speak English, don't they? It's probably just the kids who aren't so good.'

An I don say nuthin, but I think 'most people' different from 'everybody' – specially for me because I's a kid and kids who I gonna talk to.

Then Mom look at me like she feel bad an she say, 'Sorry, Rosie. I didn't lie to you. It's just the truth is complicated sometimes, understand?'

I say, 'OK,' an shrug.

But I think Mom got it wrong.

Like, sumtimes when I go in the garden with Sasa an I pretend to be a bird, Dad come out an he say, 'What you doing, Rosie?'

An I say, 'I'm a bird, Daddy, an I fly high!'

An Dad, who like games like this, look up in the sky and say, 'Fly high, little bird, tell me what you can see.'

So I say, 'I can see the car an the shops an lions an elephants an Africa an Amerika . . . an . . . an . . .' An sometimes I run out of things I can see, because a pretendin game like this real complicated. But the truth? The truth not complicated. Iss jus the truth.

8

Fadzai's kitchen was in Mbare, near Magaba market, south of the city centre, a small stall with a counter where she locked her pots and plastic plates at night. There was space out the back where she cooked on an open fire.

She travelled there daily from Sunningdale, either catching an ET or, if he was not too busy, Patson took her in the cab. She cooked *sadza*, vegetables and a meat dish – mostly chicken, sometimes beef, occasionally goat or pork, depending on what was available. A plate cost a dollar and, on a good day, she might serve sixty or seventy customers and clear up to thirty dollars' profit. But business was slow today, as it had been for months, and she wasn't sure she'd break even.

The kitchen was under pressure from several angles. Chipangano thugs now taxed all stallholders a dollar a day. They said this was to raise funds for the Party in the forthcoming election. But nobody truly believed this any more than anybody was reckless enough to dare argue.

The cost of meat was also soaring. If she'd had the capital, Fadzai would have bought some poultry or goats to rear. But she didn't have the capital.

The development with the worst financial implications, however, was the competition. Six months ago, hers had been the only regular kitchen in the vicinity. Now there were two others within a stone's throw. She had met the women who ran these new enterprises and she didn't resent them personally: everyone had a right to earn a living. But there simply weren't enough customers to sustain three kitchens so close to one another.

Part of the problem was the currency. Back in the days when Zimbabwe had its own money, she'd have been able to reduce her prices. But since the move to the US dollar, that was impossible: there were no coins in circulation, so there was no change and a dollar was the baseline for everything. One of the other women had begun giving out a free cup of Mazoe orange with every plate, but Fadzai wasn't convinced that this drummed up extra custom.

She remained confident that the working men liked her food, confident, too, that she'd been doing this long enough to outlast the others if she could just survive the next few months. But the next few months were a worry. People always want to try something new.

Gilbert had come to help out. At first she'd been grateful for his offer, because she'd been working alone the last six weeks since she'd had to let Juliet go. It was difficult to dish the food, take the money and ensure that none of her plastics went astray. Unfortunately, she soon remembered how irritating he could be.

Fourteen years younger than her, Gilbert was the brains of the family, but he was also the baby, and that combination seemed to have cursed him with a cocksure attitude. Once, she'd found it funny and charming, but now it just seemed too incongruous with his circumstance. He was the one with seven good O levels and the potential to do so much – much more, certainly, than loiter outside her stall, joking with the customers.

Gilbert had rejected the chance to attend sixth form at the school in Mubayira where their father taught and had somehow persuaded the old man that he should go directly to business college in Kadoma. He'd always been full of big ideas and their father – ordinarily a strict, but sensible man – had a blind spot when it came to his youngest son. While neither she nor her elder brother, Clifford, would ever have dared question their father's judgement, Obert Chiweshe seemed to regard Gilbert's willingness to answer back and the eloquence with which he did so with something like pride. Fadzai knew this was partly because, after her mother had miscarried so many times (five? six?), Obert had given up hope of further children, and Gilbert was regarded as a particular blessing. However, she also suspected her dad recognised something of himself in Gilbert – that quick wit and vivid imagination – and, while he had chosen largely to rein in these aspects of his own character in favour of a stable family life and secure, conservative career in education, he secretly liked the idea that his son might live more freely. And that, Fadzai thought with no little bitterness, was exactly what Gilbert had done.

Within two months of starting at KBC, her brother had met Bessie, a high-school girl, and made her pregnant. The consequent furore surrounding the pregnancy and their eventual marriage had aged her father a decade.

It was Clifford who had negotiated *lobola* and she remembered his ashen face when he returned from the first meeting and outlined the price Bessie's parents were putting on their daughter. She remembered her father's expression too. Gilbert had tried to lighten the mood with some facetious remark, but even Obert had not felt able to allow this to pass and had blasphemed, under

39

his breath but audible to all. The family had sat in shocked silence for several minutes, on account of the rarity of such an outburst.

The initial plan had been that Gilbert would return to KBC as soon as the marriage was formalised and Bessie was settled at the Chiweshe family home. But it quickly became clear that the girl's bride price left no money to pay college fees.

The headmaster at her father's school agreed to employ Gilbert as caretaker. But he spent most of his time in the library, reading anything and everything, and neglected his duties, often, for example, forgetting to lock the classrooms at the end of the day, much to his father's embarrassment.

After an appeal from her mother, Fadzai had rung Clifford to discuss Gilbert's behaviour. But Clifford had his own family and his own problems. 'I don't have time for this. I wash my hands of him,' he said.

'You can't wash your hands of him, Clifford. He's our brother.'

'He thinks being a caretaker is beneath him. He will learn.'

Fadzai understood Clifford's viewpoint, but considered it unduly harsh: there was nothing consciously malign in Gilbert's actions. She explained it to herself like this: when you raise a child to believe they are special, perhaps they will achieve great things. But perhaps that child will simply believe they are special. This was her younger brother's cross to bear and the responsibility for carrying it could hardly be left to him alone.

The two lights in this unfortunate situation were the birth of Gilbert's daughter, Stella, and Bessie herself. For Obert, it was as if Stella made up for all the disappointment he now felt for his last-born, so he took great delight in his granddaughter, playing with her endlessly with a patience and sensitivity that was un-recognisable to Fadzai (or, indeed, her children). And Bessie was a revelation, throwing herself into her new role in an unfamiliar household with common sense and good humour. If the daughter-in-law had been initially regarded as the millstone that would sink Gilbert's potential, she was soon a vital cog in the family machinery, and everyone agreed that the ingrate was lucky to have found such a girl.

Nine months after the wedding, Bessie approached her mother-in-law and told her she wanted to go to the city to train as a maid. Harare was half a day's bus ride away, so she would have to leave Stella in her grandmother's care.

Mrs Chiweshe supported the plan. Of course, the additional income would be useful but, more than that, it might shake Gilbert out of his inertia. So, as Bessie had persuaded her, she now set about convincing her husband. It took some time, but eventually Obert, too, saw the wisdom of the proposition. In fact, Gilbert was the last to know and, when he finally found out, he quickly understood his whole family was arrayed against him and no amount of eloquent argument was going to help. That had been a year ago.

9

Fadzai checked the time on her phone. It was almost three. There would be no more customers now. She began to scrape the pots into plastic containers. Gilbert was still talking to a pair of men, a *mudhara* she knew by sight and a younger fellow she didn't. She could see several of her plastics, stacked on the upturned oil drum around which the men liked to congregate. This had been her brother's only job: to collect the plastics. She watched Gilbert say something and the young man seemed to glance her way before laughing heartily.

'Gilbert!' she barked. She recognised her tone. It was the one that Patson always complained about, but she couldn't help herself. 'Gilbert!'

He looked at her absentmindedly, but if he had heard the urgency in her voice, he was choosing to ignore it. He turned back to his conversation and clapped the old man on the shoulder. Fadzai carried the pots out to the back and began to wash them at the communal tap.

She scrubbed the saucepans vigorously. She had noticed before that, if she fought with Patson (when he had stayed out all night or returned smelling of perfume) and drove him away with her anger, she tended to clean with uncommon fury. Of course, all this meant was that her husband came back later – probably drunk, certainly oblivious – to a pristine house. She considered her behaviour a peculiarly female tendency, both weakness and strength: it had little practical purpose and changed nothing, but nonetheless signified her private triumph that the household continued no matter what.

Fadzai realised that her brother was standing over her. He was smoking a cigarette that he must have begged from one of the men. The noisome stink of it hardly improved her temper.

'Business good?' Gilbert asked.

'No,' she said. 'No thanks to you.'

'It was bad no thanks to me? Does that mean I made it better?'

She looked up at him darkly. 'I thought you were going to help.'

'What do you want me to do?'

'Collect the plastics. At least you can do that!'

He nodded and disappeared to pick up the plates. Fadzai attacked the *sadza* pot again – she could almost have scrubbed a hole in it.

Her brother returned, deposited the plates next to her and flicked his cigarette lazily away. 'I don't know what you're angry about,' he said. 'You know men don't want their food served by another man.'

Fadzai sniffed. That was probably true. 'What were you talking about?'

'I told them you're a good worker and I might even keep you on if you learn to control your temper.' She paused in her cleaning. Her brother laughed. 'Don't be so touchy! We were just discussing!'

'What were you discussing?'

43

'Rex Nhongo. That's all anyone is talking about. Theories of this and that. The old man? He says he knew him from the struggle, but I think he was just talking too much. The other one said it was the wife who killed him. Me? I said, "Why will the wife kill him?" I said it was the Cee-tens. I told them about what happened with Patson the other night – the gun and so on.'

Fadzai stood up abruptly. She stared at her brother. 'Are you joking? Please tell me you're joking.'

Gilbert returned her stare. He shook his head, unsmiling. 'Of course I'm joking,' he said. 'Do you think I am an idiot?'

'I know you're not an idiot,' she said. 'But you don't think about the consequences of what you do.'

Her brother ran his tongue over his teeth and pushed out his lower lip. She'd struck a nerve. 'I have made mistakes,' he said. 'What about you? Do you not make mistakes?'

Fadzai was briefly dumbstruck, not by the question but by his admission. She ran a finger under her *doek*, loosening it a little. The cloth felt hot and heavy and was pulling at her hairline. 'We all make mistakes,' she said softly. 'It's what we do afterwards that's important.' She began to pack the pots and pans into her bag. 'Can you help me?'

'Wait. I want to ask you something.'

She straightened up. She raised her eyebrows. Gilbert appeared nervous, shifting from foot to foot.

'I want to stay with you,' he announced. 'I want to be in town.' He saw she was about to speak and promptly cut her off. 'Don't say anything. There is nothing for me at home. What am I going to do there? I'm away from Bessie. It's no good for Stella and it's no good for me. I will stay maybe two months – that's all. Until I can afford a place of my own.'

'And then?'

'Then I will work until I have money to bring Stella. And maybe Bessie can come and stay and commute to her job. Or maybe she can find a new job. I don't know. But I know it's what I have to do.'

'There are a lot of dreamers here who would like to think otherwise,' Fadzai said, 'but the city is hard.' She returned to packing the bag, but she knew that her brother was right: there was nothing in Mubayira for someone like him. He would become a wastrel. But to have him stay, to take responsibility for a grown man with no job? It would be OK if it was for just two months, but who could possibly give such a guarantee? It was a risk, especially considering the state of her relationship with Patson.

She suspected she already knew how her husband would react. He would listen in silence, his expression unflickering, then he would sniff, stand up and say, 'I don't think it's a good idea.' And he would go out and stay out and not answer his phone, expecting her to have resolved the situation upon his return.

If that was Patson's attitude, she had to admit it was largely her own fault. Her husband had always liked her brother until the fiasco of Gilbert's marriage to Bessie. Then Fadzai had been so angry and had bad-mouthed Gilbert so consistently that Patson's opinion of his brother-in-law had plummeted. Of course Fadzai had subsequently softened, but not before she'd poisoned her husband's mind, so much so that even this week's visit had prompted Patson to shake his head and remark, 'He is good for nothing. You said so yourself.'

'Fadzai?' Gilbert was insistent. 'What do you think?'

'I will talk to Patson. I can't make the decision alone.'

He smiled. 'I'm sure it will be fine. He is my big brother. We get along famously. You know I have my licence now? I can drive for Patson sometimes. We can keep the car on the road twenty-four hours and earn more money. I will work hard, I promise you. I can help at the kitchen. Like today.'

'Like today? And what help have you been today?'

'I have been thinking,' he said. 'It's what I do best. I have an idea.'

Gilbert told her his idea while they stowed the pots in the stall, locked up and walked to the ET rank. He told her the problem was competition. She automatically scoffed – did he think she didn't know that? But her brother just waited patiently for the objections to finish before continuing. She should, he announced, buy a loose-leaf notebook or two, sign her name on every page and give a sheet to every customer. She would sign it again any time they returned for a meal, and after they had received, say, five signatures, their next plate would be free.

Fadzai, ever sceptical, ran through the logistics in her head – the possibility of forgeries, guys sharing the piece of paper and so on. But there was nothing too problematic. She told Gilbert she would think about it, even though she knew it was a good idea.

'And you'll talk to Patson?' he asked.

'I'll talk to him,' she said.

IO

April looked at herself in the mirror. She washed her hands and splashed her face. Even in the embassy, the water smelt bad. She said aloud, 'This wasn't what I signed up for.' She had lately read a self-help book that required her to speak her emotions to her reflection. She wasn't sure it self-helped. She wasn't sure what she was referring to – job? Marriage? Motherhood? Probably all three. She looked pale and unwell and a lot older than thirty. She thought about Jerry. She looked in the mirror and she said, 'Fuck you, Jerry.' Doing so had no impact on her emotional state. Instead, she became preoccupied by her teeth: their pale yellow colour, that small brown mark at the top of one canine that had appeared some time ago and now seemed to be a permanent fixture, and the recession of her gums that gave her mouth a somewhat equine look. She took a small pot of day cream from her handbag and began to apply it liberally to what an online skincare diagnosis had described as her 'problem areas'. April never wore make-up to work. She wondered if she should start.

At their wedding reception, April and Jerry had both given speeches. This break from tradition was partly because April's father had drunk himself to death when she was sixteen years old and partly because she felt it was right and proper for her to have her say. She had spoken first and mentioned meeting Jerry 'at Cambridge'. When it came to Jerry's turn, he made reference to this and pointed out that, while they had indeed met 'in' Cambridge, he hadn't been 'at' the university. April was, he said, quite the brightest person he'd ever met and that was one of the things he loved about her most. He said he was the 'eye candy' in their relationship and everybody had laughed. April had laughed, too, but she also felt a slight, but pointed, irritation, the source of which she couldn't identify. Was it the mild, mocking suggestion that she might have fabricated something from embarrassment at his relative lack of education? Was it that his self-deprecation seemed to derive from some kind of compulsion to be perceived as lovable? Or was it simply that his speech, delivered off the cuff, got a lot more laughs than hers, which she'd spent days writing and practising?

April and Jerry had met in Cambridge two days after she had completed her final viva for an MPhil in Development Economics and two months after her affair with Professor St John Vaughan had ended badly, when April had opened her door to find Mrs Vaughan standing on the step. She was holding her infant daughter in her arms and declared April the 'latest in a long line of stupid, clever cunts'. Moments later, St John had pulled up in the family Volvo and coaxed and cajoled his wife into the car, saying things like 'Not here', 'Let's talk about it at home', and 'Jesus, Mary, I'm sorry, OK?'

April had watched Mrs Vaughan get into the passenger side and St John buckle his daughter into the child seat behind. Then, as he opened the driver's door, he had looked at April and lifted his right hand to his ear – I'll call you. As the Vaughans pulled away, April had realised that she hadn't actually spoken a word from the moment she opened the door. St John never called and she was largely thankful.

April completed her time at Cambridge by working, crying and self-medicating with a combination of alcohol and speed. It worked well enough.

April and Jerry had met at an end-of-year party in student digs on Trumpington Street. The first moment she saw him, she knew he had nothing to do with the university. He was wearing a T-shirt, jeans and Converse, and his hair was cropped to the same length as his beard. But it wasn't his appearance that gave the game away so much as the self-evident lack of artifice behind it. He laughed openly and often, and as she watched him in conversation with her friends and acquaintances, he appeared genuinely to be listening to what they said.

Later, when she was one bottle of rosé and a gram to the good, she spotted him dancing in the living room. Again, everything about him spoke of a life outside the university. While the anthropology students danced wildly, indulging some shamanic ceremony of ritual abandon, Jerry moved in a rhythmical but conservative white-boy shuffle – the mark of someone who had been in environments (nightclubs, for example) with people who actually knew how to dance. Fuelled by booze and amphetamines, April shimmied towards him and they shuffled together, she shielding any embarrassment by occasionally mimicking the more outrageous moves of her peers. At one point, he caught her round the waist and asked her what she did. She told him she'd just finished her master's, that she had a job to go to at Oxfam. He raised his eyebrows as if he'd misheard, then shouted in her ear, 'You don't look like a student.' He told her he was a nurse. 'Just qualified,' he shouted.

'That makes two of us,' she shouted back.

They left together and went back to hers. She was more fucked than she'd realised and threw up on the way. She told him he should go home and she'd be fine, but he wouldn't hear of it. He sat her up in bed and she watched the room spin while he made coffee. They talked into the small hours, a conversation neither of them remembered.

She woke up early to find him sleeping next to her. They were both still fully dressed. Her throat was parched and she was too hot. She drank a glass of water, brushed her teeth and stripped to her underwear. She felt unbearably lonely and pushed herself against him until he woke up. They had sex. Afterwards, he made more coffee and they sat up in bed, sharing their way through his last three cigarettes.

She said, 'You don't want to get involved with me. I'm a fuck-up.'

'Do you want a second opinion?' he asked. 'You know I'm a qualified medical professional, right?'

She told him all about Professor St John Vaughan, his most celebrated papers, his pioneering work and horrific experiences in Darfur. Jerry listened and nodded and said, 'Sounds like an impressive guy.' Then, 'But you knew he was married, right?'

'Yeah,' April said. 'I knew.'

'So why did you keep doing it?'

'I don't know. I didn't think about it,' April said. Then, 'The sex. It was just . . . it just felt like ascension.'

Jerry snorted with laughter and pulled on his cigarette. 'Fuck!'

he exclaimed. 'If you ever get another boyfriend, don't tell him that!'

April laughed, too, and took the cigarette. 'No,' she said.

As it turned out she never did get another boyfriend.

I I

April hurried out of the embassy into the car park. She was running late. She'd forgotten that Jerry had taken their car to the clinic again, so she hadn't thought to book a driver, and she cursed her husband under her breath (since she wasn't in front of the mirror). She sympathised with Jerry's need to work, of course she did, and she was privately impressed with the get-up-and-go that had made him take on something so challenging for no recompense. Nonetheless, the fact was that she was the one with the salary and, therefore, surely the needs of her job had to come first. Had Jerry even considered the amount of petrol required to drive their three-litre Land Cruiser to Epworth every day? Did he see that his desire to work was actually costing them money?

April approached Benedict, the senior driver, in the prefab booth in the car park and requested an embassy vehicle. He asked her if she'd booked one, and when she said she hadn't, he made a great show of looking at his clipboard before telling her, 'I have nobody.'

'What about you?'

'Then who will tell the people needing a driver that there is nobody available?'

'I'm sure they'll figure it out.' April was struggling to control her irritation. 'Look, I'm running late. Just take me to Avondale and drop me there. You can come straight back and when I'm done I'll get a taxi, OK?'

Benedict looked at her, unimpressed. She might as well have asked him to saddle up and carry her on his own back. 'Next time, you remember to book,' he said, but he reached down a set of keys from the wall.

April had arranged to meet Peter Nyengedza at Sopranos, a café near Avondale shops. Nyengedza was the local lawyer representing Henrietta Gumbo, the cleaner who'd been fired by April's predecessor, Jeff Shaw. In her experience, it was best to schedule meetings with those outside governmental and NGO sectors off-site. The British Embassy was a grandiose structure in Mount Pleasant – a high-tech monolith of electric gates, sliding doors, epic solar panels, back-up generators, bullet-proof glass and secret bunkers. Its whole construction spoke of keeping some people out and other people in (with never the twain to meet); consequently, those with little experience of extravagant bureaucratic folly tended to find it a threatening place to visit.

April spotted Nyengedza at once, sitting at an end table on the veranda. He was in his sixties, wearing a navy three-piece suit with a handkerchief poking from the breast pocket. On the table in front of him was a battered briefcase and a full glass of water. He was sitting bolt upright, as if to attention, waiting.

April found something unnerving about the way this generation of Zimbabweans could wait. Younger locals or any expat of any age would have been talking on their mobile or tapping at its keypad; they'd have had their laptop out, or some papers or a newspaper or, at the very least, they'd have ordered a coffee and be sitting back repeatedly checking a watch – their whole demeanour signifying pressing time, distracted attention, extreme busyness. But the older generation just seemed able to wait with a kind of impassive, centred stillness that suggested authority over time or resignation to its vagaries, unless those two were the same thing.

As April approached, she regretted her choice of venue. If Nyengedza might have been put on the defensive by the embassy, Sopranos was, in its own way, just as bad, with its three-buck lattes and obese mothers indulging obese children in bucket-deep milkshakes. As she approached the lawyer, though, and he looked up at her a little rheumily before standing, taking her hand and pulling out a chair for her, she relaxed: Nyengedza looked less defensive than somewhat cowed by the surroundings and that suited her just fine.

April ordered an Americano and asked the lawyer if he wanted anything else. He declined and sipped his water.

He asked her how long she had been in Zimbabwe. He asked her whether she was enjoying the country. She expressed the usual vague but warm platitudes she'd perfected over the last three months. Her coffee arrived. He thanked her for agreeing to meet him, opened his briefcase and produced a sheaf of papers. 'My client, Mrs Henrietta Gumbo,' he said. 'Have you had a chance to review her situation?'

She sighed. Then she smiled at him and leaned forward conspiratorially. She said she'd had a long conversation with her predecessor, Jeff, and, though she hadn't been at the embassy herself at the time, she was confident that all correct procedures had been followed. She said that, while Mrs Gumbo's retrenchment was regrettable, the embassy had paid her the full three-month notice period specified in her contract, which had in any case been due to expire. She said that if Mr Nyengedza had any further questions he was absolutely welcome to contact the embassy's legal team. She produced Tom Givens's business card from her purse and handed it over the table.

Nyengedza examined it. His brow furrowed. He looked puzzled. He asked her why she'd agreed to meet him if she was just going to pass him over to a lawyer – couldn't she have told him on the phone? She sighed again. She smiled again. She said that, if he recalled, she had in fact tried to tell him this on the phone and it was he who had insisted on the meeting. 'This is really just a courtesy, Mr Nyengedza,' she said.

He shook his head, seemingly more puzzled than ever. He began to say something but stumbled over his words. He sipped his water. She held her smile in place. She noticed a fleck of spittle in his greying beard, the frayed cuffs of his white shirt protruding from his suit jacket. She started to feel sorry for him. Nyengedza was, she decided, both past his prime and out of his depth.

The lawyer gathered his thoughts. He asked why Mrs Gumbo had been retrenched. April told him that the embassy's need for cleaning staff shifted on a monthly, even weekly, basis, which was why employees were only ever given short-term contracts. She said that Mrs Gumbo's services had no longer been required. He nodded. He said, 'I see.'

Then he said that Mrs Gumbo had told him that some stationery had gone missing the day before her dismissal. He said this with a peculiarly hyperbolic intonation, as if he were transmitting quite the most shocking news in the world. April had no idea what this signified, so she didn't respond.

He looked in his file. He said, 'A Mr Shaw ...'

'Jeff.' April nodded. 'My predecessor.'

'A Mr Shaw called together all the staff on the floor and said that two staplers had gone missing and that this petty theft had to stop.' Nyengedza paused, took out his handkerchief and blew his nose. He excused himself. He said that Mrs Gumbo believed she had been retrenched for the theft of these staplers, although no official accusation had been made. Needless to say, Nyengedza added, the lady denied having taken the staplers. He looked at April through watery eyes. He said, 'Did Mr Shaw tell you about these missing staplers?'

'He didn't mention them,' April said, which was more or less true. Jeff hadn't made specific reference to the staplers, but, towards the end of their conversation, he had declaimed in frustration, 'Fuck, April. Why all the questions? The woman was just another fucking thief.'

April drained her coffee. She put down the cup with a decisive clink. This conversation was going nowhere. 'Look,' she said firmly. 'Mr Nyengedza. I agreed to meet you because you insisted upon it and, as I said, as a courtesy. But I'm not sure what you're expecting me to do. If Mrs Gumbo were fired for stealing, there would have been an investigation. But that is not why she was released from her employment so there was no investigation. She was paid to the limit of her contract, so effectively her contract was simply not renewed. Do you think we have behaved illegally? If that is your determination, then you must do as you see fit. Otherwise, as I say, I really can't see what you're expecting me to do.'

Nyengedza stared at her. He appeared more than a little taken aback. April was pleased with herself. She could play tough when the situation required. Now he looked down and put his hands flat on the table to either side of his glass of water. It was a curious action, almost one of self-control, as though he were angry and only able to restrain his temper with an act of will. Either that or he believed the table might be about to take off. But Nyengedza didn't otherwise appear angry – in fact, every muscle in his face appeared entirely relaxed – and the table certainly showed no sign of levitation.

He started speaking and it took April a moment to follow. She wasn't sure if this was because he'd dropped his volume or his accent had somehow thickened. He was saying that it wasn't a legal matter – no, no, no – it was a question of human decency. He said that Mrs Gumbo had worked at the embassy for eight years, was April aware of that? He said that she was a widow with two teenage children and school fees to pay. He said he knew Mrs Gumbo was not a thief. He said, 'I am appealing to you, Mrs Jones, as a human being.' And then again, 'As a human being.'

Later, April reflected that she was entirely right to promise Nyengedza that she would do what she could. She did not know how he was connected to Mrs Gumbo, but she suspected they must have been related and he'd come to see her less as lawyer than concerned uncle or, perhaps, elder brother. He had appealed to her as a human being and she humbly hoped she'd responded as such. She considered how difficult it was to do the right thing in a situation like this, a place like this. She expressed as much to Jerry: 'I just have too much power,' she said. 'I mean, for that woman, it's not just a job, is it? In a situation like this, in a place like this, it's someone's whole life. The line between relative security and disaster is such a fine one.'

Jerry nodded in agreement, but April was somewhat put out that he didn't seem as stirred by the perspicacity of her observation as she was herself, so she asked him if he thought she'd done the right thing, just to check they were indeed on the same page. Jerry shrugged, sure. After all, he said, she'd only promised to do what she could, and if that turned out to be nothing, so be it.

April said, 'Jesus, Jerry! I wasn't bullshitting him. I'll do what I can.'

'That's what I said.'

She shook her head. She was sure her husband didn't understand. 'You don't understand,' she said. 'He was this old guy. I swear he didn't have a clue how it works. I'm just trying to do the right thing.'

'The right thing for who?'

'For him. For her. For me. The right thing is just the right thing.'

'Right,' Jerry said. 'Great.'

12

Patson was late getting home, as was usual for the weekend. Fadzai woke automatically at the sound of the door and checked the time on her phone. It was after one. Still fully dressed, she dragged herself off the bed to prepare her husband's plate. As she laid it in front of him, she sniffed around him, like a dog. This was what she'd been reduced to. She smelt nothing but cigarettes and the particular cloying body odour of a man who'd sat in a car for fifteen hours straight.

She sat opposite him while he ate. They hardly spoke: partly because Chabarwa and Gilbert were sleeping top to toe in the corner, but mostly because, these days, they hardly spoke.

Patson said, 'No meat?' She shook her head.

She watched him in the flickering candlelight, the peculiar, precise way he handled his *sadza*, rolling it carefully in his fingers until it made an almost perfect sphere, then scooping it through the gravy into his mouth with a deliberate, but somehow extravagant, relish. He had always eaten like this – slowly. When they had first met, she'd considered it a marker of gravitas; that he was a man to be taken seriously. Later, it had begun to irritate her and she'd decided instead that it described a basic, plodding aspect to her husband's character. Perhaps this was the nature of a bad marriage, she thought. In a good marriage you would learn to appreciate qualities you once loathed, in a bad one vice versa. But tonight, for the first time in a long time and for no reason she could identify, she found something reassuring in the way her husband ate.

When they had first met, Patson had been considered quite the catch and she was surprised when he'd shown interest in her. After all, as a teenager she'd had none of the skills of attraction that other girls seemed to develop naturally, while Patson had that corresponding nonchalance about him that seemed to take female attention for granted. He wasn't exactly good-looking, not tall, and darker than was generally considered handsome, but he moved with the well-ordered balance of someone who's properly assembled, he had that thoughtful smile, and his blue-black complexion was a glorious consistent monotone that could swallow sunlight.

Now she thought how shrunken he looked, his shoulders hunched, his head thrust forward, like a single knuckle. His skin hadn't changed, but it was as if there was now too much of it, creating not wrinkles but one great fold across the middle of his forehead, another on each cheek. She wondered what had made him like this. Was it just time, age, life? She considered what responsibility she might bear for the depth of those folds, the hunch of those shoulders.

She knew that Patson had been unfaithful to her throughout the first fifteen years of their marriage, but she had chosen to look the other way and had consequently never known the full extent of his betrayal. Something had snapped after Chabarwa's birth, however, and she had confronted him in a blistering attack from which neither of them had ever quite recovered. He had said that he would stop. She had said that she would take him at his word. But the decade or more since had seen her driven almost mad with suspicion and, therefore, bitterness, and her husband engaged in an inexorable process of retreat. She had hoped for more honest communication, but had been left with little communication at all.

Of course she could remember the pain she'd felt as she let his lies go unquestioned, the fear that other women in the neighbourhood were talking behind her back; and she didn't regret taking a stand. But she was also forced to admit that it had brought no resolution and no happiness.

As she watched him now, she finally believed that there weren't other women any more, not because he'd promised as much but because he no longer had it in him. It was what she'd wanted and she'd made it happen. So why did she feel almost guilty?

She remembered a weekend when Anashe was three or four and they had driven down to see her family in Mubayira. They were outside at sunset while Anashe played with the local children, and Patson had stood behind her and briefly lowered his lips to her neck in that embarrassing way of his. She had shaken him off and, in a moment of confidence, asked if he could spend more time at home.

He had looked at her without recrimination (because this was long before the recriminations began) and he said, 'You know I have to work, Fadzai. I am a man. But when I am home, I am *home*.'

At the time, she'd been disappointed and she hadn't known what he meant. But now she knew because now, even when he was in the house, he was always somewhere else, his eyes fixed blankly in front of him, his mind out on the Harare streets or, perhaps, locked in some internal maze of fundamental dissatisfaction. Sometimes she nagged at him just to get his attention, but when he gave her his standard riposte – 'Why are you always talking?' – she could hardly say that she was just checking to see if he was still there, that some hollow apparition hadn't taken his seat or made itself comfortable in their bed.

Patson finished eating. He asked for tea, but they didn't have any. She said perhaps it was no bad thing since it was so late and tea always kept him awake. He asked for water. She fetched him a cup.

She said, 'How was your day?'

For the first time he looked directly at her – what do you mean?

What *did* she mean? She meant nothing, but such was the state of their relationship that even the white noise of small-talk seemed to congest, choke and backfire. 'How much did you make?' she said, by way of illumination, because, though money was a dangerous topic, it was something about which they had no choice but to talk.

'Eighty,' Patson said.

'That's good.'

'Two hundred for the week. I see Gapu in the morning. It's all his.'

Patson paid two hundred dollars a week rental to Dr Gapu, the car's owner. He was at least a month behind. He began to excavate his back teeth with his thumbnail.

'So tomorrow is yours,' Fadzai said gently.

'A Sunday.' He sniffed. Then, 'I'll be out early and back late.'

He looked at her again. He stretched his mouth and, for a split second, she thought he was smiling, but he was just trying to dislodge whatever was wedged in his molars. 'Toothpick?' he said.

13

Patson went to the bedroom as Fadzai cleared the table. Despite the hour, she felt restless, so she made sure the kids' church clothes were ready for the morning before retiring. She expected to find her husband asleep, but he was standing over the small chest of drawers.

'Patson?'

He turned round. He was holding the gun. She couldn't see his face in the pale glow of the candle behind him, so she instinctively reached for the light switch and flicked it on. It was one of the rare nights in Sunningdale when the electricity was working and the sudden illumination of the naked bulb surprised them both. For a second Patson looked terrified, before he managed to reorder his expression. He lifted the gun in front of him and read along the barrel aloud: 'SIG SAUER, Sig Arms Inc, Herndon VA.'

'What does that mean?'

'I don't know.'

'Is it loaded?'

'He shot three times. But I don't know how many bullets it can hold. I don't know how to look.' He weighed it in his hand. 'It is very heavy.'

'Is it safe?'

'What do you mean?'

'I mean, if you pull the trigger, will it fire?'

Patson looked at her with some bemusement. 'I have no idea.' He blinked slowly. 'What do I do?' he said.

Then his fears came tumbling out of him, one after the next. Harare was a small town, he said. The CIO was drunk and might not remember him, but what if he recognised the car? The soldiers were unlikely to report the shooting incident, but could he be sure? He hadn't given the man his real name, but he'd told the other one, the young one outside the building, and what if they talked? It was a gun. It was a gun and surely Mandiveyi, the CIO, was going to have to account for it. He was going to come looking. He was going to come looking and if he found him . . . well, what then?

'What will he do to me?' Patson said. 'To you? Our children?'

Fadzai stared at him in shock. Somehow, since that night, she'd largely managed to put the whole shooting incident out of her mind. It was as if, in a life of problems, no particular one could be allowed to weigh more than any other. But now she knew that her husband was right, because this problem was just too heavy to ignore. She tried to gather her thoughts. She tried to remain calm. He had asked her what to do and it was a genuine question and she wanted to have an answer.

'Take it back,' she said. 'Hand it in at the desk. You put it in a bag, say it is something you found and walk away.'

'What if they look? If they look, they will take me. And if they take me . . .' Patson shook his head. 'I think I have to get rid of it. I'll throw it in a river. If Mandiveyi comes, I'll tell him I don't know what he's talking about. I don't know anything about a gun.'

'No.' Now it was Fadzai's turn to shake her head. 'You get rid of it and you have nothing. What if he finds you? He says, "Where is my gun?" What gun? He doesn't believe you. You have nothing to bargain with. We have to keep it.'

'Keep it where?'

'I don't know. We will think of something. We must stay calm.' Fadzai told her husband to return the gun to the chest of drawers. She told him in a way that suggested she had a plan. She spoke with enough authority that he did so without complaint. She told him to get into bed and he did, like a child. He lay on his side, facing the wall, his back to her.

She went to turn off the overhead light but something stopped her. Instead, she began to undress, lifting off her T-shirt and unclasping her bra. She put the bra in the chest of drawers – there was the gun. Her heart was beating faster as she slipped out of her jeans and underwear. She dropped her underwear and T-shirt in the washing basket, folded her jeans and slid them into the bottom drawer, taking out a nightdress. She stood for a moment, naked, holding the hem of her nightdress. The room was cold and she shivered a little. As if on cue, Patson turned over and looked at her. She couldn't remember the last time she had stood naked in front of her husband and she felt a rush of embarrassment mixed with a long-forgotten frisson of daring. She looked back at him as she pulled on the nightdress. Then she turned off the light and climbed into bed.

'You're cold,' he said, and eased her towards him, sliding one arm under her neck and the other round her waist so that they lay nose to nose. She positioned one hand in the small of his back and they stayed like that for a while, each listening to the other's breathing. She shifted her position so that her thigh was between his legs. She felt the thickening weight of him push through his underwear against her bare flesh, simultaneously alien and familiar. 'I thought we had no meat.' She giggled softly. 'You should have told me you brought some.'

Patson said nothing, but his hips pushed forward and some muscle memory allowed her simultaneously to extract a trapped arm and roll on top of him. Now, brazenly astride him like that, she felt a wave of nervousness, but her husband made an involuntary guttural sound that told her she was doing OK.

'Let me cook it for you,' she whispered.

Later, as they lay side by side, she said, 'I have to ask you something.'

He grunted his assent.

'It's Gilbert. He wants to stay in Harare.' There was silence. It was pitch black and she couldn't make out a single feature of her husband's face, just hear the in and out breaths, long and slow. She wondered if he was asleep. 'Patson?' she said.

More silence. She felt Patson move his arms so that he was no longer touching her. She didn't know what that meant. He might have been simply resting his hands behind his head to be more comfortable, to give her question due consideration. She couldn't tell.

'So what do you think?' she said.

'Is this how you soften me up?' he asked quietly. 'The first time in months and now you ask the question you were afraid to ask.'

'No!' she exclaimed. 'No! Really! I've wanted to ask you these last few days, but when do we ever talk?'

Patson rolled out of bed. 'I want to smoke,' he said, and he fumbled for his cigarettes and matches. He went out to the lounge without another word and she heard him unbolt the front door.

She got up herself, heavy-hearted. She put on her slippers and

67

wrapped a *chitenge* around her waist. She followed him outside. This was their pattern – flight and pursuit.

She was relieved to find him standing on the small concrete veranda, leaning on the pillar. She sat on the far side of him on the edge of the step, hugging herself. She didn't speak.

Eventually, he said, 'With what has happened, perhaps it is good to have another man in the house, in case they come and I am not here.'

Fadzai didn't look up. She didn't want to show her surprise. She said, 'You know Gilbert has his licence now? You could keep the car out twenty-four hours if you wanted.'

Patson sniffed, but it was a sound that, she thought, contained at least as much consideration as dismissal.

'I was worried to ask you,' Fadzai said. 'You told me he was good for nothing.'

Patson denied it. 'That's what *you* said. How can I talk about your family? He is your brother.'

'But we don't have room. And we can't afford to feed a grown man.'

He chuckled softly. 'He is your *brother*.' He stubbed his cigarette on the pillar and squatted behind her, enveloping her at the shoulders and nuzzling his face into the back of her neck.

Fadzai resisted the tendency to break away. She said, 'I thought you didn't love me any more.'

'When I am home, I am *home*,' he whispered into her ear, and his breath was hot and wet and, in spite of herself, she made a reflexive sound of mild distaste.

14

Iganyana summoned Mandiveyi personally. Mandiveyi was uneasy. After all, the original order had come from Phiri, his immediate boss, and he had carried it out without question: he had collected the gun from the bottle store on Simon Mazorodze Road.

Sure, the death of Rex Nhongo the preceding night and the subsequent gossip that had engulfed the city had given him suspicions (about both the order and its origins), but he had squashed them. Mandiveyi knew all too well that those who succeeded were those who acted, not those who questioned. He knew that in the hierarchy many smart men played stupid while only stupid men played smart.

Phiri accompanied him to the interview. The two men were shown into *Iganyana*'s office and instructed to take chairs opposite the empty desk. They did not speak. *Iganyana* came in a few minutes later and took his place. He walked from the door to the desk with that peculiar dainty dancer's gait. He made an extravagant sighing noise as he sat down, then shifted his position to get comfortable so that the leather of the chair squealed in protest beneath him. He sniffed enthusiastically and dabbed his eyes with a handkerchief. Mandiveyi had never met him in person and struggled not to stare at the patches of hyperpigmentation that mottled his face and had given him his nickname.

Iganyana greeted Phiri warmly and Mandiveyi hardly at all. He ordered coffee from his secretary and, when it arrived in a pewter coffee pot, said, 'I will be mother, as the English say.'

He served them, then took his own cup and saucer and swivelled in his chair so that his back was to them and he was looking out of the window. Mandiveyi glanced at Phiri. His colleague looked straight ahead.

After a moment or two, *Iganyana* enquired after Phiri's son at university in South Africa. Phiri hesitantly thanked him for remembering and said that, as far as he knew, all was fine.

'As far as you know?' *Iganyana* said. 'Do you not know about your own son?'

Phiri prevaricated. He said that the boy had passed all his exams so far, but he was a young man away from home and who could say what he might get up to?

Iganyana made a noise that might have been a laugh. He said, 'Which university?'

'Pretoria.'

'It's not a party university that one, is it?'

'I don't believe so, sir.'

There was that noise again. 'But a young man will always be a young man.'

'A young man will always be a young man,' Phiri repeated.

There was more silence. Mandiveyi sipped his coffee. It was cold and bitter. He should have taken more sugar, but he didn't want to draw attention to himself. *Iganyana* seemed briefly captured by something happening outside his window in the street below. He leaned forward and touched his finger to the glass. Then he swivelled in his chair again, placed his empty cup on the desk and his eyes fell on Phiri, as if he were surprised to find him still in the room. 'Leave us,' he said. Phiri did as he was told.

Iganyana turned to Mandiveyi. It was the first time he'd actually looked at him. He sat forward with his hands clasped on the desk and sniffed. 'You like to drink,' *Iganyana* said.

'Excuse me, sir?'

'You like to drink.'

Mandiveyi shifted in his seat. His mouth was dry. He contemplated the bottom of his coffee cup. 'Not so much.'

Iganyana stared at him fixedly until Mandiveyi had no choice but to look up and meet his eye. Then he nodded smartly, bent down to his desk drawer and produced a bottle of whisky and two glasses. 'You like to drink,' *Iganyana* said, for a third time. 'It was not a question. I make it my business to know about those who work for me. Do not lie to me again.'

He poured a large measure into each glass. He slid one across the desk. 'It is OK. A man should drink.' He raised his own glass as if in challenge and waited until Mandiveyi did the same. 'Cheers,' he said, and downed it. Mandiveyi had taken only a small sip, but the other man was waiting, so he, too, drained his glass. *Iganyana* poured another two tots and finally sat back, fingering his glass thoughtfully.

Iganyana began to ask Mandiveyi question after question, though his interest in the answers was cool and affected. It was an obvious tactic – a show of knowledge and, therefore, strength; one that Mandiveyi had used countless times himself. Still, it felt uncomfortable to be on the other side of the game, not least because the very nature of this game required both parties to know it was being played.

Iganyana asked Mandiveyi about his daughter in form four. Was she preparing well for her O levels? What were her plans for the following year? He said that he had good connections at some of the sixth-form colleges in the city if that would help. He asked about his son, 'the cripple'. He expressed sympathy that the boy had to suffer in such a way and admiration for his fortitude. He asked about his wife's Mercedes, and were they still struggling with the starter because he knew a guy who imported genuine parts at a reasonable price? He asked about Mandiveyi's mistress in town. Was she happy with her job at Tel One? Did she cause him problems with her demands for money? Did he know that her uncle was an 'agitator'? No? This was, *Iganyana* said, the kind of thing Mandiveyi should know.

'People fear me,' *Iganyana* said. 'They tell stories that I have this man killed or another one disappear. That is a very small part of my job and not the real reason they are scared. The real reason they fear me is because of what I know. Everything that happens in this country, I know about it. Do you understand what I am saying?'

'Yes, sir.' These lines were so familiar, but what choice did Mandiveyi have except to play his part? That was the brilliance of the game.

Iganyana nodded. Then he said, 'I believe you have conducted important business on our behalf. Is there anything you would like to tell me about it?'

Mandiveyi thought for a moment, then shook his head. 'No, sir.'

Iganyana stared at him, as if giving him a moment to change his mind, then nodded again. He took a swallow of the whisky. Again, he patted his eyes with his handkerchief, before folding it carefully. Mandiveyi waited. He knew there was more to come.

'Let me tell you something, Comrade,' *Iganyana* said. 'This business is not concluded. It will not be concluded for a long time. Perhaps it will never be concluded. Your part was just a small one, but I need to know that I can trust you. Do we understand each other?'

'Yes, sir.'

'And can I trust you?'

'Yes, sir.'

'So there is only one problem.' *Iganyana* smiled, those curious patches on his face shifting like a Rorschach test. 'I don't trust you. Not at all.' He paused. He poured himself another measure. This time he didn't offer the bottle. 'Phiri tells me you are a man of ambition. Is that so?'

Mandiveyi considered his options. 'I want to do my best, sir,' he said eventually. 'I believe if I do that I will progress.'

'Good answer. Ambition is not a virtue for men like us. He also told me that you are efficient and you are not a talker. Is he right?'

'He is quite right,' Mandiveyi said.

'But these are not the reasons I put this business in front of you. Do you know that? Do you know why I put this business in front of you?'

Mandiveyi felt helpless. He said, 'No, sir.'

Iganyana strained his whisky through his teeth and effected the same curious noise he'd made when looking out of the window. It was not a laugh, more like a snarl. 'I chose you, because you are a weak man with many vices and much to lose.'

Mandiveyi said nothing. There was nothing to be said.

'Of course, you know my nickname, isn't it?' Mandiveyi didn't know how to acknowledge as much, but it seemed his acknowledgement was not required. '*Iganyana*, the painted dog, on account of this —' he splayed his fingers and gestured down across his face. '– discoloration. But I like to think I have grown into the description. Do you know how the painted dog kills his prey?'

Mandiveyi was at a loss. 'He is a pack hunter, sir,' he mumbled.

'Of course he is a pack hunter!' *Iganyana* exclaimed. 'But that is not my point. The painted dog will pursue his prey over several kilometres. He is not particularly fast, but he is dogged – excuse the pun. A wildebeest, even an impala, has only so much energy. Eventually he will tire and then the dog is vicious, he will tear the animal apart.' *Iganyana* smiled. Mandiveyi saw a pair of gaping chasms in the ink blot. 'Nothing can outrun the painted dog.'

15

I knew I done sumthin wrong only Sasa tell me not to worry about it. He say he tell me nuthin gonna happen to the baby an, for sure, nuthin happen to the baby so he don know what all the fuss about. That what he say only he don say it that way. Sasa don speak English an he don speak Shona. He speak his own language what only me unnerstan. He say this when we on our way home from the party an Mom an Dad fightin in the front seat (Dad say, 'We not fighting, little bird. It's just a frank exchange of views.' Momma say, 'Why are you lying, Shawn? Why are you always lying?').

I tell Sasa to keep quiet cos I wanna hear, but he jus keep on like he does – when Sasa got sumthin to say he jus keep sayin it until you gots no choice but to listen, even if you don wanna. Mostly he jus say, 'Look at me! Look at me!' An he spread his wings wide and show off his belly, which so black you feel like it not really there an you could put your whole hand right inside.

After what happen, after Dad get out the pool and change into a T-shirt and short he borrow from Theo's dad, he go, 'OK, it's time for us to leave right now!' An he take me by the arm an he hold it so tight I starts to cry.

Theo's dad walk behind us, goin, 'Don't worry. It was an accident. He's OK.'

But my dad know otherwise an when we gets to the car he put me face down on the seat an he smack my backside an he shoutin at me only quiet an I can feel his spit on my ear. He go, 'I saw you, Rosie. I saw what you did. You could've killed that boy, you know that? You could have killed him.'

An I know he seen what I done an the tears sting my eyes cos I real shamed, but he dint see Sasa standin next to me on the edge jus sayin, 'Do it,' an 'Do it,' an 'Do it,' until I gots no choice but to listen.

Altho it's me what dun the sumthin bad an Dad smack me cross my behind, he still real angry wid Momma, tho she angry first. Momma get in the car an she jab a finger at him an she go, 'I ever see you raise a hand to our daughter again, Shawn, I'll . . .'

An Dad jab a finger right back. 'You'll what, Kuda? You'll fucking what?'

'I'll kill you,' Mom say, an that make Dad stay quiet for a bit an then shake his head an stare at the road in front.

Sasa sayin to me, 'Look at me! Look at me! Look at me!'

Dad sayin to Mom, 'You're sick, you know that? You're sick in the head. You're mentally ill.'

Sasa sayin, 'Sick in the head! Sick in the head!'

Dad sayin, 'You think I didn't see you watching her? What were you doing? Praying? Jesus, Kudakwashe! You do know what just happened, right? And you're off with the fucking angels!'

Sasa jumpin up an down now an flappin his wings real fast. He goes, 'Crazy bitch! Crazy bitch!'

An Momma turns round and goes, 'What did you say?'

An Dad goes, 'I said you're a crazy bitch!'

When we gets home, it's Gladys who give me my bath an dress me. She know sumthin wrong cos she can tell from Mom and Dad, so she go, 'Have you been naughty, little bird?'

An I go, 'I dun sumthin bad, Gladys. But Sasa told me do it.' An Gladys look at me very hard and then shake her head.

76

Gladys put me to bed, then Dad come an say goodnight. He sit on the chair next to me and he put his hand on my shoulder. He goes, 'I'm sorry I smacked you, Rosie. But you have to learn that what you did was very dangerous. Do you understand that?'

An I go, 'Yes, Daddy.'

An he smile an he go, 'You know I love you, don't you, little bird?'

An then Sasa there on the end of the bed an he go, 'Yes, Daddy.'

An I go, 'Yes, Daddy.' Then suddenly I feel sad an I go, 'Where's Momma?'

'I'm right here.' This is Momma an she standin by the door. She smile an she go, 'Good night, my love.'

I say, 'Gimme a kiss.'

An she come and she still smilin but her eyes look kinda spooky. She kiss me on the forehead and she smell like Momma even tho her lips are cold like glass. Dad says, 'Sleep now,' an he turns off the light.

I can see Sasa's eyes in the dark an he says, 'You wanna go flyin?' An even tho I know he naughty, it real excitin when we go up in the sky an he look after me real well. He go, 'I'm kinda like your dad's family, you know that? He call me up when he come home to Afrika, tho he don even know it hisself. You think I gonna let anythin happen to you when we related? No way!'

Up in the sky he point his sharp little ears forward an he say, 'I can hear evryone. Look: there's your momma prayin.'

An I go, 'Is anyone lisnin?'

An Sasa laugh an I see his teeth pointed like a Halloween pumpkin an he say, 'Well, I lisnin. I lisnin good.'

16

Gilbert arrived early. He had taken a kombi to the city centre, then another to Glenara shops, where he bought two Cokes and some chicken pieces. He walked from there, following his wife's instructions. Still unfamiliar with Harare, he hadn't known how long the journey would take so there he was, standing outside the gate of number forty-five with an hour to spare.

He was nervous. This was only partly because he was going to see Bessie for the first time in almost five months. Mostly it was because he was specifically going to see where she lived and worked and the kind of life his wife had built for herself on her own.

Besides, he had never been into a *murungu*'s house before; he wasn't sure what to expect and, from the outside, he already found something vaguely threatening. It wasn't the heavy iron gate, with the sign saying 'Armed Response', that bothered him, or the looming walls topped with an electric fence. Rather, it was the neat flowerbeds planted with climbing yellow bougainvillaea overlooking a pristine two-metre verge of lawn to the kerb. The artfulness spoke to Gilbert of a manic, controlling attention to detail that he found unsettling. How much time and effort had it taken to create this effect? And what conviction was expressed in the commitment? He couldn't imagine a life of such certainty.

He sat on the kerb at the far corner of the property, away from the gate. He took out his phone. He had no airtime, so he sent Bessie a free 'call me back', so that she'd know he'd arrived. But she didn't finish work until one p.m., so he'd just have to wait. He idled back to the airtime seller on the corner where two gardeners were playing checkers. He watched for a while and made vain attempts to engage them in conversation, but they were unfriendly and engrossed in what was clearly a regular challenge match. He tried talking to the airtime seller, but the kid was every bit as sullen. Gilbert had the sense that the workers in this rich neighbourhood banded together against any outsiders who might compete for jobs or customers.

By the time he returned to number forty-five it was five past one and, from a distance, he saw Bessie standing at the gate. He quickened his pace and, when she turned to look in his direction, instinctively raised his arm in a broad, excited arc of greeting. Her response was a brief, low-key twitch of her right hand and he felt suddenly embarrassed. The specific nuances of this small exchange signified, for Gilbert, everything that was wrong with their current situation. His love for his wife burned consistently hot but, in his absence, she had begun to resort to a kind of pragmatic frigidity that would take time to thaw even in the full glare of his passion. He sometimes worried that, one day, he would no longer be able to warm her up and she would cool him down instead.

He had told her this the last time she visited Mubayira and she appeared immediately crestfallen. 'I'm sorry,' she said. 'But when I am not here, do you believe I must think about my husband and daughter all the time? I can't do that. If I do that I will become depressed.'

Gilbert promptly regretted his comment and suffered one of those sudden reversals of sentiment common to the love-struck. 'No!' he gushed. '*I* am sorry. I will always have enough love for us both.'

She then looked at him – somewhat sadly, he thought – and said, 'You cannot have enough love for two people. That is not how it works.' At which his heart turned over once again and he wished he'd said nothing at all.

Bessie was still wearing her maid's uniform and in it she seemed all the more unfamiliar: the shapeless dress, gathered at the waist, robbed her small frame of its natural undulations, while the headscarf low on her brow made her look unusually stern. She greeted him formally, tentatively, and he, suddenly racked with uncertainty, did likewise. But, he couldn't help taking her hand in his and she smiled up at him with a brief, familiar flash of personality that made his stomach tighten.

'You have been in Harare . . .' she began.

'Almost two weeks,' he said.

'How is our pumpkin?'

'She is fine. She is speaking, you know.'

'No! What does she say?'

'*Gogo*. To my mum. Well. Almost.'

Bessie nodded slowly. Gilbert felt his clumsiness and insensitivity. He watched his wife swallow her sacrifice as she surely did every day. She waited for it to settle. She asked, 'And how is everyone at Sunningdale?'

'They are fine. Everybody is fine.' He let go of her hand so that he could adjust his small knapsack. 'Shall we go inside? I bought some chicken.'

She smiled. 'I also bought chicken,' she said. She looked back at the gate. 'Madam is having a party. There are some guests. Later I may have to help with the dishes.'

'I thought you were off this afternoon?'

'I am,' Bessie said, and shrugged. She turned, took out her keys and opened the small door in the heavy iron gate.

17

Gilbert looked around the plot. It was large: perhaps half an acre in front of the house, a driveway running up the right-hand side to a twin garage, and then at least double the space behind. The house, though, was surprisingly old and modest, perhaps eight rooms in all, and Gilbert considered that, if these people were so rich, which they must be, it was strange that they hadn't rebuilt. He said as much to Bessie, who replied, 'It is not their house; they are renting. They're from UK. I told you.'

As they skirted the garage, Gilbert heard the sounds of chatter and soft, unfamiliar music. The back of the house opened onto a large covered veranda, raised a metre or so above the lawn and overlooking a swimming pool. Half a dozen kids of various ages were splashing in the water, the youngest bobbing reluctantly in the arms of a white woman. A *braai* was in full swing on the far side of the veranda, burning too fiercely to be cooking the meat nicely. Around twenty people were gathered in clusters here and there, talking somewhat seriously. It was hardly what Gilbert would have described as a party.

Bessie told him to wait and approached the nearest group, all men, who were seated on cane chairs around a low table.

She stood at a couple of metres distance until she caught the attention of a burly man in T-shirt and shorts. He stood up, even looking slightly relieved by her intervention, and joined Bessie on the grass. She led him over to perform the necessary introductions.

Bessie's boss was tall, as tall as Gilbert and twice as wide. He had short dark hair, a broad, open face and a poorly trimmed beard that cracked easily into a smile. He transferred his beer bottle from right to left so that he could shake Gilbert's hand.

'This is Mr Jerry Jones,' Bessie said, in English. 'Sir, this is my husband, Gilbert Chiweshe.'

Gilbert took his hand. 'It is a pleasure to meet you, Boss,' he said.

The man said something incomprehensible and Gilbert was thrown until his wife prompted, again in English, 'He is greeting you!' and he grasped that the *murungu* was speaking broken Shona.

'*Ndaswera. Maswera sei?*' Gilbert said.

'Fine, fine. It's good to meet you.' The man reverted to his own tongue, swigged from his beer, then adopted a grave expression. 'I'm sorry that we keep Bessie away from you. Though I don't know what we'd do without her. She's been a godsend.'

Gilbert didn't know how to reply to this. He glanced at Bessie for help, but she was looking at her feet. 'Thank you, sir,' he tried, and it seemed an acceptable response.

There was no need for further conversation, but Mr Jones appeared determined to continue and he asked after Gilbert's family and the journey from the 'rural area'. Gilbert said that the journey had been fine, that his family was fine. Mr Jones shifted from foot to foot as if uncomfortable. He drank from his beer again. 'And what are you doing in the city?' Mr Jones asked.

'I am looking for an opportunity. But at the moment I am driving a taxi with my brother-in-law.' Gilbert took out his wallet and found one of his new business cards. It had his phone number and Patson's. It read, 'Gapu Taxis. Your journey is our business. We go in peace.' It had been Gilbert's idea to print the cards and it felt good to hand one over.

A hint of a smile twitched around Mr Jones's eyes. 'You go in peace?' he said. 'Is that a promise?'

Gilbert felt foolish. It had been Patson who'd insisted on the motto. 'It is a promise,' he said. 'Not a contractual obligation.'

Mr Jones raised his eyebrows. 'That's good to know,' he said. Then, 'Well, we're a one-car family, so I often need a taxi. I'll call you. At least now you can find the house.'

'No problem, Boss.'

Gilbert's attention was taken by what was happening over Mr Jones's left shoulder. The white woman he'd noted before was hurriedly getting out of the pool and, in the absence of any other takers, handed her child to a tall, light-skinned black guy, wearing a loose, short-sleeved shirt and light trousers – he looked, Gilbert thought, like an American singer. The woman then wrapped a towel around her waist and hurried over, busily arranging her curly hair into something like order. She was too pale to be revealing so much skin to the afternoon sun and her shoulders and upper arms were marked with countless small freckles as if by way of protest. As she approached, she jabbed out her hand like a spear and Gilbert took it to avoid being run through.

'Hello,' she said.

'Madam,' Bessie said quickly. 'This is my husband.'

'Gilbert,' Mr Jones said blithely. 'He is visiting.'

'Visiting?' Mrs Jones said, at a pitch that made her own

84

husband's eyes dart towards her, the last to cotton on to her obvious displeasure.

'Yeah,' he said, making no attempt to conceal his own irritation. 'Visiting. Bessie. His wife.'

'Tomorrow we will go to church,' Bessie said.

There was a heavy moment of silence. Then Mrs Jones said, 'Well, this is a nice surprise. Good to meet you, Gilbert.' Then, 'Bessie? Can you come back around six to clear up?'

She turned on her heels and strutted back to the party. Mr Jones sniffed and gave Gilbert a conspiratorial look, which the latter didn't entirely understand, then turned and said over his shoulder, 'Nice to meet you. Have a good weekend.'

'Thank you, Boss.'

At the domestic housing, Gilbert stood in the doorway of the small kitchen while Bessie prepared the chicken. He sipped a Coke. They didn't talk much, but that was OK. He enjoyed watching her busy herself and, besides, he knew that, though there were no words or gestures of affection, the diligence with which she cleaned and cut the meat was its own kind of intimacy.

They ate in Bessie's room. He sat at the small table on the single chair. She sat on the floor. He told her his plans. He wasn't sure how she would react, but he tried to speak as if it were all decided and brooked no argument. He told her that there was nothing for him in Mubayira. There were no jobs and he was no kind of farmer. He was proud that she had taken the initiative to come to Harare, but what kind of husband would he be if he just sat at home and let this situation drift indefinitely? He told her that Patson and Fadzai had agreed that he could stay in Sunningdale until he found his feet. He showed her the business cards. He would share responsibility for the taxi until he found

85

work of his own. It might take some time, but eventually they would bring Stella and have a house and build a life as a family. He said, 'What do you think?'

Bessie fetched the second Coke and divided it equally into two glasses. She smiled at him. She said, 'I think it's a good plan.'

18

Later that evening, around half past seven, when everyone had gone home, having expressed sufficient horror about the day's central dramatic event, and when he'd finally finished the dishes and been able to dismiss Bessie for what was left of her weekend, Jerry found April cradling Theo on her lap on the couch. Theo was in his pyjamas and half asleep, but April was still wearing her swimming costume and the same loose shirt and trousers she'd thrown over it hours earlier. Her hair was similarly unkempt, her eyes still wide with maternal terror.

Jerry said, 'Everything OK?'

She took a moment to look at him, and when she did, she shook her head, not so much to answer his question as to signify, as if there could be any doubt, the full extent of her distress. She said, 'That's the kind of thing he'll never forget, Jerry, never fucking forget. That's the kind of thing that will stay with him for ever.'

Hearing his mother's tone of voice, Theo looked up at her from beneath her chin and sneezed. Jerry made some wordless noise of agreement, but couldn't help thinking that the likelihood of his son remembering this for ever was more down to April's reaction than the incident itself. He said, 'Good job that guy was watching – the father. What's his name? Shawn?'

Jerry had intended this to be an uncontroversial and incontrovertible observation but, as was generally the case when April was wound like a corkscrew, such observations were hard to come by.

'Fuck, Jerry, fuck,' April breathed. Then, 'We've got to be sure we know where Theo is at all times. You do know that, right? You *do know that*?'

Jerry bit his tongue. He did know that; of course he knew it. But he also knew that if he rose to the accusation he was sure was present in the question (and how could it not be? Her brief dalliance with the word 'we' was clumsily disingenuous) it would only lead to a fight. And he was either too tired to fight or simply tired of fighting.

Instead, therefore, he made another vague, indecipherable noise and retreated back to the kitchen where he stood, propped against the counter, draining an open bottle of warm, flat beer and reflecting on the day. It had been, he decided, an unequivocal disaster – a party he hadn't wanted to throw, attended by people he didn't much like, pivoting around a public row with his wife and culminating in Theo's near death. As he phrased it like that in his head, he issued a brief, amused snort for the benefit of an imaginary audience.

Jerry's perspective was undoubtedly coloured by how things had turned out. Because, though he wouldn't now admit it, he'd enjoyed himself for at least the early part of the afternoon. It was coloured, too, by living in a relationship under constant strain, which chafed, frayed and squealed, no matter how much he tried to anaesthetise, bind or lubricate its moving parts. And by the end of every day, a dull, chronic pain had always returned to ensure he felt short-tempered, hard-done-by and misunderstood.

Of course the *braai* had been April's idea. Perhaps because she spent so much time dealing with personnel issues at the embassy, she now seemed to regard herself as some kind of de facto social secretary for the expatriates of Harare; initially just the Brits, but, latterly, all-comers. But if April considered a hosting role part of her professional remit, it was really Jerry who had the social skills to pull it off. Whatever Jerry thought about the motivations, perhaps even the morals, of Harare's expat/diplomatic/NGO population, he also had a kind of impulsive and irrepressible gregariousness that, at least temporarily, swamped his cynicism. Consequently, though he had dreaded the *braai* in advance, he was soon hanging coats, cracking bottles and small-talking vacantly with the woman from US AID and her husband, who looked about eighteen but was some kind of hotshot in governance. After a couple of beers, he even found himself regaling the wide-eyed cultural director of the Alliance Française with the story of his first patient at the Epworth clinic. As she variously winced and exclaimed at every gruesome detail, thereby drawing walk-ups to their conversation, so Jerry began to relish the gruesomeness himself and even to elaborate unnecessarily (and not entirely truthfully) for effect.

Later, in the kitchen, by now feeling short-tempered, hard-done-by and misunderstood, he reflected with shame on his behaviour. He considered bitterly that he'd somehow been infected by these people and the peculiar, incongruous, outdated lifestyle that saw two dozen white foreigners gather in a luxury that couldn't have been familiar to them in London, Paris, Rome or wherever they hailed from, but to which they now appeared to feel instinctively entitled. There was even, he decided, something in the way these people behaved that acknowledged the absurd inequity of their situation: their superficial piety a kind of justifying token, and the politesse of their conversations reflecting an understanding that, for reasons of taste and, possibly, security, they should not be overheard by the rest of the city, however strong their desire to drive around with windows wide, screaming, 'Look at me in my big fucking car.' And, of course, there were very few black people present; just Bessie making potato salad, Tapiwa from the embassy, Tom Givens's trophy girlfriend (Esther? Young, bored, popping bubble-gum like a teenager), and Shawn, the New Yorker April had met at yoga, his silent Zimbabwean wife, Kuda, and their eight-year-old daughter, Rosie, who'd ended up at the centre of the dreadful incident.

The afternoon had begun to go wrong with the arrival of Gilbert. Jerry had quite forgotten he'd OKed the visit, not least because he hadn't considered himself in a position to OK it or otherwise. However, while he was being, he thought, no more than appropriately friendly, April had stalked over, dripping from the swimming pool, and he could tell from the jut of her jaw that something was amiss. Ten minutes later, when he had been en route to the *braai* to poke sausages and turn steaks, April, who'd appeared deep in conversation with three or four women, had caught his arm. She'd bombarded him with a loosely strung invective: what did he think he was doing saying it was fine for Bessie's husband to visit when they'd never met him and didn't know anything about him, and, besides, this was Bessie's place of work, and was he really comfortable having a total stranger on the property with their two-year-old son?

Jerry looked from his wife to the other women and saw at once that this was what they'd been talking about and now, if not before, April was utterly confident in her indignation. He found himself staring at her, frozen in something like astonishment. Over recent months, he'd frequently found April's anger, attitude or opinions shocking; so frequently, in fact, that he now wondered whether his shock could really still be blamed on changes in her behaviour rather than his own obstinate refusal to acknowledge them.

Jerry attempted a mild remark about how he hadn't known it was his decision as to whom Bessie could or couldn't see in her spare time. He kept his voice calm, slightly jovial, cautiously stripped of any note of irritation. His comment didn't have the placatory effect he'd hoped.

This was partly because April had lately learned to read the absence of irritation in Jerry's voice for precisely the irritation it was intended to mask, and consequently reflected it right back. And it was partly, and more surprisingly, because his comment had provoked forthright opinions from the other women, which, in turn, attracted the attention of most of the rest of the Joneses' guests. In fact, Jerry soon understood that he was more or less alone in thinking that Bessie's husband visiting for the weekend was no big deal. What was more, everyone else seemed to have the personal experience, professional knowledge, cultural legit-imacy or plain brass neck to lend weight (if not reason) to their opinions.

The woman from the Alliance, for example, told a horror story of discovering her maid selling the kids' hand-me-downs at the flea-market, which prompted the fresh-faced American govern-ance expert to announce, expertly, that a Zimbabwean domestic worker had familial responsibility for an average of three other adults. Tapiwa, from the embassy, said, 'Seriously. You let a stranger on your property?' She shook her head and issued a high-pitched hum of doubt, followed by a relished 'Uh-uh!' as if to seal her authenticity. 'You are asking for trouble! Did you not read what happened to Rex Nhongo? And he was the former armed-forces chief and his wife is vice president!'

'The problem is,' Tom Givens opined, 'they just don't plan long term. You might think, Why would they rip me off? They're on to a good thing with me. But that's not how they are. They don't plan beyond hand to mouth.'

Givens was the embassy's head of legal. Jerry stared at him, bewildered – was this truly how the head of legal spoke? And who was this *they* he was referring to? Domestic workers? Zimbabweans? *Black people?* But if he expected Tapiwa, for one, to jump in and defend her race, nation or at least the working class thereof, he was going to be disappointed. Instead, she just nodded vigorously and said, 'You see now?'

April looked at him directly, gave a prim little sniff and said, 'It's just common sense, Jerry.'

And now the mildness of her husband's tone didn't even pretend to conceal his growing anger. 'I never knew you were such a natural madam,' he observed, and it was a remark that horrified the lot of them to silence.

Jerry was vexed and he was being intentionally insulting. But not until he'd spoken the sentence did he fully comprehend the degree. He'd have been better off if he'd just told his wife to stop being such a cunt. To call an expat the M-word was the lowest of blows, and it offended not just April but the sensibilities of all present, who widened their eyes, looked at one another conspiratorially and regarded Jerry with a mixture of pity and thinly veiled hostility.

The atmosphere was only broken by Shawn, the New Yorker, who, apparently oblivious to the political niceties that had just been recklessly trampled, took a swallow of beer and said, 'Where I come from, you find a nigger you don't know on your property? You shoot first and ask questions later, for real.' Then, when nobody responded, he smiled slowly: 'My bad. What shock you more, my language or my attitude to gun control?'

The cultural director of the Alliance made a curious shrill noise in the back of her throat. It might have been a laugh. Tom Givens coughed into his hand. He said, 'So, where you come from, you'd have shot the maid's husband?'

Shawn shook his head. 'Where I come from, Tom, I ain't got no maid.'

He chuckled softly, and now the rest of them were confident, more or less, that Shawn was making a joke, possibly even deliberately defusing the atmosphere, they laughed too, their amusement augmented by both relief and the exhilarating sense that they were with a black guy who felt comfortable enough to use the word 'nigger' in their company. Only Jerry and April didn't join in.

19

Shawn Appiah had met April the first and last time he went to yoga at the Ubuntu Natural Health Centre in Rolf Valley. Shawn wasn't especially surprised to be the only man at the class, but he was taken aback to be the only black person, as he said later to Kuda, 'This being Africa and all.'

The Ubuntu Natural Health Centre was run by a woman called Toney ('with an *e-y*'), who had a nose ring, a wiry middle-aged frame that spoke of excessive exercise, and a clientele that was exclusively white, apart from Shawn and a light-skinned Indian called Natasha, who turned out to be Canadian Indian and married to a Zimbabwean Indian, who owned the local Mahindra tractor franchise.

At the end of the class, Toney offered around green tea in delicate china tumblers. Shawn and April were the only takers. Shawn had no pressing reason to get home and it seemed April had a pressing reason not to, since her husband had agreed to put their son to bed and she didn't want to interrupt the process.

While the two of them sipped their tea, Toney began a long and elaborate monologue of a kind Shawn recognised as ritual for white Zimbabweans when engaging for the first time with foreigners of any hue. It was a testing of the water, a play for one voice, a sophisticated sonar establishing the shape and substance of nearby obstacles: 'No, but this place, it's the lifestyle, hey? You don't get this lifestyle anywhere else, I swear. But it's a beautiful country.

'Of course, it's not like it was before. I mean, killing each other? Even in the government. That general he was, like, right at the top of the whole bloody thing!

'But listen to me. How long have you been here, Shawn? You like it, isn't it? I wondered if you are one of those ones who left after Independence. I mean, there were black ones as well as white ones, hey? I'm telling you.'

Shawn looked at her with amused bewilderment and said he wasn't one of *those ones*. In fact he was from Queens, New York, but his wife was a Zimbabwean. 'I'm an American by birth and upbringing, if not ancestry.'

Toney said, 'Is it?', an idiom Shawn thought he'd never get used to (the way it offered the courtesy of a question without any requisite interest in the answer). Then she launched into a convoluted and incongruous recommendation of a trip to the Eastern Cape where she'd spent much of her twenties, only now it was more touristy, but that was no reason not to go, hey? And there were some radical music festivals, and last year she'd taken acid with some trance DJs from Antwerp . . .

As Toney went to refill the teapot, April made an apologetic face at Shawn. He wasn't sure what she was apologising for – presumably her race or gender unless she felt particular ownership of (and responsibility for) the yoga class. When she spoke, however, he clocked that she was English, so perhaps she was apologising for that. It was a familiar, insincere trait he'd noted among English colleagues at Brown Brothers Harriman.

She said, 'Have you done much yoga?'

'Never.' Shawn shook his head. 'But we moved here and I thought, you know, it's a new start. Let me try out a few things.'

April smiled. 'When I saw you, I thought, He's done some yoga. Then I glanced over when we were doing the full boat and I was, like, Maybe not.'

'Gee, thanks.'

'It's a compliment!' April protested. 'I mean, people who do yoga look like they're in some kind of shape.'

Shawn raised an eyebrow and the corners of his mouth twitched. 'You and me just in the same class? I mean, no disrespect, but that German lady, Astrid or whatever? What she going to look like if she *don't* do yoga? Man! And I thought the US patented the fat motherfucker!'

April laughed in spite of herself and told Shawn that she was having a *braai* at the weekend and he should bring his family.

He'd mentioned this to Kuda when he got home and she said she didn't want to go – of course she didn't. He might have hoped that bringing his wife back to the city of her birth would relax her, maybe even build a few bridges between them, but the opposite had happened and she'd just retreated further behind those eyes that seemed to speak of nothing but her hurt. However, he'd let news of the 'party' slip in their daughter's presence and she'd nagged her mother hard and long enough that she eventually agreed.

Rosie almost burst with excitement. She said, 'Can Sasa come? Can Sasa come?'

'Who's Sasa?' Kuda asked.

'You ain't met Sasa, Ku?' Shawn exclaimed, in faux surprise. 'He's Rosie's best friend, these days.' And when his wife looked at him blankly, he said, 'Just invisible, that's all.'

'An imaginary friend?' Kuda said flatly. Then, with some animation, 'I don't want our daughter to have an imaginary friend, Shawn. I don't know who that is. Sasa? What does he want?'

Shawn looked from Kuda to Rosie, who was wide-eyed, confused. Her lip was trembling. He felt his temper rise. He took the little girl by the wrist and led her out of the room, simultaneously calling to Gladys, the maid. When he returned to his wife, she was wearing the familiar look of wronged defiance and he struggled to control his voice as he hissed, 'Jesus, Kuda! Jesus! You need help, you know that? You really need some help!'

'*I* need help?' she spat back.

'Yeah, you do,' he said. 'The fucking African queen.'

The *braai* was nothing special: the Brits, apart from April and her husband, were kind of dicks. But Shawn enjoyed having a beer with some fellow foreigners and was pleased that they seemed as thrown by Zimbabwe (even if they claimed the opposite) as he was himself. It wasn't like he'd expected his first trip to Africa to be some kind of spiritual homecoming (after all, Kuda's parents and sister had visited them in New York so he'd already experienced the full breadth of the cultural chasm), but he hadn't expected to feel quite this alien either. There was a simplicity in talking to his fellow countrymen, the French woman, that Italian couple, even the British, which made him feel like he was relaxing for the first time in a month. And, of course, it wasn't just a break from Zimbabwe, but a break from his wife too – Kuda just sat on her own, sipped her juice, kept herself to herself and only spoke when spoken to.

Shawn told the other guests about his background at NYU Stern, his time at BBH and his plans now he was branching out on his own with a little seed capital. He said, 'There's money to be made here. I know there is. I mean, the mineral potential in this country's just crazy. But the way they got the law set up so you need a local partner – I already had meetings and it's, like, who you going to work with? The trouble is, you never know who's in whose pocket. And everything's so hand to mouth. They make fifty dollars, they not figuring how to turn it into a hundred, they already working out how to spend it.'

The others applied this to their own situations, whether in embassies, NGOs or day-to-day in the supermarket or wherever, and they all enthusiastically agreed. Soon after, the English lawyer (Tom?) even borrowed Shawn's turn of phrase in the midst of a quasi-racist diatribe about his staff.

The lawyer's clueless rant was an unwitting contribution to a bigger argument between April and her husband. Even coming to it cold, Shawn recognised the tension between them at once and couldn't believe it wasn't obvious to everyone. Then again, perhaps for him it was all too familiar and he sympathised with both, even cracking a quasi-racist gag of his own in a futile attempt to defuse the situation. It was a technique he'd learned on Wall Street: dropping a 'nigger' onto a white argument was like hosing a dogfight. All parties stopped and stared at you with horror and new-found respect. On this occasion, though it shocked the onlookers, the couple in question remained locked in their anger. Their shit was deep, Shawn thought.

20

Later, when Shawn was devouring a plate of salad, April approached him. She said, 'You don't want a burger? Or ribs?'

Shawn answered through a mouthful of carrot and beetroot. He said he was keeping it ital. She raised an eyebrow. 'Ital,' he said. 'You know. Like, vital. Just natural foods. It's Rasta.'

'Are you a Rasta?' she asked doubtfully.

Shawn smiled, 'Only like I do yoga,' he said.

April smiled too, nodded, then looked around, like she was scared she was being watched. She told him she'd been listening to what he'd said about needing a black Zimbabwean to comply with indigenisation; someone honest, down-to-earth and, you know, politically acceptable. She said maybe she knew the guy: a lawyer she'd met, older, kind of an idealist, war vet, but seemed like his heart was in the right place.

Shawn said, 'Cool. Thanks,' and asked her why she looked so nervous. She shrugged. She said she didn't know. She reappraised that: hooking up business deals wasn't exactly part of her job description at the embassy, though she kind of wished it was since her job was somehow conspiring to be stressful and tedious all at once and what was that about?

Shawn dropped his chin a little and looked up at her. 'Well, thanks.'

'No problem.' She shook her head as if she were trying to loosen her curls. For some reason she couldn't identify, she felt momentarily embarrassed. 'I'll call you.'

'Great,' Shawn said. Then, 'I'm sorry about Kudakwashe.'

'What?'

'My wife.' He glanced over to where she was. 'She's not usually like this – antisocial. She's not been well.'

'I didn't think anything,' April said. She was lying. 'What's ...' she began, then reconsidered the question and asked another instead. 'Is that why you came back to Zimbabwe?'

'Something like that,' Shawn said, and he was lying as well, only better, and he experienced the light-headedness that told him he'd entered the realm of deception, a comforting world where he could make sense of everything with a few unimport-ant untruths. 'Yeah,' he said, confirming it. 'That's why I brought her home.'

April now regarded him with such sympathy that he had to look away, back to Kuda, who was sitting alone on the corner of the veranda, staring straight ahead. He followed her line of vision and saw Rosie leading Theo, April and Jerry's two-year-old son, by the hand. A smile played on his lips and fixed there as his daughter opened the gate to the pool fence, which should have been locked shut. Everything slowed as she closed the gate behind them. Shawn looked to his wife, the closest adult, but she was still just staring. Later, he told everyone that he'd shouted, but he wasn't sure if that was true. He wasn't sure what was true. Certainly, he watched, seemingly transfixed, as Rosie took the little boy to the water's edge and then, with a mixture of pulling and pushing, heaved him quite deliberately into the pool.

Shawn said, 'Jesus,' and before the child broke the surface he was moving at a run. He shouted, 'No!' and he heard voices behind him, April's scream, the shift of group attention.

He reached the fence. For some reason, he couldn't open the gate. He could hear his breathing. Rosie was looking up at him from the poolside. Her expression said nothing. She was unmoved by her daddy's panic. The little boy was under water. Shawn stepped back. He tried to vault the fence, caught his trailing foot, flopped heavily onto the paving around the pool and then rolled into the water. He opened his eyes and there was Theo below him, not thrashing around, just sinking. Shawn kicked down, grabbed an arm and pulled. The boy was dead weight. Shawn tried to control his rising panic. He was at the bottom of the pool, perhaps ten feet down. He put his shoulder into Theo's midriff and pushed off from the floor. It must have been less than a second before the two of them broke the surface, but it felt much longer. And now there were hands reaching for the boy and hauling him easily out of the water.

Shawn clung to the side of the pool, choking snotty fluid, sucking deep breaths. He opened his eyes and they stung with chlorine. He found he was millimetres from the boy's small, pale foot. The foot twitched. He heard the sound of retching. He heard Jerry say, 'He'll be all right.' And then again, only sounding this time as if he actually believed it: 'It's fine. He's fine. He'll be all right.'

Shawn was pulled out of the pool by two or three of the other guests. They slapped him on the back. They said things like 'Thank God!' and 'Fuck, man. I mean, fuck . . .' He wrung out his shirt. He sniffed. He emptied his ears of water. He looked to where his wife had been sitting and there she was still, apparently unmoved.

PART TWO

21

Jerry Jones drained his beer and ordered another while Dr Tangwerai was in the Gents. Jerry had never met anyone who needed to piss so much. Tangwerai was on his fourth piss after a fourth Castle. Jerry was coming close to outpacing him two to one on drinks and had yet to spring a leak.

He looked around the Jameson Hotel's public bar. He checked the time on his phone: half six. The bar was probably around peak capacity: ninety per cent men at the end of their working day, ten per cent prostitutes at the beginning of theirs. At five thirty it had been more or less empty and in an hour it would be thinning out, but right now it was heaving with what Jerry identified, admittedly projecting for all he was worth, as a kind of desperate, booze-fuelled garrulousness.

In recent weeks, particularly since the *braai* fiasco, Jerry had taken to regular heavy drinking, a pattern of behaviour that April had decided to counter with a contained fury in which the effort of containment was all too plain. Although her chosen attitude had unarguable moral superiority, it meant that she had directly addressed his drinking only once: in a sustained volley during which she blamed it for the state of their relationship, which had unquestionably slipped to an all-time nadir. Of course, Jerry knew this was ridiculous and said as much with (somewhat drunken) moral superiority of his own: if one insisted on establishing a sequence of events, there was no doubt the failing relationship had driven him to the bottle rather than vice versa. But later, in the self-imposed exile of the spare room while staring dazedly at the mysterious paisley shapes of pitch darkness, he had had to admit that playing the game of cause and effect amid the complexities of a collapsing marriage was inherently deceitful, and the only thing that could be said with any certainty was that his current behaviour was resolving nothing and helping nobody. Consequently, he became a regular at various bars around town, recruiting a variety of drinking buddies, since the only possible outcome of his late-night moment of clarity (other than to stop drinking) was to drink more, and more often, in the company of the like-minded.

He soon discovered that Harare was full of these: every bar stool was seemingly occupied by some fellow, somewhat inebriated, who would happily swap anecdotes about wives, girlfriends or both in a tone that was sometimes frustrated and sometimes lascivious but always contemptuous. Jerry didn't know if this phenomenon of clubbable male estrangement was specifically Zimbabwean or if his experience of it simply reflected his new circumstance (after all, back in the UK, he couldn't remember ever sitting in a pub alone), but he took guilty pleasure from his membership of what felt like a louche and daring secret society.

His guilt stemmed both from the misogyny he revealed, and from the fact that nothing he said even touched upon reality, except in so far as to express his general discontentment with his wife. Once, for example, at the Maiden, the pub in Harare Sports Club overlooking the cricket pitch, he told a complete stranger how his wife was always in a bad mood and, using a mixture of euphemism, insinuation and mumble, managed to convey his belief that this was because she didn't have sex with him enough and, what was more, that this exemplified the crucial point that she – like, in fact, all women – didn't know what was good for her. Much to Jerry's surprise, his companion not only took his story at face value, but had experienced the very same trend in his own marriage, a discovery that even had Jerry briefly believing his own bullshit.

Tangwerai emerged from the Gents. When it came to Jerry's drinking companions, the doctor was the exception to whom the Englishman never mentioned his marital problems. This was partly because the pair worked together and Jerry instinctively (if not consciously) knew better than to pollute an ongoing relationship with untruths that might one day require justification or denial. It was mostly, however, because Tangwerai was a widower. For Jerry to start bad-mouthing his wife in the company of a man who'd lost his seemed ... well, it seemed lots of things, but foremost among them was *wrong*.

Jerry had found out the raw facts of Tangwerai's status within a couple of days of their acquaintance: he had asked the doctor if he was married and been told plainly, 'My wife is late.' However, in the subsequent weeks, he had uncovered little further information. He knew that the bereavement was recent ('Last year,' Tangwerai had said, when asked in that same exchange) and that the doctor now lived with his sister and six-year-old son, but he had no idea how the woman had died and, for some reason, struggled to ask. Jerry considered how he might feel if April had died in the last twelve months and imagined it would be something ever-present: a chronic pain, a weight in his stomach, a desperate breathlessness that would roll through him in peaks and troughs and regularly reduce him to tears or strike him with panic or leave him stultified. 'And I don't even like her,' he said to himself, drunk and bitter.

But Tangwerai, at least superficially, seemed to have moved on from his wife's passing: never pausing mid-consultation to look away, never dabbing at a welling eye, never taking a moment to sit alone and wallow in the horrible injustice of it all. And, for some reason, Jerry thought this apparent lack of emotion simultaneously intriguing and somehow threatening; particularly when drunk, he found question after question crowding the tip of his tongue, like commuters at a rush-hour bus stop.

Jerry held up his beer bottle by way of an offer. Tangwerai shook his head. 'Enough for me. I want to get home before my sister puts Bradford to bed.'

'One for the road,' Jerry pushed.

'You don't want to go home or you are trying to get me drunk.' The doctor smiled. 'You know, my boy doesn't like it when I have been drinking. "Daddy, you smell of beer," he says. Just like that.'

'There's nothing wrong with drowning your sorrows once in a while.'

'True enough, my friend.' Tangwerai nodded. His eyes, magnified by the thick spectacles, betrayed nothing. He gave Jerry his hand. His grip was firm and his palm warm and dry. He said, 'Till tomorrow.'

Jerry watched the doctor's exit, the confident grace with which the small man negotiated the crowded bar despite the somewhat comedic flapping of his over-sized suit, and felt suddenly and profoundly ashamed of himself. Jerry knew why he felt ashamed, but the reason the feeling had chosen that moment to surface so poignantly was beyond him.

22

'May I?'

A thick-set man, late forties, suit, was hovering by the seat Tangwerai had just vacated.

'Be my guest,' Jerry said.

'Thank you.' The man struggled to manoeuvre himself onto the bar stool, huffing somewhat and exuding the sickly smell of flesh and booze. 'You're drinking alone? Nobody should have to drink alone.'

'My friend just left.'

'But you decided to stay. I will keep you company. Two tots of Scotch whisky, that's my poison.' He settled onto the stool and looked at Jerry closely, a thick furrow above his brow. Jerry looked right back at him, unblinking. He'd spent enough time in the city's bars to be familiar with these macho games of pressure and obligation, even if he couldn't quite figure out their rules or precise purpose. He wasn't in the mood. The man cracked a smile that revealed pale pink amphibian gums and reached into his jacket pocket to produce a silver money clip. 'I am joking. What will you have?'

Jerry shrugged. 'A Castle. Thanks.' He stared at the money clip.

It was thick with bills, though he had no idea of the denominations. Jerry had never met anyone who carried a money clip before and for a moment he thought he might burst out laughing. It appeared to crystallise something he'd been thinking, which hadn't previously cohered into words. The bar's décor, the waiters' bow-ties, the clientele's moustaches, cigarettes and polyester suits, the money clip: Jerry had the sensation that he was in a 1970s cinema ad – 'For a swinging night out, visit the Jameson, adjacent to this theatre.' He found that he was smiling. He picked up his fresh beer, clinked with his new companion, and they dropped easily into conversation, the man opening with the usual questions and Jerry wheeling out his usual replies – 'Leatherhead'; 'Not London exactly, kind of like a suburb'; 'Almost five months'; 'My wife's work'; 'The British Embassy'; 'Me? A nurse'; 'No, never my ambition'; 'No, haven't got a visa. I'm just volunteering at a clinic'; 'Just one. Theo. He's two'; 'Greendale. You know Arcturus Road? Just off there.'

The man asked how Jerry found Zimbabwe and Jerry said he liked it very much and it was certainly an easy place for a Brit. The man nodded, and observed that this was unsurprising, considering almost a century of colonial rule: 'More British than the British.'

Jerry studied his expression for signs of hostility but found none. He said he knew what the guy meant but, actually, the longer he stayed, the more foreign he felt. 'Everyone speaks good English and watches American TV and listens to bad rap music – just like the UK. But whenever I scratch the surface I find I just don't get it.'

The thick-set man patted him matily on the arm. 'We are Africans,' he said, less explanation than marker to allow the conversation to move on.

But now, fizzing with fizzy lager, Jerry didn't want to move on and he heard himself say, 'Take death, for example . . .' And he launched into an expansive explanation of his colleague Dr Tangwerai's situation (so far as he understood it), a detailed description of his behaviour and a thorough account of what he, Jerry, found peculiar about it.

Jerry's companion listened politely, then said, 'What is it you expect this colleague of yours to do?'

'I don't know. Nothing. Something. We've become friends. We have a drink together. I'm just surprised he doesn't talk about his wife.'

'To you. He does not talk about her *to you*.'

'No.' Jerry shook his head. 'I'm sure he doesn't talk about her at all.'

The man shook his head too. 'She is dead, isn't it? What do you want him to say?'

'I don't know.'

The man drained his Scotch. He flashed the glass at Jerry, who ordered him another. 'Here in Zimbabwe,' he said, 'I don't think we see death like it is in UK.'

'I know,' Jerry interrupted. He'd heard this before. 'Death is part of life, I get that. And I know in the West we all think we're immortal.'

'It is not just death. It is catastrophe. The whites I have met don't know what to do when there is catastrophe. They think it will never happen. Zimbabweans, blacks, we expect a catastrophe and we know what to do. We don't panic. Our economy collapses, money's worth nothing, HIV, angry ancestors, failing crops, crashing cars, all of these things . . . and still we get up in the morning and still we have to feed ourselves and our children, isn't it? You guys with your insurance and credit and pensions and welfare state, I think you have plenty of time to worry. Whites . . .' Jerry wasn't looking at the man. He was examining the hair on his knuckles, picking dry skin from around his fingernails. But this repetition of 'whites' made him glance up and, though there was no visible change of expression, he was sure he hadn't mistaken the contemptuous tone; and now it came again. '. . . whites. It is the mark of how civilised you are, your freedom to worry.'

Jerry sipped his beer. Now it was his turn simply to want to move the conversation on. He looked the man directly in the eye. 'You know what Gandhi said about Western civilisation?'

'What's that?'

'That it would be a good idea.'

His companion smiled and any tension was gone. There were those pink gums again; not amphibian, Jerry thought, but piscine. The man examined the ice cubes in the bottom of his glass as if he expected to find something there.

23

'My youngest son is a cripple,' the man said. 'Ten years old and he walks with a frame. The doctors say that, as he grows, maybe he will not be able to walk at all. You are a nurse, isn't it? What is that?'

'I don't know. Could be lots of things. Was he sick when he was younger?'

'No, he was not sick.'

Jerry shrugged. 'I don't know.'

The man studied his face, as if checking whether he believed him. Then he said, 'Genetic. That is what they say: a genetic disorder.' He drained the rest of his whisky. He spat out an ice cube.

He lifted a finger at the barman and an eyebrow at Jerry, who said, 'I'm fine for the moment.'

The man took a second to consider whether this was acceptable. Then he nodded. 'My wife found it very difficult,' he continued. 'She believed people looked at him and thought we must have done something wrong. In the end, we took him to the *n'anga*. You know this word? It is what we call a spirit medium, like a traditional healer.'

'Sure.'

'We took him to the *n'anga*. We discovered the source of the problem. We made some sacrifices.'

'What was the problem?'

'What was the problem?' The man repeated the question and considered Jerry ruefully. 'Issues in the family. The problem is always issues in the family. But we consulted the *n'anga*, we made some sacrifices and we solved the problem.' The man blinked, too slowly, in a manner that seemed to convey deep, albeit unknown, significance. 'And do you think it has improved my son's legs?'

'Doubt it,' Jerry said.

'No. And yet we have solved the problem. Do you see?'

'Not really.'

The man gave a short, unamused chuckle and exclaimed, 'Ah! You are very English, my friend!' Then he shook his head and sat back on his stool. 'Come on, man, keep up. Everything about being an African is right there! You people? You are free to do what you want, for better or worse. But we are superstitious people. Africans are superstitious people, so we are always caught up in these webs of obligation and blame and, even if you run away, you can never escape, you know?' Now Jerry's companion leaned in and held his left forearm, thick fingers tight on the shirtsleeve. 'Family, friends, *work*. You cannot see these . . . these . . . What are they? These *restraints*. But you feel them holding you back and rubbing you raw.'

'Even now?' Jerry said.

'What do you mean "even now"?'

Jerry freed his arm to lift his beer. 'I mean even now. In 2011. This is a modern country.'

'Ha!' the man exclaimed. 'Yes! Even now! You know, my boss, he's a very important guy. He is an important guy because he knows how to create a situation of duty and debt. He's a very clever guy, very modern. You think I could ever go against my boss? No way.'

His companion was looking at him so intently that Jerry felt he had no option but to be flippant. 'Perhaps you need a new job,' he remarked.

The man stared at him momentarily, then smiled: those gums. Jerry was drunk. He found himself picturing Bessie, standing at the sink, efficiently gutting bream. He needed to eat something.

'You're right,' the man said at last. 'Perhaps I need a new job.'

Jerry said he should go. The man nodded and slid off his bar stool. 'Back to the wife,' he said.

'Yeah,' Jerry said. 'Something like that.'

They walked outside together. Jerry found himself swaying slightly, struggling to avoid the pedestrians on the busy city street. He was drunker than he'd realised.

He was looking for Patson's cab, the navy blue Raum with 'Gapu Taxis' in bright yellow on the side. He couldn't see it. He was now using the cab on an almost daily basis: to take him to and from the clinic, to take him to or from whichever bar – it was easier than arguing with April for use of the Land Cruiser. As a rule, he preferred it if Patson were driving, because when Gilbert – Bessie's husband, Patson's brother-in-law – had the wheel, he talked incessantly, telling Jerry his plans and, particularly, his business ideas with puppyish enthusiasm. Worst of all, he seemed to believe that Jerry might be prepared to advise or even invest. Patson, on the other hand, was largely silent. The downside was that the older man had a tendency to go AWOL if he got the offer of another job, even if he'd been asked to wait. And then they had to go through this whole rigmarole of lies as Jerry threatened to find another taxi and Patson swore he was only seconds away.

Jerry dialled and lifted the phone to his ear: 'Where are you?'

'I am very close, Uncle,' Patson said. 'I will be there just now.'

Jerry tutted and cut the call. He turned to his companion from the bar, who was looking at him quizzically. 'Your driver?' the man asked.

'Cab,' Jerry said.

The man opened an arm into the street. 'There are plenty of taxis.'

'I know this guy,' Jerry said. 'I like him.'

The man raised an amused eyebrow. 'And he is taking advantage,' he said. He offered Jerry his hand. 'It was good talking to you.' The two men shook. 'You were saying you were having trouble with your visa. Perhaps I can help. I can help with lots of things. I know some people.'

'Thanks,' Jerry said, 'but I know people who know people. No luck so far.'

The man smiled. It was, Jerry thought, a sinister expression. He decided he didn't like the guy much. 'Perhaps you know the wrong people,' the man said. 'Or perhaps they know the wrong people.' He opened his arms – *Who knows?* 'In this country, you need to know people. But I'm sure you understand that. I am lucky to know a lot of people and I would always be happy to help a visitor like yourself.'

'Thanks very much,' Jerry said. 'That's kind.'

'What's your name?' the man said. 'We have been talking all this time and I don't even know your name.'

'Jerry. Jerry Jones.'

'Mandiveyi,' the man said. 'Albert Mandiveyi. Take my number.'

The two men shook hands again. They swapped mobile numbers. Mandiveyi made sure that Jerry entered his name correctly. He admired Jerry's iPhone. Jerry slurred some vague small-talk about how the iPhone wasn't all it was cracked up to be. They shook hands a third time. Mandiveyi said, 'It was good to meet you, Nurse Jerry.'

'Likewise.'

Mandiveyi flagged down a taxi and was gone. Patson pulled up seconds later, profusely apologetic. They barely talked on the way out to Greendale.

The house was dark and silent. The guard – Petros? – was asleep. The Land Cruiser was in the driveway. Jerry checked his watch: eight – April was home early. For once, she wouldn't be able to complain of a lack of sleep. Jerry struggled with his keys. He stopped in the kitchen. There was no food out for him. He cut a piece of cheese and looked for bread. There was no bread. He ate the cheese with his fingers. He turned on the alarm and turned off the lights. He was about to go straight into the spare room, but saw the light under the master-bedroom door. He had an unlikely, drunken vision of his wife waiting up for him, eager for his return. He opened the door. April was sitting up in bed, reading. She didn't acknowledge his arrival. She turned a page. Jerry stripped off his jeans and exchanged one T-shirt for another. April's attention didn't flicker. Jerry climbed into bed. Without looking up, April said, 'You're not going to brush your teeth?'

'No,' Jerry said.

'Are you drunk?'

'Yes.'

Jerry lay on his side, watching his wife. She kept reading until eventually he turned over. He closed his eyes. He could feel April's presence behind him and he couldn't relax. He imagined how it would feel if she buried a knife in his back. He was just drifting into inebriated sleep when she said, 'I wanted to tell you something.'

Jerry opened his eyes. He found the room was slowly starting to move around him. He focused on the cupboard door to concentrate his mind. He said, 'So tell me.'

'I can't talk to you when you're drunk,' she said.

'So talk to me when I'm sober.'

He heard her shut her book. She said, 'Do I need to make an appointment?'

Jerry heard his wife slide out of bed. He didn't look up as the bedroom door opened and closed. April had gone to the spare room. He felt fleeting vindication, which even his drunken self couldn't ratify. He rolled over and switched out the bedside light. He spread himself on the bed as if this was what he'd wanted all along. The pitch darkness didn't stop the room spinning; quite the opposite. He slipped into unconsciousness but was awake again within minutes when he knew he was going to vomit. He stumbled to the bathroom and was sick. He tried to be sick quietly. He hoped that April wasn't hearing this.

24

When Patson spotted the *murungu* emerging from the Jameson bar arm in arm with Mandiveyi, the CIO who'd dropped the gun in his cab, his heart stopped beating. The *murungu* scanned this way and that, looking for him. Patson slipped the car into gear and, without turning on the headlights, swung left along Samora Machel and ignored the angry horns until he could pull in a hundred metres further up the road. He then stopped, got out and lit a cigarette, which gave him a sharp pain in his chest. He held a palm to his sternum and his heartbeat was fast and irregular.

His phone rang in his pocket. He took it out and answered. 'I am very close, Uncle,' he said. 'I will be there just now.'

He moved onto the shadowed step of an office block from where he could just about see the two men. They were talking like old friends. This was just a coincidence – it had to be a coincidence. Harare was a small town and he was always going to run into Mandiveyi again at some point.

By the time he saw Dr Gapu two days later to pay his weekly rental, he had removed the 'Gapu Taxis' stickers from the car. He should have done it before. But he'd figured that, on the night of the incident, the CIO had been so drunk that he would surely remember nothing about the cab he'd taken or its driver. Only when Patson saw him again, in the flesh, did he understand with a sudden and breathtaking certainty that this was an assumption he couldn't afford to make.

Of course, Gapu was none too pleased to discover that the stickers he'd had custom made by Starlight Adhesives Msasa (PVT Ltd) had been so recklessly abandoned. However, Patson pointed out that the doctor hadn't paid for a municipal taxi licence. Consequently, Patson was consistently pulled over by the cops and forced to spend half an hour arguing his poverty or otherwise pay a fine. 'It is better this way, Uncle,' he told Gapu. 'This way I just use clients on the phone. It is much, much better.' Any doubts the cab owner had about Patson's argument were mollified when the driver paid not just the two hundred dollars' weekly rental, but a further twenty towards his long-standing arrears.

Patson was home in Sunningdale by seven thirty. This was his new routine. Four nights a week, he ate with Fadzai, Gilbert and the kids, before Gilbert took the car out again for the night shift. Patson was loath to admit it, but his brother-in-law was proving a blessing, with a seemingly limitless work ethic that belied his feckless reputation. Gilbert helped at Fadzai's kitchen from Monday to Thursday before taking the cab out in the evenings, then drove the day shift in the taxi on Friday, Saturday and Sunday. It was no exaggeration to say that Gilbert's contribution had revolutionised the household – Patson's taxi was making almost double money, and Gilbert's loyalty scheme seemed to have eliminated Fadzai's competition, letting her clear up to a hundred and fifty dollars at the end of each week.

Most of all, something had shifted between the married couple, a shift of which Patson had long given up hope. Where for years they had moved in separate orbits – around the house, around their children – Patson and Fadzai now, suddenly, found synchronicity. There were little things that signalled this – the way she served his food and made his tea, for example, or the fact he now allowed her to bathe before him in the morning and felt no inconvenience. But there were big things, too: they now sat on the veranda when Chabarwa and Anashe were asleep and the silence was companionable and his wife would even light a match for his last cigarette of the night.

And, of course, there was the rekindling of their sex life. So recently the act of going to bed each night had been a statement of war, whoever made the first move seemingly saying, 'You see? This is what I think of you.' Now they seemed to melt beneath the blankets simultaneously, silently folding into one another, and within seconds it was as if each didn't know which limb, which mouth, which hand was their own; and all was hot, lubricious and unidentifiable sweat and spittle and juice.

On one occasion, afterwards, Patson said to Fadzai, 'We are like newlyweds again.' Fadzai said nothing, then murmured a vague but conclusive affirmative. In that instant, Patson understood his wife perfectly. Because they both knew that it hadn't been like this at all when they were newlyweds. Where their sex life as a young couple had been frequent and urgent – brief and memorable acts of explosive copulation – it was now of a different order entirely: soft, slow and strangely, dizzily, all-consuming. Fadzai's murmur, therefore, was one of assent, but it also told him not to talk further. Because she understood – and, now, he understood too – that this new synchronicity was a magical thing, which shouldn't be explained, analysed or discussed for fear of breaking the spell.

Secretly, Patson considered he might know the source of the magic, and early the next morning, when his wife was bathing, he went to the chest of drawers and took out Mandiveyi's gun. He tried to grip it, to see how it felt in his hand. He read and re-read its mysterious inscription: 'SIG SAUER, Sig Arms Inc, Herndon VA'. He then buried it at the very back of the drawer and vowed not to look at it again.

Since the first night he and Fadzai had discussed his options, Patson had turned them over in his mind again and again and he had quickly concluded that his wife's position on the matter made little sense. She had told him not to dispose of the gun in case Mandiveyi came looking and he was left with no bargaining chip. But Patson knew that, if the CIO came looking, admitting he'd had it all along was less bargaining chip than admission of guilt. What was more, Patson felt his subconscious working through a terrifying equation that he didn't dare allow to crystallise. He knew the rumours surrounding Rex Nhongo's death: about those in government who would benefit, about the gunshots heard before the fire. But he reassured himself that there was no reason to assume a connection and he ignored the concomitant implication that there was also no reason to assume none. Either way, it was surely better to throw the weapon into the river as he'd originally planned and, if it came to it, deny any knowledge of its existence. And yet he couldn't bring himself to do it. Because Patson had come to believe that it was the gun that had transformed his marriage, its magic the magic of fear that bound the two of them clinging together in the unspoken thrill of a shared threat that could take away everything they had. And all they had was each other.

25

Sasa and me in the TV room. In Amerika, Momma only let me watch one day a week, but now I watch evry day. An evry day Mom come in an she say, 'You watch too much TV, Rosie.' An I say, 'I don!' An she look at me an it like she don know whadda say next an fold her arms an jus stare an, long as I stare right back, I know that she gonna look down and give up in the end. This time, tho, she come in wid Gladys an they both stand there, arms folded, lookin at me an then each other like I already done sumthin naughty.

Momma say, 'Isn't this scary, Rosie?'

I turn to the TV. Iss a cartoon about the puss in boots what got a sword an fight against an evil ogre by stabbin his toes. 'Iss not scary.'

'Watching on your own . . .' Momma say.

'I not watchin on my own,' I say. 'I watchin with Sasa.'

Momma look at Sasa, but I know she can't see him, even though he flappin his wings, an sayin, 'Look at me! Look at me!' Then she turn to Gladys with eyes like a question an Gladys shake her head an walk in front of the TV so that her big backside in the way an she say, 'Enough TV for today, little bird.'

Sasa start jumpin up an down an his mouth all little sharp teeth an he sayin all kinda curse words like Daddy when he angry, an I giggle cos I the only one can hear them.

Gladys tryin to turn off the TV only she don know how cos she jus the maid. So I slide off the couch an I start to scream – 'No! No! No!' – an I hit Gladys hard as I can.

Mom say, 'Rosie! Stop it!'

But I don stop it and Mom come over an try an pick me up. So I struggle an flap my wings jus like Sasa, an he goin, 'Bite her! Bite her!' So I do. I bite Gladys jus as hard as I can on her leg, an now she scream too. An it sound so funny that I laugh an Momma holdin me under my arms, right up to her face, an she say, 'It's not funny, Rosie! Stop it! Stop it!'

An I say, 'Iss funny!'

She whisk me through the house an put me on the naughty step by the kitchen door an I start cryin and she say, 'You stay there till you learn how to behave, Rosie. Ten minutes. On your own.'

I cry harder cos, whateva Sasa say, I don want Mom to hate me. But she wrong cos I not on my own an Sasa go, 'There, there, little bat.'

Even though I don want to cos I still sad, I laugh an I say, 'I'm not a little bat! I'm a little bird!'

An Mom turn round an she go, 'What you say?'

So I jus bow my head an make a sad face again.

On Sunday, it jus me an Momma cos Gladys don come Sundays an Daddy away workin again like always. She give me bath time and breakfast all by myself an then she cornrow my hair an, even though I complain cos I don like all that pullin, I like it too cos Sasa not there for a change an it jus me and Momma an she look at me like she use to when I was a little girl in Amerika. She put on my best dress with the purple butterfly on the front, which Aunty Dionne sent me by post on my birthday, an she go, 'You look smart, little bird!'

We early at church cos Momma say she gotta talk to the pastor. We go to a house behind the church an the pastor meet her at the door an hold her one hand in his two. He look down at me with one of them big smile that don mean nuthin an he say, 'Look at you, Rosie! Growing bigger every day!'

Him and Momma talk in his office while I sit outside on a plastic chair. The pastor's wife, who wear make-up like a clown an kinda scary, bring me orange juice. Altho I do bad things, I'm a good girl, so I tell her that I not allowed juice before lunchtime. She go an aks my mom who say iss OK jus this once. Thas how I know that what she talkin about with the pastor sure serious.

When they come out, pastor got his arm round Momma's shoulders an she been cryin. But I know not to say nuthin, cos when she cry an I say, 'You cryin, Momma?' she always say, 'No, little bird. Not crying.' So wos the point if she gonna lie?

The pastor look at me with those same eyes like a question. He turn to Momma an say, 'It'll be OK, Kuda. We are a strong congregation here at UFIC and the holy spirit works miracles.'

Tho Momma talk to the pastor for ages, we still sum of the first people in church – we real early. Generally, we sit near the back with Gogo, but today we right at the front behind the choir. I say, 'Momma? Am I goin to Sunday school today?' Cos I like to play wid other kids even if they don speak no English.

But Momma say, 'Not today, little bird.'

Church go on for ages an I so bored I can't keep still an Momma get cross, but she bring my crayons an paper so I draw a picture. I draw a picture of Sasa wid his big wings, pointed teeth an sharp claws. I try to show her but she all busy wid church an don look.

Then the pastor say sumthin an Mom pull me up an suddenly we right at the front an evryone lookin at us. I don know wos happenin but the pastor got his hand on Momma's shoulder an I can feel her shakin. He go, 'Many of you know our sister, Kudakwashe, recently returned from the States.' Then he say sum other stuff I don unnerstan, but I unnerstan the people real excited all right.

The pastor tell Momma to let me go an she do like he says. I scared now an I start cryin – why Momma don like me watchin the puss in boots but do this? The pastor say, 'It's OK, Rosie. Don't be afraid.' He touch me on my forehead an my chest, even though my dad say no man allowed to touch me there but him.

I don know what happen after that. Nex, I jus outside the church an Momma holdin me an she still shakin an evryone comin up to her an goin, 'God bless you' an 'Trust the power of the spirit.'

Momma say, 'How do you feel, little bird?'

An I say, 'Fine.'

The pastor come up an he go, 'This is a . . .' I can't say the word. '. . . spirit, Kuda. I haven't seen it before. It's not from Zimbabwe. Did you hear its language? Maybe Twi.' Then, when Momma look shock, he go, 'It's gone now, Kuda. It's gone. Everything will be OK.'

When we get home, Momma different. Iss like she had hiccups an now they better. She say, 'What do you want to do, little bird? Let's do some baking. Cookies.'

An I say, 'I wanna watch TV.'

But it don make her angry. She smile at me. She go, 'OK.' An turn on the TV for me even tho I know how to do it my own self.

Sasa sittin on the couch. He say, 'Where you been?'

'Church,' I say.

An he say, 'How was it?'

An I say, 'Fine.'

He look at me like I already done sumthin naughty an he start to bounce up an down an shout an scream until I don hear nuthin else.

26

Late afternoon, Shawn Appiah sat in the driver's seat of the battered Isuzu *bakkie*, legs splayed out of its open door, smoking a cigarette and shading his eyes against the bright orange sun making a rapid descent over the golden hills of . . . wherever the fuck he was. He resented the fact he was smoking, because he didn't like the taste and it made his lungs feel like shit. But he needed something to do with his hands, something to pass the time. At home, in New York, he'd have been tugging on a reefer, enjoying the calm wash right through him. He'd heard the local grass was good, but he'd decided early on that he couldn't be seen buying weed and such-like. He'd already concluded that, in the absence of sufficient water and electricity, Harare ran largely on gossip.

Shawn was all about business, and business here meant playing the game. Playing the game was why he was smoking cigarettes, why he was driving this crappy truck, why he was watching Peter Nyengedza, his geriatric co-director in the recently formed NA Holdings, standing on the *stoep* of some shitty shebeen ten klicks north of Mazowe Dam in intimate conversation with three gold-panners who, to judge by the threadbare state of their clothes, were hardly an advertisement for their industry.

Shawn watched the old man in his three-piece suit explaining the finer points of the deal. Every now and then, the panners looked towards the large American lounging in the truck, as if to confirm both their worst suspicions and best hopes. In the end, Shawn couldn't resist waving a smoke signal of greeting. 'Hello, motherfuckers!' he said loudly, confident they'd only half hear him and wouldn't understand anyway. One, the youngest, who was wearing a torn Lakers vest over a pair of denim shorts that revealed muddied ankles above filthy, bare feet, raised a nervous hand and half-smile by return. 'I fucking hate the Lakers,' Shawn announced to nobody.

This was the easiest way to make money that Shawn had ever discovered, so why was he finding it so hard? The principle was simplicity itself. Gold fetched around forty dollars a gram on the Harare market, while the desperate panners who were, frankly, often two-thirds of the way to starvation would accept as little as twenty-five, sometimes less. All Shawn had had to do, therefore, was buy a Gold Purchasing Licence from the Chamber of Mines, form a company and find an 'indigenous' Zimbabwean to take fifty-one per cent. This was where Peter Nyengedza came in – thanks to April Jones of the British Embassy, no less. Shawn had invested twenty-five thousand dollars, Nyengedza nothing but his name. Still, at the current rate of progress, NA Holdings was looking at an official return of a quarter of a mill in the first year and exponential growth thereafter. So, what was so hard about that?

Primarily Nyengedza. Shawn liked Nyengedza – respected him, at least. But Nyengedza laid down ground rules for the business that, even as they made sense, ticked Shawn off (because this was *his* idea and it wasn't like Nyengedza was risking jack). The old man, for example, had told Shawn he had to trade in his top-of-the-range Pajero for this piece of crap Isuzu, the reason being that a fancy car would lead to all sorts of fancier expectations from the panners selling gold in the fields. Fair enough. But Shawn couldn't help resenting the principle as he ground through the truck's gears on crummy dirt roads and seemed to spend as much time with his head under the bonnet as over the wheel.

Likewise, Nyengedza had insisted on making first contact with the panners. He would facilitate a relationship, which would allow Shawn to buy on his own thereafter. It was a plan that had already borne results with four 'collectives' in the Mazowe area. But if Shawn couldn't fault the old man's reasoning – Nyengedza spoke Shona and struck up a good rapport with the locals, which, in turn, enabled them to trust Shawn – the long-winded, ritualistic process of ingratiation drove him to distraction. Wasn't it simpler to just make these guys an offer, say, twenty bucks a gram, with twenty-five as your final position? Didn't they understand the basic principles of capitalism – supply and demand? Why all this need for soothing and buttering and false respect?

It was, in fact, the negotiating process that seemed to crystallise what Shawn was finding most difficult of all – simply, he was really starting to find himself hating Zimbabwe or, rather, its people.

Shawn stubbed out his cigarette. Nyengedza was approaching. Everything about the guy was meticulous, even the way he walked, picking his way through the dusk like Bambi through a minefield. Shawn swigged from his water bottle. He considered lighting another cigarette. He didn't. Instead, he reached under the passenger seat for his fanny pack, which held the cash. He switched on the interior light, so that he could see what he was doing. When Nyengedza eventually arrived, he said, 'Yes, Peter. How much have they got?'

'Quite a lot,' the old man said. 'They say they can bring a hundred grams tomorrow.'

'Tomorrow?'

'Tomorrow.'

'They haven't got it with them?'

'Yes.'

'Yes, they've got it with them or yes, they haven't?'

'Yes,' Nyengedza said. Then, sensing his partner's irritation, 'Yes, they haven't got it.'

'Fuck!' Shawn said. 'So now what?'

Nyengedza took his handkerchief from his breast pocket, carefully unfolded it, and blew his nose. 'The dust,' he said. 'This is a dusty place.' Then, 'They say there is a motel on the main road. We will come back in the morning when we can see what we are doing. We will buy groceries?'

'Groceries?'

'*Hupfu*, vegetables, chickens. These are hungry fellows. They will give it to us for groceries. Just give me one hundred. It will show we are serious.'

Shawn looked at Nyengedza. He shook his head. He said, 'A motel? I'm supposed to be back in H Town.'

Nyengedza looked back at Shawn, shook his head too, and his voice became impatient: 'It is one night in a motel. We give them a hundred dollars tonight and maybe we buy them two hundred dollars' worth of groceries and we have their gold. I thought you wanted us to make money?'

Shawn was taken aback. He stared at the old man while he did the sums in his head. They didn't make any sense. Even if the gold was shitty quality, they were looking at three and a half

K profit on a three-hundred-dollar investment. Was this even market economics? He wasn't sure any more. He peeled a single hundred-dollar bill from the roll in his fanny pack. He said, 'You're right. Of course you're right.'

It was now dark. In fact, it was so dark that Nyengedza walked three steps and vanished into the ink. Shawn laid his head back on the headrest. He took out his cell. The signal had been coming and going, but right now he had three bars. He made a call. 'Look,' he said, 'I'm not going to make it back tonight, OK? I'm still stuck out in Mazowe.' Then, 'I know. I'm not taking nothing for granted, believe me.' Then, 'I'll see you tomorrow.' He clicked the 'end' button. He checked the time in the light of the display. He considered calling his wife, but figured the maid would already have Rosie in the bath by now and he risked Kuda's accusation of interrupting his daughter's routine. Instead, he rejoined a game of Tetris he'd started an hour or so before. He lit another cigarette without thinking about it.

27

Shawn's hatred of Zimbabweans had, of course, started with his wife, and it predated their arrival in her mother country. But somehow, back in New York, he'd mistaken it for some kind of love.

Sure, Shawn knew he'd been a dog, and when Kuda had found out some details, he was racked with guilt and vowed to change before she found out any more. But as his weeks of good behaviour had turned to months and still he was given the cold shoulder, his patience had evaporated. Kuda had retreated into herself, spent hours on her own and wouldn't talk to him, except to confirm the most practical details of the school run, utility bills and the like. Eventually Shawn felt forced to conclude that this withdrawal was less about his behaviour than some deep-seated fissure inside her; that she had, in fact, been waiting for just such an opportunity for disappointment.

He had tried confronting it directly, but she'd looked at him sadly and said, 'You're not the man you pretend to be.'

He'd lost his temper. He said, 'Fuck that! Who the fuck you think I pretend to be? I don't pretend shit!' It didn't help.

Kuda began to find fault in everything he did and, worse,

everything about their lifestyle. Where once, for example, she'd puffed and passed with Shawn and his buddies, now she declared their house a weed-free zone – for Rosie's sake, she said, so that he couldn't argue the point.

She forbade their daughter to watch more than half an hour's TV a week. 'All the advertisements!' she declared. 'Everything in this country is sex! Sex to sell shampoo! Sex to sell soda! It's too much!' She began to complain about their neighbours, at first specifically – the unfriendly yuppies on the ground floor or the crackhead mom who lived opposite – then as a point of cultural principle: 'You people are so isolated. If there is a problem, who do you go to? There is no one.' She even began to hate the available shopping: the cereal was full of gluten, the tomatoes too watery, the milk laden with hormones.

Once, he'd got home to find her sitting at the kitchen table, contemplating two chicken legs, uncooked on a plate in front of her.

He tried to make a joke of it: 'You gonna cook those, boo? Or just stare at them?'

She spun round to him, eyes firing indignation. She picked up a leg and waved it at him like a ratchet. 'What chicken is this? What chicken is a size like this?' Then, 'How can I ask you? You don't even know what a chicken looks like. In Zimbabwe ...'

In Zimbabwe ...

That did it for Shawn. The last time Kuda had come back from a solo trip home in 2007, she'd returned with horror stories of the collapsing economy, empty supermarket shelves and shortages of just about everything. 'In Zimbabwe?' he repeated. 'Like it's the land of milk and fucking honey? Shit! You think there's one motherfucker in Zimbabwe who wouldn't trade for our life here? You want to go back there? That it?'

And Kuda froze, the chicken leg still raised above her head. 'Yes, Shawn,' she said. 'I talked to my mother. She said it is not so bad, these days. She said I should come home. That is what I want.'

They managed the move within six months. The way Shawn told it to his coterie at the time, this was a heroic, last-ditch attempt to save the failing marriage. The idea exemplified the most successful of Shawn's lies, since at some deep-seated level he almost believed it himself. The truth, however, was much more prosaic. The truth was that he had enabled the move because it sat comfortably in a false personal story he'd been cultivating since his teens.

Shawn was a conscious brother. At high school, this had mostly meant listening to the right music – PE, Dead Prez, Marvin and Nina. At college, he'd discovered that everybody listened to the right music, even the white kids. So he'd had to re-up. He joined groups that signified radicalism without compromising employment prospects. He briefly became a vegan. He briefly stopped drinking alcohol. He researched his family history and discovered a many-times-great-uncle who'd worked on a Georgia plantation for a man called James McClaren. He promised himself that he would lose the slave name, though it could wait until he had both feet securely on the career ladder.

Shawn had got the job at Brown Brothers Harriman. He was the nigger who said 'nigger' and a lot else besides. He accepted invitations from New York's public schools to talk about the possibilities for a young black male in the world of high finance. Some teachers fell in love with him and he memorably fucked one of them – a Jew called Ruth – two days before his wedding.

He married Kuda, and his boys, white and black, said, 'Of course! You going deep, bro.'

'You don't even know,' he replied. 'I paid *lobola*. Like, bride price. Cows and shit.'

He got a little drunk at a Christmas party and upbraided the BBH senior management for the fact that he was the only black guy at his level.

He found out about a project at NYU where they were testing African Americans' DNA to give answers about precise origins. He went along and discovered that the majority of his ancestry, albeit including a distressing white streak from mainland Europe, was from what was once called the Gold Coast – probably Akan, speakers of Twi or Fanti.

28

With Rosie now going to elementary school, Kuda completed her postgrad in community-health administration and learned enough to know she didn't want a career in it. Instead, she got a part-time job at a hippie jewellery store in Fort Green. One Saturday she got home early, just as Rita and her son, Angel, were leaving. Rita played it cool. She offered Kuda her hand. She said, 'You must be Kuda? I heard so much about you. Rita Perez. Angel and Rosie are in the same class. We thought we'd organise a play date.'

Kuda played it cooler still, insisting, now she was home, that Rita and Angel should stay for a cup of tea. 'I bought cookies,' she said.

Shawn went to the bathroom and washed his hands, but when he was sitting at the table, only half listening to the idle chat about Pine Hill and Rita's husband, Ronnie, and his current struggles as a realtor, he lifted a cookie to his mouth and he could still smell pussy on his fingers.

Shawn thought he'd got away with it. He was used to getting away with it. But that night, out of the blue, when he was brushing his teeth, Kuda said, 'You think it's fine to bring a married woman back to our home when I'm not here?'

Shawn swilled a mouthful of Listermint Total Defence and spat it into the basin. 'What?' he said.

'Because where I come from, it's not fine at all.'

Shawn stared at her. She was wearing a face mask and looked like a ghost. 'Yeah,' he said. 'It was a play date for Rosie. Yeah, I think it's fine.' Then, 'We're not where you come from. This is New York. You do know that, right?'

BBH hired a Nigerian called Ayo as the vice president of Shawn's group. She was fastidious, with a high-pitched voice, and she would never rock the corporate boat. He took the appointment personally. One thing was for sure: so long as she was there, playing the black card with her neat little dreadlocks and her white husband called Stuart, who was some big shot at Morgan Stanley, his career at the bank was going nowhere.

He called a summit meeting with his boys at Paddy's, a downbeat Irish pub in Midtown. He said, 'Jesus Christ! What is it about locks, man? You meet a high-flying sister with locks and you *know* she's hooked up with some white dude. How fucked up is that?'

His boys were drinking bourbon on his tab. His boys agreed with his analysis. His boys said it was 'time to make moves'. Malik downed another shot and said, 'So there's no room for a black man at Brown Brothers.'

'For real, bruh,' Shawn said. 'The irony isn't lost on me.'

He announced that he was done with BBH, that he was going to start putting feelers out, speaking to head hunters.

In his rush for fraternal support, Shawn had left his cell on the kitchen table at home for the first and only time. He arrived home to find Kuda had gone through his emails and read a couple from Rita, which, though hardly graphic, were revealing enough. He tried to front it, but he was too drunk for semantic subtlety and his denial simply petered out.

While Kuda broke shit, slapped him, clawed at his chest and drew blood, Shawn experienced a bizarre sense of detachment, like he was watching the discovery of an affair on some daytime soap. He felt regret, that he'd given Rita his personal email. He felt relief, that he'd not given his personal email to any of the others. He said, 'I'm sorry, Kuda. I'm so sorry. I made one mistake.'

Shawn didn't contact any head hunters. For a while it looked like he might be paying for a divorce and that was no time to be moving jobs. He kept his head down at work and his head down at home. He was the model employee and the model husband.

Ayo called him into her office. She told him they were letting him go. She told him that it was no reflection on his work, just a symptom of contraction throughout the sector.

Just a few weeks previously, Shawn would have cried foul, but he didn't have the energy. He wasn't at the top of his game. He was low on confidence. He was feeling remorseful.

He chose this moment to change his name from McClaren to Appiah. He'd imagined doing this at a point of maximum certainty, but somehow the opposite felt appropriate too. He told Kuda that she was now Mrs Appiah. She looked at him with something close to hatred. He didn't tell her he'd lost his job.

In fact, Shawn didn't tell anyone he'd lost his job. Being knocked off his career path by something as mundane as 'contraction throughout the sector' just wasn't who he was. Before he could admit as much, he needed a sub-plot that would sit comfortably within his broader narrative. Then, after a particularly depressing meeting with a recruitment consultant who pulled off the neat trick of simultaneously talking up his client's experience and talking down his imminent prospects, Shawn returned to the apartment to find Kuda brandishing a chicken leg and declaring her intention to go home.

Shawn thought about it for twenty-four hours. He thought about how far his generous severance might go in Zimbabwe. He thought about the opportunities for an educated brother like himself in the land of his ancestors. He said to Kuda, 'Let's go. To Zimbabwe, I mean. It's a last chance. Or a new start. I don't know. It's something. We gotta try something, right?'

His wife sat quietly. She started to weep. Then she looked up at him and said, 'Thank you,' before retiring to their bedroom and closing the door.

When Shawn told his boys, Malik held up his glass in a toast. He said, 'I always knew it. You always on the real tip. And now you the first nigger I know who gonna set foot in Africa.'

Shawn said, 'What you talking about, bruh? You know Kuda, right? She born there.'

'Yeah, but you know what I'm saying, though.'

'Sure I know what you're saying,' Shawn said. 'You're saying, "I'm an ignorant motherfucker." '

Malik laughed. 'You know it, baby. New York for life.' He offered Shawn skin and the pair touched knuckles.

Less than a year later, Shawn sat alone in the bar of the Mazowe Star Motel, nursing a beer. He was the only customer, but he'd introduced himself to Constance, the barmaid, and they'd made the usual small-talk about her desire to visit the USA some day before she'd retreated to the fridge at the other end of the bar, idly to polish glasses. Shawn was now so used to this kind of exchange that he could do it in his sleep.

He lit a cigarette, drained his beer and lifted the bottle towards her. He said, 'Constance!'

She came over. She said, 'Unfortunately we are now closed.'

He stared at her. He checked the time on his phone: ten past nine. He said, 'The receptionist said the bar would stay open until I was finished.'

'No. Monday to Thursday we close at nine p.m.'

'Constance!' Shawn said, dangling his beer bottle in front of her.

'We are now closed,' she said. She lifted her chin and looked at him along the length of her nose. Then she returned to the fridge. He thought she was going to get him a beer, but instead she turned off the lights and retreated to a back room.

Shawn sat in the dark. He tried a small laugh for no one's benefit. He said, 'Fuck!' He pictured Constance's face: that upturned chin, the flaring eyes and flaring nostrils. How quickly an instinctive, false obsequiousness gave way to disappointed, self-righteous belligerence. It was so fucking familiar.

29

Bessie now visited Gilbert on Sundays, unless the *murungu* woman decided to cancel her day off (something that, to Gilbert's irritation, his wife seemed to accept without protest). She'd begun attending New Vision Church in Sunningdale with Fadzai, so would generally be by the house in the afternoon when Gilbert returned home to eat. The couple had little time to themselves before Gilbert took out the taxi for the afternoon and evening, generally managing no more than a short walk after the meal, but it was better than nothing; better, for sure, than the months spent apart.

Initially, Gilbert had sensed that Fadzai had had some difficulty persuading Patson that her brother should stay for a prolonged period. The older man had said nothing – he wasn't much of a talker at the best of times – and had not been actively unwelcoming, but Gilbert noted a vague contained impatience if Patson found him sitting in his place or reading his newspaper. Gilbert wasn't sure if this was because Patson had active reasons for not wanting him there or simply because a pride of lions generally has room for only one adult male, but he made sure that he avoided his brother-in-law's place and newspaper thereafter. And, before long, Patson's impatience gave way to something like warmth, albeit expressed every bit as intangibly, in silence.

In fact, Gilbert quickly understood that everyone – Patson, Fadzai, the kids, Bessie – was comfortable with the new routine; everyone except him. Gilbert was frustrated. He had moved to the capital with specific intentions: to find a job and his own place; to bring Stella to Harare as soon as possible and to live with his wife and child. Instead, he had simply replaced his layabout life in Mubayira with one of seemingly endless toil for no reward. After all, despite all his work, he had no money to call his own beyond the occasional twenty Patson gave him at the end of a particularly good week.

Gilbert had no desire to return to Mubayira, but part of him missed his father's school library and the chance to read for hours at a time. For sure, his life there had been racked with guilt and the pressing burden of parental disappointment, but at least the books made him feel like he was improving his mind and allowed him to dream. Here in Harare there was no time to dream, let alone to fulfil whatever dreams he might once have had.

He tried to explain this to Bessie on one of their Sunday-afternoon walks. She listened patiently, but her response, reasonable and considered, was not what he'd hoped for. She said, 'We cannot run before we can crawl, isn't it? How long have you been in Harare? Just three months. I told you, I like your plans, but they will take time. We must pray for what we want and, if it is God's will, it will happen.'

Gilbert was irritated by that and failed to hide it. This failure was partly because he didn't understand his irritation and there-fore didn't recognise it as such in time to conceal it. Of course it would take time to get what he wanted, but he'd been looking for reassurance from his wife – that he was better than what he was doing, that he could achieve what he wanted, an affirmation of faith. Instead, she had affirmed her faith only in God, which was no use to him, so it was that he railed against. 'Do you know how many people pray for what they want?' he asked. 'Do you think God answers every prayer? Two people pray for the same job, which one gets it? The most faithful? I don't believe it. These prayers are just superstition.'

His wife looked at him with such shock that Gilbert immediately regretted the outburst. She reached for his hand and entwined her small fingers with his. She said, 'Our pastor, Pastor Joshua, he says that Zimbabwe is on the threshold of a spiritual awakening. He says that there are now so many Christians in this country that every prayer will soon be answered.'

Gilbert stared at her, dumbstruck. He wanted to ask her if she saw all the fat cats in their big cars and big houses. He wanted to ask if these men were aware of her 'spiritual awakening'. But he said nothing.

Bessie cleared her throat. She thought she was seizing the moment. She said, 'You should come to New Vision. I'm sure you would find the answers you are looking for. And ... and I would be proud to go to church with my husband.'

Gilbert looked at the ground. His anger suddenly fell away and he was so overwhelmed with love that it was almost painful. 'You know I have to work,' he said quietly.

'I know you have to work.'

'I just want to live with you and Stella,' he said. 'I just want to live as man and wife. I want a job, I want a house, I want more children. Is there anything wrong with that?'

'No,' Bessie said. 'There's nothing wrong with that.'

There were no calls from their regular customers so, at nightfall, Gilbert drove Bessie back to the *murungu* house in Greendale.

They hardly talked on the half-hour journey and Gilbert wondered if she was still offended by what he'd said. But as they pulled away from the city on the Enterprise Road, she rested her head on his shoulder and, after a while, began to knead his thigh with one hand. When they turned onto Arcturus Road, Bessie said, 'Stop here.' Automatically, Gilbert pulled over. They sat for a couple of minutes in the darkness. She pressed her lips to his ear. She said, 'This is a busy road. The next one is a dead end, isn't it?' Gilbert restarted the engine, slipped the Raum into gear and turned down into the pitch-black side-street.

He said, 'Maybe there are security guards.'

'Not in the road,' Bessie said, as she eased herself astride him.

Gilbert knew what she was doing. He knew what she was thinking and he did not believe problems could be so easily solved. But he loved her for her tenderness.

30

Fadzai put Gilbert in charge of the kitchen while she went to buy airtime. Generally, there was no way she'd leave him alone to serve at their busiest time of day, but that morning she'd forgotten to tell Patson that he had to pick up Chabarwa from school at half past twelve and take him directly to band practice at New Vision.

It wasn't that she didn't trust her brother, but she'd discovered that what he'd said on his first day was absolutely true – her customers liked their *hupfu* served by a woman; either that or they simply preferred the familiarity of her face and the fact she didn't try to engage them in idle conversation. Gilbert was too jolly, full of jokes and banter. Most of her customers didn't want jolly: they wanted something that would sit in their stomachs and tide them over through the long afternoon. Besides, for all Gilbert's efforts, he didn't have her economy of labour. The speed with which she could dish, take payment and make change was a skill she'd developed over years.

Fadzai bought her dollar airtime, scratched off the pin and juiced her cell. She called Patson, but the network was patchy and she had to redial half a dozen times before she could confirm he'd got the message. The whole process took a lot longer than she'd hoped and she must have been gone almost ten minutes when she turned the corner back to the kitchen and saw her brother squaring up to three shaven-headed youths – Chipangano.

She broke into a trot. She said, 'Gilbert.'

Gilbert turned at the sound of her voice. He looked angry, but unworried. For all his recently acquired urban nous, he had no experience of Chipangano, the militant gang that had grown up to support the government in the elections a decade ago and had terrorised Mbare on and off ever since. Besides, Gilbert had a good head in height and three years of muscle over every one of the young thugs. She took in their faces. She knew the leader: a nasty, sly creature whom people called Castro.

Gilbert said, 'They took three plates, these *kids*, and they don't want to pay. They say we have to give them ten bucks. I was just telling them I'd fuck them up. Ten bucks doesn't go far at the hospital.'

Fadzai looked directly at Castro. She said, 'Ten?'

Castro's expression was simultaneously cocky and ingratiating. He said, 'It is a mark of your success. A month ago, there were three kitchens on this stretch, now it's just you. What are we to do? As your profits increase, so do your responsibilities – that is how Big Jimmy puts it.'

A small crowd was gathering: a mixture of the impatient and hungry and those who were just impatient and hungry for distraction. Fadzai wanted to defuse the situation as quickly as possible and she reached for the cashbox and dug out a ten. She handed it to Castro. She said, 'No problem.'

Gilbert said, 'What are you doing?'

Fadzai flashed him a look – *Not now.*

Castro pocketed the ten and scooped a lazy mouthful of *sadza* and gravy. He chewed slowly. He said, 'Chicken again. Every time I come here, it's chicken. You should vary your menu. You will lose business.'

'Thank you,' Fadzai said. 'That is good advice.' She would have said anything. She just wanted them to go.

Castro looked at her. He nodded. He said, 'You know what they say: the customer is always right.' He took another mouthful. He was in no mood to hurry. He gestured idly at Gilbert. He said, 'Who's this?'

'My young brother,' Fadzai said. 'Don't worry about him. He has just come from home.'

Castro finished his food thoughtfully. He said, 'I know the type. Thinks he knows everything because when a cow shits in the river it's going to rain.' He handed Gilbert his plate. Castro said, 'There aren't many cows in Mbare, my brother.'

Gilbert took the plate. A peculiar smile teased the corners of his mouth. He said, 'And I know your type, too: playing the big man in front of your friends. I wonder if you have that swag when you're on your own.'

Some of the assembled men began to laugh. Fadzai made as if to take the plate from Gilbert, positioned herself between him and Castro, then tried to usher her brother away.

Castro said, 'Do you think you are smart?'

Gilbert answered, over Fadzai's shoulder, 'Why do you care what I think?'

'I can find you, country boy.'

'You're very smart,' Gilbert said. 'I'm here every day.'

Castro smiled very slowly. He took a matchstick from his pocket and pushed it between his teeth. He turned and walked away.

Fadzai waited until they were packing up to raise what had

happened. She said, 'You don't know Chipangano, Gilbert. I pay a levy every week. It is what we have to do.'

Her brother was belligerent. He said, 'You think I am stupid? I know what's going on. But that doesn't make it right.'

'So, you are going to change the way it is? I don't think so. Those same guys, the ones who stand around laughing at your jokes, they will be laughing when they find your bloody body by the road too. I can't afford this kind of trouble.'

Gilbert stopped drying the pots. He said, 'They beat me and you can't afford the trouble? That is what you are saying?'

Fadzai stopped, too, and took his hand. She said, 'They beat you and I have to pay for the doctor and still I have to keep working and still I pay ten dollars every week. *That* is what I am saying.'

Gilbert stared at her. He blinked. He said, 'He called me country boy. You should have told him about the time I lost Daddy's goats. *Country boy?* Me?'

Fadzai started laughing. She caught herself. She said, 'Next time, you just give him ten bucks, OK?'

'You're the boss,' he said.

When they got home, Gilbert made tea and sat on the step, waiting for Patson. Fadzai came outside and asked him if he didn't want to eat something before starting the night shift. He shook his head, and she said, 'Suit yourself.'

As soon as Patson pulled up, Gilbert approached the car and got in the passenger side. Patson said, 'What are you doing?' But Gilbert stared straight ahead through the windscreen. Patson looked at him for a moment, shrugged and opened the driver's door. Then he thought better of it and shut the door again. 'What's the matter?' he asked.

'You know that Fadzai is paying Chipangano.'

Patson sighed. He wanted a cigarette, but he was out.

'Ten dollars a week,' Gilbert said.

'Ten?'

'Ten dollars a week. It's a lot of money.'

'It's a lot of money,' Patson agreed. He reached across to the glove compartment and rummaged inside. Sometimes he left a cigarette there and forgot about it. No such luck. He sat back. He said, 'What's this all about?'

Gilbert turned to look at him for the first time. It was clear the boy was rattling with fury. 'Aren't you angry?'

Patson rubbed his face with his hands. He said, 'No, I'm not angry. When I was your age, I was angry all the time. But now? No.'

'What happened?'

'I got older.'

Gilbert dropped his chin. 'You have been very good to me. I didn't mean to be disrespectful but . . .'

'You are angry.'

'Yes.' Gilbert stretched his neck to lay his head back on the headrest. 'I was talking to some of the guys, the other drivers, at the rank. They were telling me about this lease-to-buy situation. You know, you pay the owner two hundred and fifty dollars a week and in a year the car is yours.'

Patson said nothing, but when Gilbert didn't continue, he felt he had to encourage him. 'I have heard about this,' he said.

'I want to do it,' Gilbert said. 'Find an owner and get a car for myself. In a year, it is mine. I will pay you rent at the house, isn't it? Two cars on the road. We will be growing a business, you see?'

'I see,' Patson said. He looked at Gilbert. He was moved by the young man's anger, moved, too, by his intentions, and he knew he needed to weigh his words carefully. 'I know you are frustrated. But I must say two things. The first is that I have heard about this deal many times. But I have never met a driver who has done this deal and now owns his car. Why is that? Because the deal is too hard. The second thing is that you and me are now driving this taxi twenty-four hours, isn't it? And we pay Dr Gapu two hundred dollars a week and we hardly have enough to feed us all. Before you came? I was struggling for even that two hundred. What you are saying? I don't think it is possible.'

The young man looked at him and Patson recognised the despair all too well. 'I am married,' Gilbert said. 'And there is Stella. I have to do something.'

'I know,' Patson said. Then, 'When you are a farmer, you work hard and you plant and, if the rains are regular, you're a lucky man. And if you are unlucky and there is no rain? You work harder and you know you are doing your best, even as the family is suffering.'

'I don't understand.'

'I am telling you, you are doing your best, Gilbert,' Patson said. He opened the driver's door again. 'You must get on the road if you want to meet the Bulawayo bus. It will be there by eight. You'll find work, isn't it?'

31

Mandiveyi was sitting with Nature in the Zim Café, a large and boisterous outside bar on the corner of Fourth and Fife. He was sipping his whisky, idly picking at a plate of ribs and considering how strange it was that the very things that had first attracted him to this young woman now repelled him. Nature was all excitable sociability, and where once this had made a pleasant change from his wife's stony silence, it was now giving him a headache. She had made him chase her and he'd enjoyed the challenge. Better that than the placid acceptance of most of these bar girls. But he had neither the energy nor the inclination to continue the pursuit. Even her undoubted physical attributes were now a negative. Once, he had enjoyed the fact that every other man would stare at her and wonder whom she was with; now such attention made him nervous.

He was going to have to be rid of her. He hoped she was sensible enough to understand his position – or, more to the point, her own – and that she wouldn't make a fuss. He had no desire to hurt her. Then again, he had no fear of doing so either.

Nature was sipping a Smirnoff Lemon straight from the bottle.

He didn't understand why she couldn't use a glass like any decent human being. She was leaning forward with her elbows on the table and the bottle in two hands, so that the curve of her lower spine lifted her round backside almost out of the seat, as if presenting herself to all-comers. Somehow she was managing to pin him down with her chatter even as her head darted this way and that, checking who was coming and going and, every now and then, greeting some passer-by with a familiarity he resented, both personally and professionally.

'You don't call me for almost two months, Albert,' she was saying, 'and now we are here like nothing has happened. That's some bullshit.' She raised her eyes to a passing whore: 'Yes, yes, sister. *Zviri sei?*' Then, back to him: 'I thought I was the Small House, isn't it? But you treat me like some street girl. Is that what you think of me? I am a professional woman. I earn my own money. What have you done for me lately? That is what I am asking you. Like the song. "What Have You Done For Me Lately"? Janet Jackson.'

The DJ dropped an old-school classic: Shalamar. Nature began to snap her fingers to the music and gently gyrate her hips and buttocks. 'My groove,' she said.

Mandiveyi bit into a rib and a dollop of barbecue sauce dropped onto his tie. He examined it irritably. He said, 'A tissue,' and the girl automatically got up and went to find a napkin. As soon as she left the table, Mandiveyi's cell rang: Phiri. He answered.

'You are with the Tel One chick, isn't it?' Phiri said. 'I thought you had more sense. After you spoke to *Iganyana.*'

Mandiveyi stiffened. He resisted the urge to look around. He sipped his drink. Then he said, 'Where are you?'

'Meet me outside.'

The darkness of the street was so complete that it seemed

almost viscous. Mandiveyi got into the back of the Range Rover to sit next to his boss. Phiri neither greeted nor looked at him. He just said, 'You are busy.'

'What do you mean?' But there was no further clarification forthcoming, so he added, 'We are all busy. Mostly these directives from the Chamber of Mines. There is a lot to do.'

'Our other business,' Phiri said. 'Do you think it is concluded? It is not concluded. I know *Iganyana* told you as much.'

'He told me. But on my side it is finished. I am not thinking about it.'

'You are lying,' Phiri said flatly. 'Please do not lie to me.'

Mandiveyi said nothing.

'What gun did you collect?' Phiri went on.

'What do you mean? The gun the guy gave me.'

'What gun was that?'

'A SIG.' Mandiveyi shifted in his seat. He regretted his drinking. He could hear his own breathing. He could smell it. He was thankful for the darkness.

'And what did you do with it?'

Mandiveyi almost answered immediately, but managed to hold his tongue. He had been on the other side of enough such interrogations to know their rhythms. If Phiri knew how a lie sounded, so did he. Instead, he held a moment's pause, then played naïve defiance. 'I got rid of it,' he said, as if that were the most obvious thing in the world.

Phiri's mouth made a wet, ruminative tutting sound. Mandiveyi's senses were at their most acute. It was a situation with which he was comfortable. It was why he was good at his job. It was as if the world outside had stopped and everything that existed was in the small, hermetic space of the car. And, in fact, for him, that was more or less the truth of it.

'Why did you do that?' Phiri asked.

Mandiveyi played casual. 'It made sense. What was I supposed to do? I don't see the problem. The police have found no bullets, no evidence of gunfire. Nothing.'

'Police? Gunfire?' Phiri exclaimed. 'I don't know what you are saying.'

Mandiveyi's heart skipped. He'd made a mistake. He'd thought he and his boss were at least deep and long enough connected to share the supposition of the gun's use. But Phiri's protested ignorance claimed otherwise and, worse, cut him loose on the implications of his assumption. Although he couldn't see, Mandiveyi was aware of the other man turning towards him for the first time. He could smell Phiri's breath – it carried as much alcohol as his own. He realised that Phiri was scared and his own fear intensified. 'I am not saying anything,' he said. Then quickly, in spite of himself, desperate to say something, 'I buried it.'

'Then you can fetch it for me.'

'Sure.'

'So get it,' Phiri said. 'Bring it to me.'

Mandiveyi was frantically trying to control his thoughts, the situation. Controlling situations was what he did. He said, 'Sure, but it's safe, you know? We're on the same side, isn't it?'

Phiri's index finger buried itself in his sternum. 'You're not an idiot, Mandiveyi. There are not two sides. There are many sides. Even us: you, me, *Iganyana* – it is already three. And I will make the gun disappear myself. Otherwise you can see what happens. You will bring me the SIG, isn't it?'

'Of course.'

Mandiveyi got out of the Range Rover. His mind was racing.

He didn't go back into the bar, but caught the nearest cab. He wasn't thinking about Nature. If the worst came to the worst, she could disappear just like that. If the worst came to the worst, so could he.

32

A Sunday evening in October: it was oppressively hot. With Bessie off-duty, Jerry and April spent the whole day together, more or less: a lazy breakfast followed by shifts watching back-to-back *Teletubbies*; lunch with the Americans Terri and Derek Sedelski and their two kids, then a trip to Greenwood Park; delight in Theo's delight at the train ride, laughter at his reluctance to get on the trampoline, photographs on Jerry's iPhone of the happy family – Dad holding Theo's hand on the climbing frame, Mum with Theo on her lap eating ice-cream, the three of them smiling brightly into the sunshine at Derek's insistence. They got home at five and Jerry bathed Theo while April made scrambled eggs on toast. They ate in silence punctuated by their son's demands for more ice-cream. They put Theo to bed together: Jerry sitting on the floor, carefully making sure the sleepy child could see every single page of *The Very Hungry Caterpillar*, April on the bed, eyes closed, her hand resting lightly on Theo's back. Only when he dozed off could they finally go their separate ways: Jerry to the office and his laptop to catch up on the latest releases on Tru Folk, April to the living room by way of the kitchen.

April poured herself half a glass of white wine and settled

on the sofa, her legs tucked under her. She stared at her mobile phone, as she had been doing surreptitiously all day. She was behaving, she realised, like a teenager, and the thought gave her a light shiver of excitement. She sent a thank-you text to Terri to pass the time. She sipped her wine. She clicked the phone to light the screen, as if it were somehow possible that in sending a text message she could have missed an incoming call. She clicked the phone back to sleep. She told herself that she didn't need a call, that the anticipation was enough excitement. She laid the phone on the coffee-table. It rang – or, rather, vibrated – almost immediately. It was an unfamiliar number. 'Hello?'

'Yes, hello. Is that April? April Jones?' The voice came in staccato: a woman, clearly agitated. April experienced a sudden swell of terror.

'Yes. Who's this?'

'April Jones . . .' the woman said. 'I'm sorry to disturb you at this time, April. It's Kuda. Shawn's wife. Shawn Appiah.'

'Hi! Kuda. Yes. You're not disturbing me at all. How are you?' She heard her voice as if from a great distance. It sounded ridiculous: too friendly, too *hearty*.

There was a great sob from the other end of the line. The effort it had taken to make the call, to get out the opening exchange, was clearly spent.

'What is it?' April said softly.

She found Jerry buying albums on iTunes. It was an extravagance of which she disapproved – the double expense of the album and the ludicrous price of a data plan in Zim. At the sound of her at the door, Jerry automatically minimised the window. April shook her head. 'I had a call,' she said. 'Kuda.'

'Who's Kuda?'

'Shawn's wife. The American. The guy I met at yoga. They came to our *braai*. The guy in the pool.'

Jerry turned around in his chair to look at her. 'What did she want?'

'She wants you to go over. She remembered you're a nurse. She said Shawn's not there and she's had an accident. Her maid's away and it's just her and the little girl – Rosie. She says she can't drive to a hospital.'

Jerry blinked at her and shut his laptop. 'Right.'

April looked on as Jerry packed his bag. He asked what the woman had said about the accident, what had happened. April shook her head. She hadn't said anything. She'd sounded distressed, feeble. Jerry thought aloud as he chose what to take – a burn? A cut? A shock? April watched with something like admiration. She had forgotten how calm her husband could be, how competent.

'You have the address?' Jerry asked.

'Yeah. Newlands.'

'Write it down for me.'

'I'm coming too,' April said quickly, and Jerry looked up at her.

'Theo . . .' he said.

'We don't know what's happened,' April said. Then, 'The girl . . .'

'Right.'

'I'll call Bessie.'

'Is she here?'

'I don't know, do I? I'll call her.'

April called Bessie. The maid was in her room at the back of the property. April asked if she could babysit. By the time Bessie walked up to the house, her boss was already behind the wheel of the Land Cruiser, Madam waiting at the kitchen door. Bessie asked: 'Is everything OK?'

'I don't know,' April said. 'An emergency, it seems.' She attempted a weak smile. 'Theo's down. I'm sure he won't wake up. Have you got your phone? Good. I'll call you if we're going to be very late.'

Jerry swung the car onto Alexander towards Arcturus and Enterprise Roads. April said, 'Don't you want to go via Glenara?'

Jerry said, 'I know where I'm going.'

They drove in silence for a while. Jerry was putting his foot down, too fast. April gripped the strap above her head and bit her tongue.

Jerry said, 'She didn't say anything?'

'She didn't say anything.'

'For future reference, you need to get as many details as you can. Even if the person's distressed.'

'I wasn't expecting this,' April said. 'Fuck!'

'For future reference,' Jerry said. 'That's why I said "for future reference".' Then, 'Call her.'

'What?'

'Call her. Talk to her. We don't know what's happened. Keep her on the phone.'

April searched through her phone for the last call received. She pressed dial. There was no answer. Jerry hissed, 'Shit!' April began to feel very frightened. Less than an hour ago, everything had seemed like a game. She looked out of the window at the oncoming headlights.

Jerry turned off Enterprise Road and onto Princess Drive. He hunted house numbers in the headlights. He found what he was looking for. He pulled into a driveway and buzzed down the window to press the intercom. Nothing. He waited. He was about to press the buzzer again when the automatic gate opened. He drove inside.

In spite of herself, April found herself drinking in every detail, curious about how the American and his Zimbabwean wife lived. She noted the empty, cracked swimming pool, the slightly unkempt lawn, the swing frame with no swing. The house was nice, but smaller than she'd imagined. She wondered how it would look in daylight. She knew that Shawn liked to drink his coffee on the veranda. She couldn't see any veranda. It must be on the other side.

'No guard,' Jerry said. Then, peering through the windscreen, 'I think the front door's open.'

He cut the engine and reached into the footwell behind April's passenger seat for his bag. He touched his hand to her elbow. He said, 'I want you to wait here. I want you to lock all the doors and wait here.'

'For fuck's sake, Jerry.'

He said, 'We don't know what's happened. You can't get her on the phone. The front door's open. Wait here.'

'OK, sure,' she said.

Jerry got out of the car and disappeared inside the house. April tutted to herself, even as she was swamped by an unexpected wave of fear. She hit the central locking.

33

April waited until five minutes turned to ten. She called Jerry's mobile. It rang on the shelf beneath the steering-wheel. She composed herself for a moment before getting out of the car. She stood on the gravel driveway, listening intently. The cicadas were deafening. She approached the front door, acutely aware of the crunch of every footfall. She pushed open the door into the small dark hallway. A light was on in the room to the left. She entered a living room dominated by a large flat-screen TV and, on the opposite wall, an even larger framed seventies poster for *When The Revolution Comes*, an album by the Last Poets (whoever they might be). She stared at the poster, fascinated. It had to be Shawn's. He must have brought it all the way from America to hang it on this African wall. She wondered what it said about him. She backed out of the room. She hissed, 'Jerry!' No response. She headed deeper into the house. The hallway opened into a corridor that led left and right. To the left was pitch darkness. To the right, a lit doorway. She padded towards it. She said, 'Jerry!' again, this time at conversational volume. Her voice seemed to die in the still, enclosed space. There was no immediate reply, but she heard a noise behind the door and then, as she got closer, her husband say, somewhat breathlessly, 'In here.'

April pushed the door. It swung into a brightly lit open-plan kitchen. The first thing she saw was a small red spatter up the right-hand wall by the intercom. Her eyes widened. To her left was a breakfast bar. On top of it sat a mobile phone, presumably Kuda's, which was next to a small stainless-steel cleaver in a thick, congealing pool of blood.

April had never considered herself the squeamish type. Then again, such an assumption had never been tested and she felt a brief surge of light-headedness so that she had to support her-self on the counter. Her fingers came away bloody and she said, 'Oh, Christ.'

Jerry said, 'Are you OK? It's a bit of a mess.' And she saw him for the first time, knelt over Kuda's partially visible body, which was lying on the floor at the far end of the counter. He hadn't looked up at her – presumably he'd just heard the distress in her voice. 'A bit of a mess,' he repeated.

April now saw that the pool of blood smeared into a thick, careless streak that stretched the full length of the counter before disappearing over its end. She took a couple of steps forward and found that Jerry was kneeling in an even more impressive bloody puddle, a needle in his mouth, and a length of rubber tube in his hands.

'Is she dead?'

'No.'

'What are you doing?'

Jerry didn't have time for explanations. He said, 'I saw the girl. In bed. Other end of the house. I thought she was sleeping, but that was before . . . I didn't check. Can you check?'

'Right.'

April returned to the corridor. She ran her hand along the wall until it hit a light switch. She flicked on the light and hurried towards the far end, less from any sense of urgency than to preclude the opportunity to reflect upon what she might be about to find. She tried the penultimate door on the right, but it was a small guest toilet. She opened the last door quietly and she was in Rosie's bedroom. She stood looking down at the little girl in the half-light from the corridor. Rosie was lying on her front, her head to one side, her thumb lightly touching her lips. April watched for a moment that stretched unbearably. She thought she might scream until, at last, she saw Rosie's spine rise and fall with a deep and heavy breath.

Back in the kitchen, Jerry was pulling off a pair of latex gloves and washing his hands. April said, 'She's just asleep.'

Jerry nodded. 'Thank God,' he said. Then, of Kuda, 'She must have been waiting for us. She opened the gate and then passed out. I've stabilised her blood pressure, but we need to get her to hospital.'

'Suicide?' April breathed.

Jerry looked at her. His expression was serious but unflustered. He shook his head, not an answer so much as a negation of the question in favour of pressing practicalities. He said, 'Can you wait with her a minute? I have to check something.'

Jerry moved quickly around the kitchen. He tried the back door. It was locked and bolted from the inside. He returned to the main part of the house. April heard doors opening and closing. She stood over Kuda's body. She looked down at it. The woman was wearing a white T-shirt with 'Jesus Saves' across the front in red letters. The midriff of the T-shirt was a wide bloody stain. Kuda's arms were swathed in bandages, gauze and tape.

April guessed six or seven cuts in total. Jerry had raised her right wrist to rest on an upturned saucepan and he'd taped a drip to the counter that ran into her upper arm.

April *was standing over the body*. She felt peculiar. She wondered if this was how it would feel or, rather, how it would look if you had just killed a person. If somebody had walked in at that moment, would they assume her a murderer? She dropped to her haunches and rested her hand on Kuda's shoulder, if only for the sake of appearances.

Jerry came back into the kitchen. He said, 'There's definitely no one else here.'

April looked up at him sharply. She hadn't even considered this a possibility. She said again, 'Suicide?'

'I don't know. She's cut her radial, but the angle ... But I don't know. I'm no expert. And she called us and waited for us to arrive. It's just weird. And the other cuts? I don't know. Self-harm. Maybe.'

'Shawn. The husband. He said something about mental illness.'

'He told you that?'

'No. At the *braai*. He said she hadn't been well. That's why they'd come back to Zim. It was the way he said it. That's what I thought: mental illness. And on the phone, when she called, she said she'd had an accident and that Shawn was out of town. She didn't say anything about anyone else.'

'Right,' Jerry said. Then, 'I need to get her to a hospital. You're going to have to stay here – for the girl. I'm going to carry her to the car. Can you carry the drip?'

April looked at her husband. She didn't much like his plan, but she knew it was the only one that made sense. She said, 'You're sure there's no one else here?'

'Yeah, I'm sure.' He took April's hand and squeezed it. He said, 'I'll be back as soon as I can. Maybe you could call someone.'

'Like who?'

'I don't know. Terri? Tom Givens?'

'No,' she said. 'Let's just do this.'

34

April watched Jerry pull the Land Cruiser through a tight three-point turn and swing away up the drive. It stopped at the gate and she watched the idling car for a second or two before realising she'd have to open it from inside. She hurried back to the kitchen and found the intercom by the door. She lifted the receiver and saw the button smudged with a bloody fingerprint. She found a tea-towel to cover her own finger and pressed it. She heard the grind of the gate and the grunt of the powerful engine.

April turned to look around the kitchen. She was impressed by her own sangfroid. She considered cleaning up the blood. She believed herself equal to the task, but decided against it, because what if there was some kind of criminal involvement, after all? Surely it was best to leave it for now. She wanted to make herself a cup of tea. She opened every cupboard, but couldn't find tea. She did find a bottle of Scotch and poured herself a large one, not because she wanted it but because she had no experience of situations like this and it was the kind of thing they did in films or on TV.

She went to the lounge, shutting the door to the kitchen's horrors on her way out. She sat on the sofa opposite the TV and beneath the large poster. She took out her mobile and tried to call Shawn. That was her impulse: to call her lover. Only after she'd hit 'dial' did she appreciate that, if he answered, she'd have to talk to him as a husband and father. She felt a surge of panic until she heard the familiar automated response: 'The subscriber you are calling is not available at the moment.'

April sipped Scotch. It gave her heartburn. She stood up again. She went to check on Rosie. The girl was still sleeping soundly.

Without allowing herself to consider what she was doing, April opened the second door down from the child's bedroom. If she had considered it, she'd have told herself that she was looking for clues as to what had happened, or rechecking for intruders, or simply that she was bored. But she found that she was quite able not to consider what she was doing at all.

She turned on the overhead light. The room appeared to be a study or home office. There was a cluttered desk with a space where a laptop habitually sat. There was a daybed made up with a baggy single sheet, a crumpled quilt and pillow. Shawn hadn't lied to her about his sleeping arrangements and this knowledge gave her grim satisfaction so powerful that she sat on the bed and lifted the quilt to her face and positively revelled in the grotesquerie of her own behaviour. The quilt smelt faintly of cigarettes and armpits and arse. April wondered if this, cigarettes apart, was how all men smelt – of armpits and arse. It was certainly true of Jerry, just different armpits and a different arse.

She remembered St John Vaughan, the Cambridge academic. She remembered his curious, odourless hold over her; the bliss she'd experienced against his bare chest and gripping his hairless buttocks. She remembered blowing him in the Queens College car park and the watery, tasteless gush of his semen. She found this memory exciting, not of itself, but in the power it now seemed to give her over other, smellier, men. The idea was absurd and weightless; and, in this bizarre situation, it allowed her to float right out of motherhood and marriage in a way that she found intoxicating. When life takes a bizarre turn, she wondered, doesn't it endorse our most bizarre behaviours?

April stood up and swilled Scotch like a veteran. She left the study and made for the room at the corridor's end. It had to be the master bedroom. It was. She was no longer even positively not considering her actions: she was at the whim of her whims.

She took in the king-size bed, with the extraordinary and ornate faux-leather headboard. She wondered who'd chosen this bed; assumed it was Shawn. This thought led her to imagine the plans she knew he'd have laid out for its topography, then the all too obvious reasons these plans had been foiled. She smiled to herself. Shawn was a kind of sexual hobbyist – his desire to fuck a certain woman in a certain position in a certain venue little different from Jerry's urge to own the latest releases on Q-Topia, Partisan and Storyville. And just as there was an endless back catalogue of unoriginal ways to sing the blues that excited only the most dedicated fan, so there was an endless back catalogue of unoriginal ways to fuck.

April sat on the bed. On the bedside table, there was a Bible. She opened it at the bookmark. There was a passage marked with biro, Ephesians 6. She read, 'Put on the whole armour of God, that you may be able to stand against the schemes of the devil.' April didn't believe in God, certainly not the devil, but the words still had the power of an incantation and gave her short-lived pause. She looked up to find Rosie standing in the doorway.

'Who are you?' Rosie said.

'April. I'm a friend of your mum and dad. You came to my house once. Remember?'

The little girl nodded. She said, 'I need the bathroom.'

'OK.'

'It's dark.'

April led her to the bathroom. She switched on the light. The girl eased herself onto the toilet seat and her face took on an earnest expression of concentration. Then she smiled, said, 'Finished!' and reached for tissue paper. She said, 'Where's my momma?'

'She had an accident,' April said. 'She had to go to the hospital. So she rang me to come and look after you.'

Rosie looked up at her. She seemed to take in this information without any kind of shock or difficulty. She said, 'What kinda accident?'

'I don't know,' April said. 'She cut herself. But she's going to be OK. We should get you back to bed.'

The little girl slid off the toilet and slipped past April in the doorway. 'I don wanna go to bed. I'm not tired any more. I wanna watch TV.'

'It's late, Rosie. You need to be sleeping.'

'No! I wanna watch TV. I got DVDs. You like *Henry Hugglemonster*?'

April followed the child down the corridor to the lounge. She watched helplessly as Rosie turned on the TV and DVD player with expert ease and settled herself on the sofa. She knew she should probably put her foot down, but it wasn't her kid and it was an unusual situation, to say the least, so, instead, she sat down next to her. The girl said, 'You lemme watch TV?'

'Why not?'

For a moment, the girl looked at her in disbelief. Then, she instinctively snuggled into her and April lifted her arm to allow Rosie to settle her head on her lap. Maybe she'd fall asleep again there. The anti-piracy warning flashed up on the screen. April said, 'What's the programme?'

'I told you. *Henry Hugglemonster*.'

'Right.'

Rosie sat back for a moment and regarded her with a furrowed child's brow. She said, 'Momma had an accident?'

'That's right. But she's going to be fine. You don't have to worry.'

'I's not worried. Jus maybe it Sasabonsam what did the accident. Because he real naughty an dun all kinda accident even if I gets the blame. Like, when we at your house by the deep end an I push your baby in the water an Daddy dive in? Thas me an I know I dun sumthin bad, but it Sasa what said it, you know?'

April looked down at the girl and her heart stopped, then restarted and quickened and her breaths came short and her head filled with blood. She recalled the day of the *braai*, Theo being dragged out of the pool and lying limply on the burnished tiles. She felt something: a curious, cold, uncomfortable emptiness that swelled behind her navel and rose in her chest until she thought she might gag. She said, 'Who's Sasa?'

'He like my friend. Only I tell him he not my friend any more cos he get so angry an always gettin me in trouble.'

April felt her fingers tighten around the soft flesh of the child's belly. She said, 'Is he in your imagination?' Rosie looked at her blankly. 'I mean, Sasa, is he pretend or is he real?'

'I dunno. Pretend, I guess. I mean, thas what Daddy say an no one see him but me. He come when we move to Zimbabwe.'

'Where's Sasa now?'

'Dunno. Sleepin, probly.'

April gave her a reassuring squeeze. 'Don't worry,' she said. 'I'm sure Sasa had nothing to do with it.'

April relaxed and allowed her breathing to even out; her thinking too. She understood her physical reaction to Rosie's story reflected the sudden recollection of her greatest fear. She believed she also understood the little girl who'd moved to a foreign country at the heart of a breaking marriage and invented a friend to support her and, no doubt, justify her anger. It all made sense, as everything made sense if thought about in the right way – the urge to love, love's passing, the desire for something more.

In that instant, April experienced some kind of epiphany, believing that she fully and dialectically understood herself – educated career woman struggling with maternal instincts, child and wife of alcoholics, vulnerable loner and sexual predator, powerful and powerless, utterly controlled and at the mercy of her temperament. In that instant, she believed that she was seeing herself as she was, and the clarity of the harsh light rather suited her – even her flaws looked to her sympathetic and almost beautiful. Everything was comprehensible and, when understood, could be excused.

She was stroking Rosie fondly and, when she looked down, she found the girl was fast asleep. April considered lifting her to bed, but didn't want to risk waking her, so instead rested her head on her hand and watched back-to-back episodes of *Henry Hugglemonster*, in which small, lovable cartoon fiends taught children the value of sharing and listening and eating a varied and nutritious diet.

35

Gilbert was working all the time, more or less, whether in the cab or at his sister's kitchen. He slept no more than three hours a night. Of course, he could catch forty winks here and there when on the taxi rank. But he was finding it increasingly difficult to sleep in the car because his mind was ever restless. In fact, when he witnessed the way other drivers cut their engines and dozed off in a matter of seconds, he determined this was a mark of their weakness: resignation to their lot, stuck in a routine that left them almost delirious with exhaustion and paid them barely enough to eat. Gilbert believed he was capable and deserving of more; and if more was what he wanted, he had to do something different.

The problem was the 'something different' couldn't impinge upon his capacity to take a fare at a moment's notice. Consequently, he fell back on a familiar crutch and read avidly. He had always believed that time spent reading was never wasted. It was an idea drummed into him by his father and, though he currently couldn't see how it might happen, he held tight to the notion that books might save him.

There were several bookstalls at Avondale flea-market. For the most part they sold a mixture of tourist cast-offs (largely pulp thrillers), glossy self-help books of a more or less Christian bent, and dog-eared African adventures written by white people with double-barrelled names featuring savages whose nobility was trumped only by that of an elephant. Gilbert read them all. Browsing one afternoon, he came across Kenneth, a wiry, coloured man who chain-smoked Madison, quoted Shakespeare in an impressive basso profundo and, on Fridays, appeared at the market carrying a suitcase brimming with an eclectic selection from the literary canon. And as Kenneth came to identify Gilbert as a 'fellow intellectual', he began to allow him to exchange whatever he'd taken the previous week at no charge and even thrust books upon him with a manic glint in his eye: 'This is a fuckin' classic, *ek se*! A fuckin' classic!'

In the last month alone, Gilbert had read Dickens and Hardy, Eliot and Baldwin. He lost himself in worlds of which he knew nothing and found himself again in brief passages or even single phrases that spoke to his heart – he considered, for example, that he was paying for what he'd done, for what he'd allowed himself to become, and reflected on the best and worst of times with wisdom, foolishness, belief and incredulity.

Gilbert found an ineffable truth in these books that was almost like love. It was different, of course, from his love for Bessie, which had never been a thing of words. But if his feelings for Bessie were something he couldn't articulate – a grand passion of almost unbearable tenderness – this was love that declared itself openly, eloquently and without fear.

Currently he was reading *Candide*. He found the bizarre narrative alienating and entrancing in equal measure – perhaps not so different from his love for his wife after all. He hated the protagonist but wondered if he was only truly hating what he saw in himself. He would never have considered himself an optimist, yet wondered if his actions, his continuing hope in the face of apparently insurmountable challenges, spoke otherwise – the obstinacy of maintaining everything is best (or could at least be so) when it is . . . anything but.

When Kenneth handed him the book, he'd said, 'This is a weird one, but it's some fucking funny shit:"Let us work without reasoning, it's the only way to make life endurable." Satire. You know about satire?'

Of course Gilbert knew about satire and, defensively, he'd said as much. But he found little ridiculous in *Candide* – grotesque, certainly, but only in the way his own life seemed consistently verging on the grotesque.

It was after ten p.m. and Gilbert was parked outside the Infectious Diseases Hospital on Simon Mazorodze Road, reading by the cab's internal light. He was waiting for a Jeremiah, who'd called half an hour before and said he was one of Patson's regulars. Gilbert had never heard of Jeremiah and he was cautious about heading to Mbare for a stranger at this time of night. But the guy had his phone number and sounded genuine and, besides, the evening had been quiet so far and he needed the job. On arrival, he'd texted Jeremiah to say he was outside. '10 mns', the man texted back.

Twenty minutes later, Gilbert glanced up from his book to check the time on his phone, considered the pitch dark of the hospital entrance (not even a security guard in sight) and decided he'd best head back into town. He started the engine and flicked on the headlights. They illuminated half a dozen men in front of the car who were armed variously with crowbars, timber and, in one case, a *sjambok*.

Gilbert cursed. He checked the rear-view mirror and saw at least as many men behind the car. He put the Raum in 'drive' just as a crowbar smashed the passenger side headlight. The car lurched forward and hit something, or rather someone. He heard a pained scream. He instinctively hit the brakes and the car lost traction on the sandy verge and stalled.

There was tapping on the driver's window. Gilbert, terrified, turned to see nothing but a knuckle. Now a face bent to join the knuckle and, illuminated by a cigarette lighter, revealed itself as that of Castro, the ringleader of the Chipangano cadre. Gilbert tried to restart the car but, in his panic, forgot that it wouldn't start in 'drive' and the key turned dead. He hit the central locking. Castro lit his cigarette and, face pressed to the window, eyes wide, made a winding gesture with his right hand.

Gilbert got the engine going and the one remaining headlight was bright enough for him to see a large youth behind Castro, with a piece of two-by-four raised over the windscreen. His eyes darted back to Castro. He buzzed the driver's window down an inch. Castro was calmness itself. 'Hello, country boy,' he said, with a smile that expressed some simulacrum of sympathy. 'If you get out of the car now, we will probably not kill you. If you don't, we will kill you and we will torch the car. There we are. Your choice. Make it fast-fast.'

Gilbert cut the engine. His fear dissipated just like that – this was what it was. He recalled one of the self-help books he'd read: *Angry Men, Happy Husbands*. Its central tenet was that anger came from fear: fear that the desire to fight or flee would not ultimately be productive. Gilbert knew he could neither fight nor flee and was surprised to find exactly the 'acceptance' the book had suggested was just around the corner for all 'adult men'.

He moved for the door and noticed that *Candide* was still open on his lap. He thought that, if he was still alive after this was over, he would want to read on. He remembered Kenneth saying he couldn't return a book with dog-eared pages. He took his time, therefore, to mark his page with a receipt. He almost enjoyed the absurdity of this action. He got out of the car.

Castro took a step back. Gilbert was aware of the others circling around him, but he kept his eyes on the ringleader. Castro said, 'How much money have you got?'

Gilbert took out his wallet. He counted out the single bills. He said, 'Six dollars.' Castro gestured for the money. Gilbert handed it to him. Castro said, 'Thank you,' then punched him square in the face. Gilbert heard his nose break with a crack that echoed in his ears.

Having decided he wasn't going to die, Gilbert gave up his body as a punch-bag. He covered his head and accepted kick after kick to his back and guts. His mouth was full of a thick liquid and he thought he was choking. But he managed to gulp down his own blood and it tasted metallic and soupy. Now he felt a searing pain like fire, first on his buttocks, then across his back. He was being whipped with something that cracked the air with each stroke, a coat-hanger perhaps. He began to cry and scream, but it wasn't long before he passed out.

36

Gilbert came round with a start and a sharp intake of breath that sucked in a whole lot of dust and made him choke. He pushed himself up on his hands and coughed until the coughing turned to retching and he vomited. Vomiting hurt a lot, squeezing his battered ribs and stretching every welt on his back. He gingerly lifted himself to his feet and carefully flexed his joints. As far as he could tell, there was nothing broken except his nose, which was simultaneously numb and extraordinarily painful, sending sharp, stabbing messages directly to his brain and making his eyes water. He tried to clear his vision, but every time he wiped his eyes, they seemed to fill again immediately.

He wasn't wearing any shoes. He checked his pockets. His wallet was there, his car keys and phone, though the screen was cracked. He looked at the time. It was just after eleven. He slowly circumnavigated the Raum. Apart from the smashed headlight, it appeared undamaged. Castro was true to his word – he hadn't killed him and he hadn't torched the car. This had been, Gilbert realised, no grand show of force, no personal vendetta, just business as usual for Chipangano. The thought riled him – the ruthlessness, the easy violence. When he'd seen Castro standing at the driver's window, he'd assumed he'd got under his skin that day at the kitchen, threatened his standing. But the evident truth was that he'd simply given Castro a job to do, which he'd carried out with efficiency and little expense of energy, thought or emotion. And somehow that was worse.

Gilbert wondered what had happened to his shoes. He imagined himself lying unconscious when Castro had given the signal – *Enough*. And, as the gang moved off, one of them had thought, I want a pair of shoes. And he'd taken them. There was something so petty about it that it only fuelled Gilbert's anger. If they'd wanted his car, they'd have taken it. If they'd wanted his life, they'd have taken that too. But they'd wanted nothing from him except pain and shoes.

He opened the driver's door. He slowly eased himself behind the wheel. Sitting down was excruciating. It was the whipping that had really fucked him up and he couldn't begin to think about how his back and buttocks must look. However much his siblings insisted he'd had it easy from their father, he'd had his share of hidings to the snap of Obert's belt, and on a few occasions they'd drawn blood. But those beatings had been nothing compared to this. Every time Gilbert shifted in his seat to turn the wheel or indicate or simply try to find a more comfortable position, the material of his shirt or underpants or jeans tugged away from a raw wound and sent his head reeling.

He drove back to Sunningdale very slowly, partly because he had only one headlight, partly because his vision was still misty and partly because he was scared he might pass out from the pain. At one point, he began to cough and, finding that he was snorting blood over his shirt, he had to stop the car. He opened the door, swung his legs into the road and spent five minutes gobbing into the dirt before he dissolved into tears of pain, self-pity and fury.

He reached the house around midnight. He turned off the engine. He sat for a moment, trying to gather his strength for the effort to drag himself inside. He was sweating profusely, but shivering with cold. He was experiencing waves of nausea. He blacked out. He came to in time to open the car door and throw up. This made him feel a little better and he thought he should grasp the opportunity to try to move. He hauled himself out of the car, lugging his limbs like a labourer lugging sacks of cement. He stood for a moment, slumped forward over the roof. He saw the door of the house open and a figure emerge. A match sparked and Patson lit his cigarette and sat down on the veranda. He looked directly at Gilbert and raised a slow hand in greeting. Gilbert summoned all his energy and stumbled in the direction of the house.

'I heard the car,' Patson said. 'It's early to call it a night.'

Gilbert couldn't answer. He felt the faint coming and his eyes blackened before his legs gave out. He lurched forward and his knees buckled. Patson exclaimed but Gilbert no longer understood language.

He drifted in and out of consciousness. On the floor of the main room. His clothes being removed. His sister's voice, barking commands at the children. Gilbert was delirious and thought she was his mother. Candlelight. Face down on the marital bed. Fadzai dabbing at his wounds with a cloth. Every touch like fire and ice. Coughing and vomiting. Apologising. Aware of his nakedness. Apologising. Fadzai kneeling next to him, kissing his cheek. Patson's hovering presence: weighty, restless, impotent. The cold light of daybreak gave rise to a bout of violent shivering. Fadzai tried to cover him, but even the weight of a light sheet was unbearable. Fitful sleep. Vivid nightmares. Morning sun, waking up slowly, stuck to the mattress in a sticky mess of sweat, spit and blood. He opened his eyes. He was desperately thirsty. His sister was asleep on the floor next to him. But her eyes now snapped open, sensitised to any shift in his condition. She blinked. She touched his face. She said, 'What happened, Gilbert?'

He said, 'Chipangano.' Then, 'Water.' She nodded, stood up and left the room. His fever had passed. All that was left was the pain, which was raw and precise and bewilderingly inalienable.

He heard low voices in animated discussion – Fadzai and Patson. He imagined them considering the possible repercussions: whether to go to the police or take more personal revenge. But as his ear attuned to their whispering, he realised it was actually a mundane conversation about who should stay at home to keep an eye on him, the urgent need to fix the headlight and the potential lost income if the kitchen was closed with the car off the road.

Gilbert found himself staring at the small chest of drawers. He knew this was where Patson kept the Cee-ten's gun. He pictured Castro's face at the car window and he wondered whether, if he'd had the gun, he'd have shot him right there and then. Gilbert knew himself well enough to admit that last night he'd have done no such thing. But after what they'd done to him? Today everything was different.

37

Shawn met Feinstein at Rainbow Towers, the monolithic downtown hotel. It was just after eight a.m.

He'd never been into Rainbow Towers before and he found
something grotesque and melancholy about the building. Con-
structed in the early eighties, it resembled an alien spacecraft,
which had landed with grandiose, imperial intent only to be
abandoned by its crew when word came down from the mother
ship that there was nothing worth colonising after all.

Shawn recalled a college trip he'd made with his buddies down
to Cancún, Mexico, for spring break, sophomore year. Sure, they'd
had their fair share of fun but, as conscious individuals whose
consciousness had something of a competitive edge, they'd talked
each other into a trip inland to the Mayan city of Chichén Itzá
too. Shawn had looked down from the summit of the great temple
across the tourist-trampled site to the dense jungle beyond and
wondered how the structures must have loomed ahead of nine-
teenth-century looters chopping back the undergrowth.

Now, as he approached the Rainbow Towers entrance, with
its peeling gold paint, chipped fixtures and broken fittings, he
unpicked his mind's decision to load this particular memory.

After all, while he liked the idea of himself scything through the metaphorical scrub of contemporary Zimbabwe, he was less comfortable to be cast by his own subconscious as some kind of contemporary bounty hunter. Perhaps it was just about the aliens. Shawn remembered Malik had been reading a book called *Voyage of the Gods*, which claimed the ancient Mayan cities were of extra-terrestrial origin.

In fact, that book had provoked serious beef. Kenny had mocked Malik's interest, describing it as 'typical nigger learning, all conspiracy theories and some shit'. This had then widened into an argument about what constituted a conspiracy theory: the CIA flooding the community with crack? The Judeo-Masonic New World Order? The Holocaust? Holocaust deniers? *Slavery?*

Shawn ended up settling the dispute, at least for that night. 'Listen to us!' he'd said. 'I figure "conspiracy theories" are a "conspiracy theory": divide and rule, right there. A bunch of educated black men sitting round discussing who fucked who instead of getting out there to do some fucking of our own.'

His boys had at least been able to agree on this. 'True that.' Kenny nodded.

Shawn perched uneasily on one of the lobby's ugly armchairs. He'd set off before five from a *makorokoza* camp at Pfungwe after an uncomfortable few hours' sleep in the truck. He'd hoped to stop at home before this meeting to shower and change, but the drive had taken longer than expected so he'd had to come straight here. He was uncomfortably aware of his grubby jeans and dirty sneakers among the lobby traffic of suited middle-aged men. Rainbow Towers was located a stone's throw from ZANU (PF) Headquarters and Shawn had heard it was a spot favoured by Party bigwigs. While he couldn't be sure that all the suits shaking hands, clapping shoulders and laughing delightedly at their own importance were indeed the ruling elite, it didn't seem unlikely.

Shawn was questioning why Feinstein had chosen such a meeting place considering the nature of their business when, across the lobby, a lift opened to a festival of hand-shaking, shoulder-clapping and delighted laughter before spitting out a tall, slim guy of about his own age. He was wearing a crisp blue shirt, chinos and sandals beneath a receding Jewfro. This was clearly Feinstein and clearly he was down with the middle-aged suits. Of course he was. In fact, Shawn wondered why he'd ever countenanced another possibility.

Shawn had heard about the Israelis from Kemp, a self-described 'Rhodesian' he'd come across at a panning site on the Nyaguwe. He'd told Kemp about his partnership with Nyengedza, necessitated by indigenisation, and the white man had almost killed himself laughing. 'So, let me get this straight: it's your investment, your risk and your hard work, and this black fellow takes fifty-one per cent? Shit! These fuckers take us for mugs!'

Kemp had made initial contact and a couple of days later Feinstein had called Shawn. The principle was simplicity itself – the Israelis bought gold under the counter. All Shawn had to do, therefore, was run a proportion of his deals through NA Holdings and the rest could stay off the books. According to Kemp, the Israelis paid thirty-five dollars a gram, and while that was less than the market rate, it was free of tax and, more to the point, free of any cut for Nyengedza.

Shawn questioned the sense of acting illegally (and by 'sense' he meant, of course, 'safety'). But Kemp insisted the whole mineral trade was top down corrupt anyway, functioning solely on a system of kickbacks and bribes, and there was next to no chance of getting caught. 'These clowns don't know what's going on in their own country. How many times you see an official in the fields?'

'No risk?'

'Minimal, I swear.'

It had been reassurance enough for Shawn.

Feinstein approached with certainty and extended a hand. His grip was strong, almost self-consciously so. 'Mr Appiah.'

'Mr Feinstein.'

'I'm late. Sorry for that. I tried to call you, but I couldn't get through.'

Shawn took out his cell. There'd been no signal in the bush, so he'd switched it off the night before to save the battery. He'd bought a Chinese car charger from a kid in the street, but it had never worked. He switched the phone back on, clicked it to silent and mumbled his excuses.

Feinstein nodded and said, 'Have you eaten? My colleague's in the restaurant. The buffet's OK.'

'Sure.'

38

Feinstein introduced his colleague as Mr Cohen. He had a shaven head and polished nut-brown skin. He was simultaneously ploughing through a cooked breakfast, swilling a Coca-Cola and smoking a cigarette. Shawn put him at early fifties, but it was hard to tell on account of his grotesque obesity. He was so large that working out his age or height or anything much else about him seemed impossible or, at least, irrelevant – you'd never describe him as the 'old guy', 'bald guy' or 'tall guy', you'd just say 'the fat guy'.

Cohen took up the whole banquette of one of the restaurant's booths. At the appearance of Feinstein and Shawn, he made a show of attempting to stand in greeting but even this minor charade threatened to upset the table, so he sank back, gesturing Shawn into a seat opposite. Feinstein took another chair and sat a little distant and a little behind, crossing his legs, one knee on the other. To Shawn's New York eye, the position and posture, the chinos and sandals, gave Feinstein the mien of an Upper East Side analyst; or at least how such characters were portrayed in art-house movies.

Cohen made an expansive, lordly gesture with one arm. He said, 'Breakfast, Mr Appiah. Help yourself.'

Shawn inhaled a distinct whiff of deodorant, soap and flesh and had to consciously withhold the distaste from showing on his face. He had an instinctive disgust for obesity, which was connected to sex – what kind of man allowed himself to get into a state where he couldn't fuck properly? Despite his hunger, Shawn demurred and ordered a cup of coffee.

Cohen made small-talk. He asked Shawn about his background and Shawn told him. Cohen flashed impressed recognition at the mention of NYU Stern and BBH. 'Appiah?' Cohen mused. 'Your family must be of West African extraction.'

Shawn raised a sardonic eyebrow and pursed his lips. '*Extraction* being the word,' he said, and disclosed the decision to change his name.

Cohen considered him thoughtfully and Shawn imagined him juggling words like 'angry', 'Negro' and others in his head. But Feinstein observed blithely that Jews understood more about displacement than most and, in fact, the Israeli government encouraged returnees to Hebraise their names. 'It's not so different,' he concluded, presumably for his colleague's benefit.

Cohen asked him what he was doing in Zimbabwe and Shawn told him about his Zimbabwean wife and her desire to return home. Cohen asked him what he thought of the country, so Shawn said it was an excellent place to raise kids. This in turn led to a discussion of schools, then a brief tangential story about Cohen's nephew, David, in Tel Aviv, who was eight years old and something of a soccer prodigy.

Shawn wondered if all this chatter was heading anywhere and when they might get down to business. But he noted the way Cohen's eyes occasionally darted to Feinstein lurking on the very periphery of his vision and he concluded they were checking him out. Eventually, sure enough, Cohen sat back in the booth, lit another cigarette, and turned explicitly to his colleague with an expression that said, 'OK, over to you.'

Feinstein explained the terms. They would pay thirty-four dollars per gram and wouldn't take less than a kilo at any one time. Shawn nodded. He said that Kemp had talked about thirty-five dollars. Feinstein considered him and the Israeli's expression never altered a jot. 'We will pay thirty-four thousand dollars per kilo, Mr Appiah,' he said. 'Cash.'

'And what's the maximum?' Shawn asked.

'Maximum?'

'Weight.'

'No maximum,' Feinstein said. And they shook hands on the deal.

Shawn walked out to his truck. He was running math. Since the first conversation with Kemp, he'd accumulated approximately eight hundred grams off the company books, so it might take up to a week to secure a first sale. Thereafter? He figured that with the right excuses for Nyengedza he could set aside a kilo every month or so, risk-free. Without even growing the business, therefore, he could reasonably expect to clear five thousand dollars a month through NA Holdings, plus an additional fifteen thousand with the Israelis. And, of course, the extra capital would mean extra purchasing power and the only limitations would be logistical – he'd need a way to get the profits out of the country and probably another guy out to buy from the panners; someone he could trust. He shook his head. He was getting ahead of himself. He mustn't get too greedy too quickly.

Shawn took out his cell. He had half a dozen missed calls from a single number. It wasn't one he'd saved to his address book, but he recognised the digits. He felt a twitch of mischievous excitement deep in his gut, triangulated by his navel and his balls. He knew a lot of men who enjoyed chasing a woman but were immediately uninterested when she was hooked and landed. Shawn wasn't like that. He loved this stage of enthusiasm and helpless commitment when a chick seemed to think he was some kind of answer and pursued him with unmistakable gratitude. For him, interest generally wouldn't waver until she stopped being grateful.

Shawn lit a cigarette and dragged deep, enjoying the anticipation. He clicked 'dial'. She answered on the first ring. She said, 'Shawn! Christ! Where have you been?'

He enjoyed the desperation in her voice. He said, 'Sorry, boo. I told you I'd call soon as I got back into town. Where are you?'

'I'm . . .' Her voice broke, and for the first time he sensed her anxiety might have a source other than her desire for him. 'Christ, Shawn,' she said. 'I'm at your house.'

His cigarette froze on its lazy parabola to his mouth. The excited tug in his midriff was suddenly a heavy ice block and he shivered. 'What the fuck?' he said.

39

Shawn smoked a cigarette in the car park of the Corporate Health Clinic in the Avenues, just off Baines, before hustling inside at a kind of stepping half-trot that spoke of desperate urgency. Corporate Health's reception was quiet and almost empty. There was a Knicks game mute on the TV and he found his eyes attracted to it until he realised it was a few days old and he'd seen it already – before he'd headed out to Pfungwe on his latest trip, before his wife had done . . . whatever the fuck she'd done. This was a disquieting thought. Three days ago, he'd watched the game 'as live', sitting at home on his big sofa while Kuda had buzzed around him disapprovingly. Now here he was and his world had changed and SuperSport 2 was still showing the same reruns.

His eyes flicked across the rows of bolted leatherette easy chairs. He took in an elderly Zimbabwean, who appeared to have dressed up for her visit to the clinic and sat rigid with her handbag on her lap, as if in church; then a young, stressed white woman, foreign, no doubt, and her daughter who mewled occasionally – although whether this was because of some terrible undiagnosed ailment or frustration with her mother's iPad was impossible to tell.

There was no one at the desk, which was shielded by an opaque screen with a letterbox just below eye level. Shawn bent down to look through and spotted three figures in white uniforms, a man and two women, chatting by a water dispenser. He said, 'Excuse me,' and the man looked towards him – slowly, vaguely – before rejoining his conversation. Shawn banged on the screen. He said again, 'Excuse me!' And the man finally turned and approached lazily, as if in positive denial of any correlation between Shawn's evident frustration and his return to work.

The man sat down, lifted the telephone and listened to imaginary voices for a second before looking up. 'Yes, sir.'

'My wife was brought in here. Kudakwashe Appiah.'

'Your wife?'

'Yes. My wife.'

The man opened a large ledger and traced the entries with his finger. He furrowed his brow. He tapped at an ageing computer. He said, 'One moment,' stood up and walked away and Shawn was left, hunched over, peering through the letterbox, spitting, 'Where are you going? Where are you going?' at the man's retreating back.

'Shawn!'

Shawn straightened up to find Jerry Jones emerging from the clinic's interior. The Englishman was wearing jeans and a stained T-shirt. He looked exhausted. On the only previous occasion they'd met, Jerry's fleshy features had suggested joviality and bonhomie, but now everything sagged – his cheeks, the folds of skin beneath his eyes – like a balloon slowly deflating. In spite of himself, habitually, Shawn imagined Jerry and April having sex and the picture that jumped into his mind was of a large construction worker tacking tarpaulin to the frame of a gaping window. Only when he clicked that the stains on Jerry's T-shirt must be Kuda's blood was he uncomfortably jolted back to present reality.

'Jerry,' Shawn said. The two men shook hands. 'What the fuck happened? Where's Kuda? Can I see her?'

'She's heavily sedated,' Jerry said, and rested a hand on Shawn's shoulder, which he promptly shrugged off.

'Sedated? What do you mean? What the fuck's going on?'

'She's going to be fine. Really, she is. She's not in any danger. Just lost a lot of blood. Needs to rest. The sedative will help. While we work out what happened – you know, her mental state.'

'Her mental state?'

Jerry looked at him. He rubbed his eyes with his hands. He looked at his hands, then closer at one wrist. He went over to a small basin beneath a sign that read, 'Please observe good hygiene.' He lathered up the liquid soap and scrubbed thoroughly. Shawn stood over him, twitching impatience. Jerry said, 'Do you mind if we step outside? I could use some fresh air.'

In the car park, Shawn smoked another cigarette while Jerry recounted the whole story in minute detail: Kuda's phone call to April, the time it had taken them to get to the house, exactly what Jerry had found and what he'd done, that he'd spoken to April this morning and Rosie was fine – confused, but fine.

'The front door was open,' Jerry said again, by way of conclusion. 'But I checked all the doors and windows and there was no sign of any break-in. And it's not like your wife mentioned anything on the phone. An accident – that's what she said.'

'You think she was trying to commit suicide?'

'I don't think anything. I'm just telling you what I found. Like I said, the wounds don't look self-inflicted – the angles, the nature . . . I don't know. That's just what my gut tells me. You'll see. They're too *frenzied*.'

'So she was attacked?'

'I don't know. That's not what she said. By who?' Jerry paused. He shook his head. He bit his thumbnail. Shawn discarded his cigarette and lit another. Jerry said, 'Can I have one of those?' Shawn passed him a cigarette and cupped his hand around the lighter's flame. Jerry inhaled deeply, exhaled.

'April told me that your wife had maybe had some issues before. Psychologically, I mean. In the States. That's why you brought her home.'

Shawn stared at him. He didn't know what to say. His lie was being told back to him and didn't it sound truer than ever? Nonetheless, he was irritated at the idea of April discussing it with her husband. It had, after all, been a careless, lightweight, spur-of-the-moment untruth and now, with repetition, it weighed too much. Perhaps this man was even making it true retrospectively. For a moment, Shawn said nothing. He looked at Jerry. They were of roughly equal size. Maybe April had a thing for big guys, but Shawn's bulk was undeniably more elegantly distributed. He shook his head. He said, 'Nothing like this.'

'I don't know. I just figured, if this was self-inflicted, maybe it wasn't suicidal, more like self-harm.'

Shawn stared at him. 'Fuck,' he said. Then, 'I should get home.'

'You don't want to see her?'

'I thought you said she was sedated?'

'She is. But you can see her.'

'Not if she's sleeping. Let her sleep.' Then, 'I want to get back to Rosie. She must be terrified.'

'You going to get the police?'

'The police?'

'Maybe it was a break-in after all. I mean, what do I know? Maybe they could work out what happened.'

Shawn was suddenly swamped by possibilities, each as awful as the last. 'No,' he said. Then, 'The police? Here?' He forced out a sound approximating a laugh.

'Fair enough.'

Jerry ground out his cigarette under the sole of his shoe, then picked it up with Shawn's discarded butts and walked them over to a dustbin. As he returned, he flashed an ingratiating smile. He said, 'Don't tell April I was smoking. She hates it.'

'What?' Shawn said. Then, 'Yeah, right. Fine.' He could barely control a sneer. Who was this man, this nurse, who picked up his litter, who hid a cigarette from his wife, who couldn't fuck her right? No wonder. No wonder. He said, 'Thanks for what you did. Really. I owe you big time.'

'Sure,' Jerry said. 'It was April too. She's still at yours. She said the maid came in, but she didn't want to leave Rosie.'

'I'll send her home,' Shawn said.

40

Mandiveyi traced a slow crisscross of the Sunningdale streets. He was driving his wife's ageing Mercedes. It still had a problem with the timing and stalled on one corner in five, drawing attention to both car and driver. But, since he had little idea who he was looking for anyway, perhaps it made no difference.

He'd spoken to Chifura, the young operative who'd first collared the taxi driver for illegal parking outside the Central Intelligence Organisation building. Mandiveyi approached the conversation warily because Chifura was one of the new breed: as brazenly ambitious as he was untrustworthy, brimming with meaningless Party rhetoric. He wondered whether Chifura's crass approach spoke only of inexperience or, in fact, a shift in the very culture of the Organisation. It was, after all, a shift he'd witnessed throughout the establishment – as the ideologues had become criminals, so criminals became ideologues.

Mandiveyi chose his moment. He caught Chifura in the lift and made idle small-talk down to the ground floor. They exited the building together and went their separate ways before Mandiveyi stopped in his tracks and called his colleague back as if suddenly arrested by an afterthought. 'Chifura!' he said. Then, when the young man turned, 'Excuse me. I forgot. There is something I wanted to discuss.'

And he asked him about the taxi driver. He explained that he'd taken down his details because he'd thought he could be a contact worth cultivating, but the guy had given him a false name and number.

Chifura regarded him quizzically. He said, 'He gave me his name as well, but I don't remember. It's weeks ago.'

'What about the car? Do you remember the car?'

Chifura shook his head. 'I don't know. A Raum, Demio, Spacio. One of those.' Then, 'Why are you so interested? What did he do to you?'

Mandiveyi kept his gaze steady. 'He lied. He made a fool of me. I was drunk. I want to find him, show him how things are when I'm sober.'

Chifura smiled. It was, Mandiveyi considered, a grotesque expression that appeared to relish potential future cruelty: these young guys, the new breed – they scared even him. 'I remember he told me he was from Sunningdale,' Chifura said. 'But perhaps that was a lie too.'

'Sunningdale.' Mandiveyi shrugged, as if conceding defeat. 'Not much to go on.'

'But if you find him you will teach him a lesson,' Chifura said, still smiling, eyes widening until Mandiveyi wondered whether delight in another's pain could ever be considered naïvety.

'You can count on it.'

Mandiveyi wouldn't be teaching anyone a lesson today. He'd been combing the streets since six a.m. and had seen plenty of Raums, Demios, Spacios and so on, but none that particularly jogged his memory. Frankly, he could barely remember anything about the taxi driver's appearance either: stocky, dark-skinned, middle-aged. The only thing he recalled with any certainty was the deep crease that bisected the man's forehead. He'd know that again if he saw it.

He stopped and bought a Coke from a tuck shop near the community centre. It was just after eight. His phone rang: Phiri, demanding to know his whereabouts. 'Just off the Airport Road,' Mandiveyi said vaguely. 'I'm tracking down a source.'

'What source? Is this connected to the Chamber of Mines agenda?'

'I don't know. Just someone I'm trying to cultivate. I suppose it could be.'

As expected, Phiri gave him an earful.

The Central Intelligence Organisation's current remit was all about addressing the blight of illegal dealing in precious metals. The 2006 Marange diamond rush had seen the country overrun by chancers of every nation, creed and hue. Now that the government had imposed some kind of order on the diamond fields, the chancers were looking elsewhere and the Organisation was tasked with cracking down on the illicit trade in platinum and, above all, gold.

Phiri told him that an Untouchable was having a meeting at that very moment. He asked with unconcealed acidity whether Mandiveyi might trouble himself to investigate the lie of the land.

'Of course,' Mandiveyi said. He wasn't surprised Phiri was angry. After all, he'd intended his vagueness to be provocative: better Phiri's anger than having to field questions about his progress with the other matter.

'About the other matter,' Phiri said. 'I want the gun.'

Mandiveyi answered slowly. He told him he was on it. But he'd had little time, with all the pressure being exerted by the Chamber of Mines.

'This is not the time to tell me lies, Mandiveyi. Don't forget, as it stands, I'm your friend in this situation. That's not something you want to change.'

Mandiveyi slid back behind the wheel of the Merc, phone wedged between ear and shoulder. He turned the ignition. For once it started first time. He considered Phiri's lie. Friends? Did the man not remember what he'd said outside Zim Café – that they were already on different sides? He assumed this inconsistency stemmed from Phiri's own fear. 'I am not lying, sir,' he lied. 'I know you are my friend and I appreciate that.'

He cut the call and slipped the car into 'drive'. It promptly stalled.

Twenty minutes later, he sat across the hotel restaurant from the Untouchable. 'Untouchable' was a nickname operatives granted those at the heart of any investigation who were not to be questioned, arrested or in any way inconvenienced by the Organisation. This status derived from the individual's relationship to power, whether bought, earned or inherited. On occasion, months of legwork had come to nothing when the prime suspect turned out to be Untouchable. On occasion, the prime suspect bought such status at the very moment the net was closing. Experienced operatives didn't allow such absurdities to irritate them. They were an inevitable by-product of negotiating the geography of this political, economic and legal landscape. Besides, experienced operatives generally understood this as a quid pro quo for the likelihood that one day they would need to be Untouchable themselves.

Mandiveyi ordered coffee, but the Untouchable's meeting was over before it arrived.

The Untouchable and his colleague, presumably likewise Untouchable, if only by virtue of proximity, remained in their booth, but the third man stood up and, after curt handshakes, made for the exit. Mandiveyi followed him outside into the car park where he stopped by a battered Isuzu truck and lit a cigarette. The CIO got into his own car and watched from behind the wheel as the man made a phone call and then, apparently given pressing news, quickly discarded the cigarette, leaped into the truck and reversed somewhat recklessly out of his parking space. The CIO was caught by surprise. Fortunately, the Merc started first time and he was able to follow at a cautious distance. The truck cut through town to the Avenues where it pulled into the car park of a clinic called Corporate Health.

Mandiveyi watched the man smoke another cigarette before entering Reception. He then sat back, preparing for a long day's surveillance. But after ten minutes, the man had reappeared with company. Mandiveyi sat forward. This was unexpected and interesting. He recognised the Englishman, the *murungu* he'd met at the Jameson, the nurse . . . What was his name? The CIO scanned the address book on his phone: Jones, Jerry Jones.

Mandiveyi watched the two men in conversation. They got into their respective vehicles and drove away. The CIO went into the clinic. He talked to the receptionist, who was so indolent that it was hard to regard his attitude as anything but deliberately obstructive. However, when Mandiveyi showed him his ID, the man soon provided a name: Appiah.

41

It was a week after the beating before Bessie managed to visit Gilbert in Sunningdale. This was partly because her sister-in-law, Fadzai, had told her that he was fine – 'I am not going to lie to you,' she said. 'It is serious. But he's going to be OK. We are taking care of him.' And it was partly due to the situation at work, where Mrs Jones seemed to be spending more time out of the house than ever and Mr Jones or, more to the point, Theo relied on her care.

After talking to Fadzai, of course Bessie was concerned and asked Mr Jones for a day, even just a few hours, to go and see Gilbert. He listened attentively and appeared horrified by her description of the injuries Gilbert had sustained. At one point, he even mentioned that perhaps he should go to Sunningdale and, as a nurse, see the situation for himself. However, when Bessie raised the possibility of taking time off that afternoon, he looked almost panic-stricken. 'Yes. No. Of course you must go,' he said. Then, 'It's just I'm supposed to be in Epworth. But it's fine. I'll call Dr Tangwerai. You must go. Have we organised supper? For Theo, I mean. No? OK. Don't worry. I'm sure I can sort something out.'

As he spoke, her boss shifted from foot to foot and wouldn't meet her eye, and it took Bessie a moment to decipher any meaning from what he was saying. She wondered, not for the first time, why he didn't simply speak his mind. She'd heard him talk like this to his wife. She wondered how Mrs Jones put up with it. But no sooner did she think this than she remembered all the times she'd witnessed the woman wilfully misunderstand her husband's, admittedly obtuse, intent for her own ends: *Can you take Theo . . . /No. That's fine. I love spending time . . . You know I do . . . It's just . . ./Great. I'll see you two later. Around five.* If Mrs Jones was frustrated by the stuttering style of communication her husband employed, she'd certainly learned to exploit it.

In the end, standing in the kitchen, her hands raised in rubber gloves dripping with dishwater, Bessie surprised herself by impatiently cutting through the prevarication. 'Don't worry, sir,' she said. 'My sister-in-law, she says that Gilbert is OK. I will go on my day off.'

'No. Sorry. I wasn't suggesting . . .' her boss blustered, before petering to a halt of resignation and no little relief. Then, 'Thank you, Bessie.'

Bessie did speak to Gilbert on the phone a couple of days later, but that did nothing to allay her anxiety. His voice sounded strong enough, but there was something in his tone that disquieted her: an emptiness, a removal – she couldn't quite put her finger on it.

Before Bessie met Gilbert the first time, she'd heard talk of him. Her friends, the kind who courted male attention, described a guy who was charming and funny and smart, but way too big for his boots. They repeated stories of the things he'd said and done, his attempts to impress, his continuous boasting that would have been unbearable but for the glint in his eye that suggested he might be in on the joke. He appeared to be one of those boys whom girls discuss while constantly bemoaning the very fact they're discussing him.

'Why are we even talking about him?' one would say. 'He does not deserve our time.'

'And wouldn't he love to think he is the subject of our conversation?' said another.

'So arrogant!' declared a third and fourth simultaneously.

Eventually Bessie saw him for herself at the school gates. He was at the heart of a gang from the local business college, she on the fringes of a group of the more precocious high-school girls. He was engaged in an elaborate explanation of his future plans, which involved university in the States, Harvard Business School and something called 'intellectual property'. 'That is my future,' he announced. 'In Africa, do we not have good ideas? Of course. But we have not learned how to protect them.'

Bessie had never heard this expression – 'intellectual property' – before, but to judge by the looks on the other faces, even those nodding enthusiastic agreement, nobody else had either. But Gilbert didn't seem to mind and he expanded with enthusiasm and a limber articulacy, which Bessie could appreciate if not follow.

'In the past, wars were fought over land,' he said. 'In the future, wars will be fought over ideas. In fact, it's already happening.'

It was at this moment that he glanced at Bessie for the first time and his grandiloquence waned. His features arranged themselves into an expression that seemed to suggest he was puzzling to answer a question she hadn't posed. His friends saw an opportunity in his sudden reticence and began to fill the silence with stories of their own. But Gilbert just looked at Bessie. Later, he told her, 'For me, the clocks stopped.'

When she fell pregnant, Bessie was inevitably the subject of school gossip. When it emerged that Gilbert was the father, the students responded knowingly: wasn't this always the outcome when a boy with too much confidence charmed a girl with too little?

They speculated freely that Gilbert would deny paternity or simply run away. But such considerations never occurred to Bessie. Because, though she recognised the brittle pride, recklessness and ambition that defined Gilbert for other people, the essential quality he'd shown her from the first moment he'd looked her way was devotion, and it was deep-rooted and unfaltering.

In fact, Bessie sometimes wished Gilbert's devotion were slightly less consistent, since being the object of such passion resulted in a constant barrage of demanding flattery, requiring resourceful response. In fact, once, recently, he'd declared, 'I will always have enough love for us both.' And she'd told him that wasn't how it worked and, seeing his crestfallen expression, immediately regretted her unkindness. His love for her burned like high sun and it never dimmed, and she knew she should be grateful and for the most part she was.

All these thoughts and memories returned to haunt her when she spoke to him on the phone after the beating at the hands of Chipangano. He told her he was fine. He told her exactly what had happened and why. He told her that he would be back driving the taxi within the week, because what else could he do? He asked this last, rhetorical, question with a suggestion of bitterness.

Unsure how to respond, she said that he was lucky to be alive, that he must be careful, that she was praying for him every night and every morning.

'You are praying for me?' he said. Then again, 'You are praying for me?'

They concluded their conversation soon afterwards. But

she couldn't shake this last repeated question from her mind. His voice hadn't held any particular intonation. He hadn't, for example, disparaged her. Nonetheless, to Bessie, that very lack of intonation spoke eloquently of his fury. He was so angry and, for the very first time since she'd known him, that anger had subsumed his love for her. She needed to know the source of his anger – the beating, those who'd done it to him, his impotence, his whole situation, a broad disappointment in his circumstances, or God? And, now she thought about it, weren't all of these truly anger with God? And didn't such anger always have terrible consequences?

Bessie worked to the end of the week. She cooked and cleaned and bathed and played and washed and scrubbed and washed and scrubbed. She kept the white family going. They were having problems of their own. In quiet moments over the stove, Mr Jones told her about their friend, a Zimbabwean, who was in the hospital, and that was why Madam was out so much, between working and checking on the husband and child. In her every spare moment Bessie prayed. She prayed for the love of God, because she knew that only God's love can heal a person. When Gilbert had said that he had enough love for them both and she had contradicted him, this was in fact what she'd meant – only God has enough love. She wished she'd explained herself. She would explain when she visited on her day off.

42

April's father was an alcoholic. She was first aware of this at eight years old. Woken one night by a commotion, she went downstairs to find him kneeling on the doormat in the middle of a shower of glass. Her mother was squatting beside him wrapping a tea-towel around his bloody hand, which he'd thrust through one of the panes of the front door, assuming, for some drunken reason, that it was on the latch. He looked up at her, standing on the penultimate step, and smiled mistily. 'It's all right, Days,' he said. 'Just an accident.'

April's father always called her 'Days' or 'Daisy', because that was what he'd wanted her christened, only for her mother to overrule him. 'April', with its lack of obvious affectionate diminutive, was a compromise. After he died, nobody called her Daisy again. In fact, she had never told anyone she met subsequently about her father's pet name; not even Jerry. This was another small way in which, she felt, her husband didn't know her.

April never really discussed her father's drinking with her mother before his death, and afterwards they avoided contact as much as possible until their relationship more or less dissolved. April blamed her mother for her father's death – unconsciously, and sometimes consciously; secretly, and sometimes openly. She blamed her in that way people blame others while declaring the opposite: 'Obviously I'm not blaming you, but it can't have helped that ...' And her mother blamed her right back, albeit with an unspoken accusation: that April had condemned her to twenty years with that man.

Since she'd never asked her mother, April assumed that the alcoholism predated her own awareness of it. But she couldn't be sure. Even in his last few years, her father had managed sporadic bouts of teetotalism with the support of AA or prescribed medication, though they always ended in some or other incident, dangerous or embarrassing, but always hurtful.

By the time April was fifteen, her mother had thrown him out and secured a court order to keep him away from the family home. But when his estranged wife went to the supermarket on Saturday morning, regular as clockwork, April met him at the nearest bus stop and they sat in McDonald's for half an hour and he bought her a McFlurry. April never told her mother about these meetings and it was an early opportunity for her to discover how easy it is, how painless, to deceive those closest to you, often with a conscious, indignant negation of their proximity – *He or she doesn't understand! He or she doesn't really know me!*

Generally, her father was sober at these clandestine meetings, but not at the last. He was a sad, philosophical, sometimes violent drunk. On this occasion he was only sad and philosophical, but April was painfully embarrassed by the look and smell of him, to say nothing of the way he cried into the coffee he'd stiffened with some unidentifiable dark spirit. He put his hand on top of hers and sobbed that he was sorry. She snatched her hand away and said that if he were truly sorry he'd stop drinking.

He shook his head. He stared into his Styrofoam cup. He said, 'It sounds so simple, Daisy.'

He told her that there had been a moment a couple of years before when he'd realised he was teetering at the top of the steepest slope. He'd looked down and felt heady with the exhilaration of danger. He could see sharp rocks, jagging branches, overhangs that gaped into nothingness, but such was his state of mind that he considered himself almost weightless. He imagined that if he launched himself off the edge, he'd merely be blown back to safety by a sudden warm gust or, at worst, bounce gently downwards, like a beach ball.

So, he launched himself. And at first it was thrilling, all the more so as he began to gather speed. But as the rocks bit, branches snagged and overhangs took his breath away, he began to see that he'd achieved inexorable momentum, and the thrill turned to terror.

The terror, however, lasted only as long as he believed he might stop himself. And he had tried. Of course he had tried. He had screamed and bellowed for help. He had grasped at passing outcrops and come away with fistfuls of dirt and grass. He had skinned his knees and knuckles attempting to break his fall.

But when he had resigned himself to his fate, it had become easier. The pain was the same, but it was without fear. In place of fear was that weightlessness again, something akin to melancholy; poignant, certainly, but breathable. Naturally, as he fell, he retained the dull certainty of gravity and ground combining to conclusive effect, but the inevitability of the outcome seemed to rob it of its potency.

At fifteen, April had no idea what her father was talking about. In fact, she hated him for speaking to her in these intimate euphemisms, which she couldn't understand but which left her simultaneously embarrassed, confused and scared. She stood up and told him that she didn't want to hear this, that it wasn't what dads were supposed to do, and why couldn't he be normal and, sorry, but Mum would most likely be back from Tesco's any minute. She left her McFlurry. She didn't even like McFlurrys, but she'd never told him that. Neither did she tell him that she'd had enough of these secret meetings and, yeah, she knew Mum was annoying, but it wasn't like anybody was *making* him drink. And she never got to tell him, because he wasn't waiting for her at the bus stop the following week, or the three weeks after that. And the next Saturday was her sixteenth birthday and she had a party at the house. He wasn't invited. He was found dead in his bedsit the Thursday after.

Although April may not have understood it at the age of fifteen, her father's description of the fall stayed with her and, occasionally, broke the surface of her consciousness. After the collapse of her affair with Professor Vaughan at Cambridge, for example, she was dimly aware of her weightlessness on amphetamines – perhaps that was why people called it 'getting high'. But then Jerry arrived on the scene and pulled her back from the edge.

Now, however, she was lying in Shawn Appiah's bed in the middle of a weekend afternoon. Jerry had taken Theo to the park, so that she could lend support to poor wifeless Shawn and poor motherless Rosie. But Shawn had dispatched his daughter to the shops with Gladys, the maid, and they had retired to bed to fuck. The sex had been mechanically pleasurable – Shawn had a kind of box-checking, pornographic routine that she suspected might come to seem comical – but joyless. And now she sat up next to him sipping a glass of room temperature white wine in some kind of sordid simulacrum of romance, his semen wet, sticky and uncomfortable in the crack of her arse, a fitting signifier of her recklessness.

Now she knew what her father had been talking about twenty years before. She knew that she had been walking the brink of a precipice by committing adultery. It had been risky behaviour, but comprehensible – justifiable, even – within the parameters of a failing modern relationship. But when Kudakwashe had seemingly attempted suicide (albeit, Shawn insisted, with no knowledge of the affair), April had faced a choice between appropriate, silent penitence and the descent into a kind of base immorality lacking any possible justification. She was neglecting her marriage, her child, any responsibility to the woman who lay sedated in a Harare hospital. She was beginning to doubt whether she much liked Shawn. Certainly she wanted no enduring relationship. And their sex: he had a thick, but rather rubbery erection that he had to shovel inside her with one hand at the base, which gave her the vague sense of DIY pipe-fitting. Her orgasm when it came was Christmas lights not aurora borealis – flicked switch not natural wonder. But none of this seemed to matter because she had, like her father, launched herself off the edge and she was weightless and the plummet was thrilling. Like her father, she was now without fear. And it never occurred to her how terrified he might have been in the weeks she didn't see him before his death, or, of course, that those who claim they are not scared can only ever claim they are not scared *yet*. Catch even the devil unguarded and ask him what he fears and see the admission flicker behind his eyes before he voices his defiant denial.

43

Sunday. Patson got home after two p.m. With Gilbert still recuperating, he was back to working every hour God sent and a few more with an altogether different return address. A profitable morning carrying women and children to churches around Harare, therefore, had followed a successful night ferrying revellers from Chez Ntemba to the city's darkest corners. It had been his best shift for several months and he pulled up outside the house with a rare sense of possibility. He had even stopped at the OK supermarket in town for a bottle of Mazoe: a treat for the kids.

Fadzai emerged to meet the car in the driveway. She'd lately taken to doing this if she was at the house at the time of his return, even in the middle of the night. It was one of many small shifts in behaviour that neither of them spoke about but both knew signified much. They weren't discussing their relationship for fear of jinxing its recovery. This was less superstition than acknowledgement that they didn't understand the reasons for improvement. And both knew from long experience the potential damage of a single ill-judged or mistimed word, no matter its intention.

Today, however, Fadzai seemed distant. And though she held open Patson's door, embraced him gently and expressed appropriate delight at the night's takings, the new custom wasn't yet sewn into the fabric of their marriage; Patson assumed he must have done something wrong. In years gone by he'd concealed so much from his wife that he automatically assumed he must be doing so again, though he couldn't think what. He followed her inside, therefore, enervated by a vague but thoroughly familiar dread.

He found Chabarwa doing homework. The boy promptly cleared his books off the table and laid a place for his father while Fadzai busied herself at the stove to heat his plate.

Patson went through to the back of the house to wash his hands. Anashe and Bessie were doing dishes. Patson was always pleased to see his sister-in-law. She had a lightness about her, which seemed to elevate the spirits of the whole household. But today she greeted him with the very same absent-minded, rather sullen distraction as his wife.

He asked how she was doing, how she'd found Gilbert after 'the incident'. He made a light-hearted, feeble remark about how he and Fadzai had done their best to take care of him, but some jobs were best left to 'the better half'. Bessie said nothing, allowing herself only a small grunt to avoid being actively rude. Unacknowledged, Patson's comment seemed to hang in the air between them, opaque as smoke.

He asked about her work. He asked about her boss, Mr Jerry: was he still at the clinic in Epworth? Patson had now driven him there several times. He said he admired the Englishman who had come all the way to Zimbabwe to help people and apparently he wasn't even paid for what he did . . .

Patson tailed off. Generally, he was a laconic man who

chose his words carefully, often choosing none at all. But now, unchecked by any response from Bessie, the banalities were spilling out of him, like he was a holed bucket. He felt ridiculous.

He asked where Gilbert was. Bessie raised her head for the first time and, hands covered with soap suds, jutted her chin to the street visible beyond the fence. There Gilbert, smoking a cigarette, walked five steps one way, then five the other – a contained, imaginary sentry duty.

'Right,' Patson said.

He headed inside, more convinced than ever that the fault must be his, the sense of dread growing proportionately.

When Fadzai put the plate of *sadza* and vegetables in front of him, therefore, and sat at his side, Patson feared the worst – a question he couldn't answer, an accusation of something inexcusable he had or hadn't done. But, instead, Fadzai began to talk to him about her brother in an urgent whisper. The combination of her tone, his preconceptions of where this was heading and his relief to discover he was in the clear meant that his wife was a minute deep into her concerns before Patson even began to focus on what they were, so he held up a hand to stop her, rolled a ball of *sadza* ruminatively and asked her to begin again.

She stopped. She sighed. She wetted her lips. She told him she'd never seen Gilbert like this. Of course she knew the beating had tormented her brother, emotionally as well as physically, brutally undermining his confidence, but she'd thought Bessie would snap him out of it. Instead, when Bessie had gently chided him for not attending church with the rest of them that morning and told him Pastor Joshua had even preached on Psalm 28 ('The Lord is my strength and my shield'), he had reacted furiously, calling his wife a stupid little girl who put her trust in fantasies.

As Fadzai recounted this, she stared at Patson, as if to say, 'Have you ever heard of such a thing?'

Patson sat silently for a moment and gave the impression of deep consideration. In fact, he *was* considering deeply, but not to gather his thoughts so much as to weigh what might or might not be said. He had more than a little sympathy for Gilbert: to be told to turn to God when in a state of humiliation seemed almost further belittling. However, Patson also knew that Gilbert's outburst had been shocking. Sometimes he thought there should be a pact between women and men: the former could take responsibility for the family's spiritual needs, the latter for material needs, and neither ever question the other's domain. The trouble was, these days, a woman, in her insecurity, needed to earn money while a man, in his, needed to consolidate moral authority.

Patson nodded, as if he had reached a meaningful conclusion. 'Bessie needs to be patient,' he said. 'The young man is hurt. He will recover.'

He looked at his wife steadily. He read the smallest movements of her features at once. He should have known that such platitudes would never suffice. She said, 'I am serious. I am worried for my brother. You know what he is like — full of crazy ideas and ambition. I have never known him to be without hope, not even for one day.'

'I will talk to him,' Patson said. 'Just let me sleep first.' Fadzai stood unmoved, but for an eyebrow. Patson sat back. He shifted awkwardly in his seat. He said, 'Can I at least finish eating?'

44

Patson found Gilbert at the car. Kneeling on the driver's side, he was reaching across the handbrake to the small drawer under the passenger seat where they kept the wheel wrench.

Patson asked him what he was doing.

Gilbert sat back on his haunches, then backed out of the car. The strain such simple movements put on his injuries twisted his face into a grimace. He was holding an ancient, battered paperback. 'My book,' he said. 'I'm going to take out the car. Earn some money.'

'Now?'

'Why not?'

Patson told him that he'd had an excellent night, that Gilbert could wait until he was fully recovered, that there was no need.

'No need to earn money?' Gilbert said.

Patson sighed. He was too tired for this. He took out his cigarettes. Along with the Mazoe, he'd bought a whole pack of Pacifics – takings had been that good. He unwrapped the cellophane and offered them to Gilbert. This was a first and Gilbert was momentarily hesitant, confused by the implication of the gesture – doesn't everyone know, after all, that men bond over minor iniquity? He took the packet and extracted a cigarette. Both men lit up.

Patson said that Fadzai had told him about the argument with Bessie.

Gilbert exhaled ruefully – so this was the agenda. He remarked that it was just one of those things and, respectfully, it was between him and his wife.

Patson nodded: of course. He nodded some more. He dragged on his cigarette. He let the pause linger. He said, 'Of course. However, in this instance, it is my business, too, because you are staying in my house.'

Gilbert said nothing. He smoked.

Patson said that naturally Gilbert was angry, but it would pass and there was no value in taking it out on the rest of the family, his wife least of all. 'How often do you see her – once every two weeks? Those should be happy times. You must take comfort in your wife.'

Gilbert smoked.

Patson said that, unlike himself, Gilbert was still a young man, and that youth was both blessing and curse. 'You believe you can improve your situation.'

Gilbert exhaled. 'You say that like it is a bad thing.'

'It is what I said – a blessing and a curse.'

'So you want me to think it is not possible to get the things I want? You want me not even to hope?'

Patson dropped his head a moment and drew a rough semi-circle in the dirt with the toe of his shoe. 'It is hope that causes most problems,' he said.

Gilbert shook his head. He flicked his cigarette, even though it was only half finished. It was an act of defiance. He said, 'My fate is my own. I married my wife. Our daughter was born. She came to Harare. I came to Harare. You allowed me to stay. I have worked hard. These were my choices. If I cannot hope to improve the situation for my family, what am I doing?'

Patson stared at his brother-in-law. He didn't know what to say. He was foundering. He was just so tired; too tired. For some reason, he glanced over his shoulder and found Fadzai watching them from the doorway. He must have sensed she was there, or at some level known that she wouldn't be able to resist verifying the conversation was indeed happening. He wondered what his wife thought he was saying. If he could guess, he'd have said it. He'd have said anything to conclude this conversation and be free to lie down. He dropped his eyes to his feet once again. He added a straight line to the parabola to make a P. Then he marked an A and a T, before scrubbing out the letters with the sole of his shoe. Eventually he murmured, 'I don't know. I try to find joy in small moments.'

'Like what?'

Patson made a low, gruff noise, somewhere between laughter and protest. 'I'm not sure I can think just like that. There are many moments.' He paused. 'When I watched Chabarwa play the cornet at New Vision,' he said. Then, quickly, to counter a brief surge of embarrassment, 'When one of the guys at the rank tells a joke; my wife; hot food; even a cigarette. All these things.'

Gilbert was staring at him, almost as if he'd never seen him before. Patson was suddenly uncomfortable. Had he indeed said something foolish? But Gilbert's eyes held a near maniacal seriousness that forced Patson to look away.

'What about the times in between?' Gilbert asked.

'What do you mean?'

'In between these *moments of joy* . . .'

Patson shrugged. 'I don't know. I am not a thinker. I am a

worker. After a certain age, that is what a man does – he works. Otherwise . . .'

Gilbert interrupted by lifting his paperback to shoulder height and, momentarily and preposterously, his brother-in-law thought he might be about to clap him around the head. But, instead, Gilbert simply brandished the book at him, eyes flashing. ' "Our labour preserves us from three great evils – weariness, vice and want." '

'What are you talking about?'

'That is what he says. In this book.'

'Who?'

'The writer.'

'Who is this writer?'

'Voltaire,' Gilbert said, checking the cover as if he needed to remind himself. 'He was a Frenchman. Hundreds of years ago. You see? Nothing changes.'

Patson, utterly befuddled, nodded. 'Weariness?' he said.

The conversation appeared to be over. Where Gilbert had been morose and angry, he now seemed energised. Patson didn't know why and he was too weary to consider it. He left Gilbert two more cigarettes and returned to the house. Fadzai was waiting for him. She asked, 'Is everything resolved?'

'It is resolved.'

'What did you say?'

'It is resolved. Everything is OK.'

Fadzai kissed his cheek, resting her hand on his shoulder. It was an intimate, tender moment and Patson could smell his wife and, despite the exhaustion, feel the blood hot in his face and penis. This was, he thought, one of the moments he had told Gilbert about and he wondered if he would ever grow too old to feel enlivened like this.

Fadzai said, 'You must sleep.' And she went into the bedroom and prepared the bed for him lovingly.

Gilbert went to Bessie. He apologised for what he'd said. Initially, Bessie was unreceptive, but he was so animated, so sure of himself, that his very manner trampled her reservations. He was talking in abstractions. He said things like, 'I will not fight a war I cannot win.' And 'I have mistaken hope for joy.' He said, 'I know what we must do.'

And Bessie, who had never imagined herself joyful and considered hope, at least in abstraction, a fatuous luxury, didn't ask what he was talking about, but only, 'What must we do?'

'Go home,' Gilbert said.

'Home?'

'Mubayira.' He held both her hands briefly.

She thought he would kiss her, but he didn't. Instead, he smiled brightly and said, 'I will go to work. We still need money.' She smiled too and patted him amicably on the elbow, even though she now felt an acute if nebulous concern.

Alone at the car, Gilbert lit one of Patson's cigarettes. He knew he was not supposed to smoke in the car, but sudden certainty often prefaces recklessness, especially in young men. He slid himself behind the wheel, cigarette in hand. He leaned over to the passenger side and opened the small drawer beneath the seat. He looked at the gun that he'd taken from the bedroom and stashed earlier. He knew now that he wouldn't use it. Even if he saw Castro or the Chipangano guy who'd stolen his shoes, he wouldn't use it. But there was no harm in keeping it there. Just in case.

217

45

It was a typical day at the clinic, as busy as it was unproductive. In the morning, for example, Jerry saw a middle-aged woman brought in by her husband. She was suffering acute joint pain. Upon examining her, Jerry discovered a distended abdomen, and gentle palpation revealed a knotty growth approximately the size of a tennis ball, just below the transpyloric plane, most likely on her pancreas. He assumed it was cancerous and terminal. His only doubt was because of the size of the tumour and the fact she was still alive. He had never before come across a tumour that had been allowed to grow gleefully unchecked for so long.

In the UK, cancer was a drug war, a beating back on several fronts in the battlefield of the body. Here it was a walkover. The woman needed a scan she couldn't afford followed by treatment she couldn't afford followed, inevitably, by death.

He asked her husband why it had taken so long to seek medical help. The question came out sharper than he'd intended and the man looked shaken and terrified. He replied that they had been to Outpatients at Parirenyatwa the previous month. He said that his wife had been given some pills that had helped somewhat but were now finished, so they were hoping for a renewed prescription. He passed Jerry a large medicine bottle and Jerry read its label. It was high-dosage diclofenac.

Jerry said, 'I see.' Then, 'Of course.' He went to the clinic's small medicine cabinet and refilled the bottle. He carefully totted the number of pills, so he knew how much he would have to pay for the anti-inflammatories. His action was both illegal and immoral, but it was also, he considered, indisputably the right thing to do. He had never before experienced circumstances that so frequently required him to square that and other circles.

When the man asked how much the drugs would cost, Jerry waved him away with a reflexive smile of generosity. The effusive, humble gratitude of the man and his dying wife made Jerry briefly think he might cry.

In the afternoon, the power was cut off. This was unusual for a Tuesday, but everyone knew the schedule for load-shedding was euphemistically described as 'a guideline'. The clinic would need the generator to power lighting and, especially, the borehole pump. However, Jerry found that they were out of petrol, so he had to dispatch Bongai, the receptionist, to the nearest garage with a container and twenty bucks from his own wallet. The patients sat and waited in resigned silence.

At one point, Tangwerai emerged from his office, stood next to the queue and lifted his face to the sky ruminatively, as if considering a prospective investment. Then he announced, to nobody in particular, 'The rains, they are late this year,' before specifically addressing a young man in the queue: 'Do you think they will come soon?'

'I think so,' the young man replied.

Tangwerai nodded as if reassured and headed back inside. This was, Jerry thought, the doctor's way of rallying spirits – of saying,

'I am here and I am waiting too' – and he admired him for his subtlety.

He caught Tangwerai by the arm. He said, 'The light's OK. Maybe we could see a few – you know, anything that's not acute?'

'With no water?'

Jerry shook his head, frustrated. 'We should have a water tank,' he said. 'Ten thousand litres. For when there's no power.'

'You're right, we should have a tank.' Tangwerai looked at him with the hint of a smile peeping from between the lapels of his oversized suit. 'Will you buy us a tank, Jerry?'

At some or other recent expat do, Jerry had found himself describing his role at the clinic, a little drunk, to Derek Sedelski, the cherubic American governance expert. 'I feel a bit like that Dutch kid,' he said. 'You know, the one who stuck his finger in a dam.' But that was a lousy metaphor, because at least the Dutch kid, however temporarily, had stemmed the flow.

Increasingly, Jerry had no idea what he was doing here: here at this clinic, here in Zimbabwe. He had wanted to work, to be useful, to play a small part next to April's larger part in the UK's altogether grander scheme to save Zimbabwe from itself. But now April was only pushing paper, complaining about pushing paper and complaining about Jerry. And Jerry was paying for painkillers for the terminally ill. Jerry was no longer sure whether Zimbabwe could be saved, required saving or, indeed, wanted it. But the one thing he knew for sure was this: if there was any saving to be done, he wasn't the man for the job.

Jerry came to work only to have a reason to leave the house and, perhaps, collect horror stories that might have capital back in the UK. He was in danger of becoming everything he'd sworn he'd never be: a man of wide and interesting experience and dull and narrow mind, possessed of a dazed, bitter, bewildered, reflexive certainty; just another expat.

By the end of the day, Jerry resigned himself to resignation, although exactly how one resigned when not actually employed in the first place was something of a comedic paradox that spoke volumes about his situation. He imagined suggesting a month's 'notice' period, so that at least the clinic could get used to the idea of losing a nurse and, arguably more importantly, his daily contributions to transport, drugs and fuel.

When Tangwerai called him into his office, therefore, Jerry assumed the young doctor had read his mind. Tangwerai had two beers on his desk. He opened the first with the other and the second with his teeth. He offered one to Jerry and they clinked glass. Tangwerai said, 'Your good health,' before swigging deep. 'I want to thank you, Jerry,' he said. 'You have been a godsend to us and I much appreciate your work and commitment.'

'No,' Jerry said. 'Really.' And he nodded reciprocal gratitude before taking a drink of his own.

'The clinic is to shut down,' Tangwerai said.

'I'm sorry?'

'Shut down. At the end of the month, we will shut down.'

'What?'

'Our funding has been discontinued,' Tangwerai said. Then, off Jerry's bewildered silence, 'Apparently it came from a budget for crisis alleviation. Apparently there is no longer a crisis. And, with the current political situation, donor policy is not to commit to Zimbabwe in the medium term. After all, we are a pariah state.'

Jerry stared at the doctor. Whatever his personal feelings, he couldn't stop the tide of indignation rising in his throat. He made an involuntary noise of rising indignation. He said, 'That's ridiculous!'

Tangwerai returned the stare, bottle paused halfway to his mouth. 'Of course it's ridiculous,' he said. 'It is all ridiculous.'

'And our patients?' Jerry spluttered.

'Our patients will go somewhere else.'

'Where? Where will they go?'

Tangwerai drank. He put the bottle on the table. 'Somewhere else,' he said quietly.

Jerry nodded. He gathered his thoughts. Why was he so outraged? Why did he care? It made no difference to be outraged. It made no difference to care. 'And you?'

Tangwerai smiled. 'I will be OK. I'll go somewhere else too. I am taking Bradford to the UK. I have a place at the University of Sussex for a PhD: "Community Health Initiatives in Prevention of Tropical Disease" . . . or, as we call it in this part of the world, "disease".'

'Right.'

The doctor raised his drink. He said, 'Don't look so worried, Jerry. Let's toast the future, whatever it may bring.' They clinked again. 'The future,' Tangwerai said.

And Jerry joined in: 'The future.'

46

Jerry was waiting outside the clinic for Patson to pick him up. He checked the time on his phone and found he had a text from April: she wouldn't be home until after eight. She wanted to stop in on the Appiahs. 'Another disaster,' she wrote.

Jerry considered the commitment his wife was showing to this family they barely knew. He was irritated that it ate into the already limited time she made available for their own son. He caught himself and tried to think more generously: perhaps the night they'd found Kudakwashe had affected her more profoundly than he'd realised. Nursing had inevitably, if sadly, inured him to other people's blood and pain, but April had clearly been shocked by it all and thrown herself wholeheartedly into a supporting role, particularly listening to Shawn, an outlet for the man's stresses, fears and loneliness.

Out of the blue, Jerry wondered whether his wife had a crush on the American. It was a thought that gave him pause and, the more he dwelled on it, the more he was certain it was true. There was something obvious about it – the amount of time she spent there, of course, but also the way she talked to him about Shawn and Rosie, filling in the latest from the hospital, the man's worries for his wife's sanity and the apparently bizarre reaction of Kuda's family to the sad situation. In fact, this was more or less the only thing he and April now talked about, a kind of conversational neutral territory where there was no reason for either to be irritated.

Jerry even wondered whether April had acted on her crush, but he quickly dismissed the idea. It wasn't that he imagined his wife morally or emotionally unsuited to infidelity. He knew that she wasn't; not like him. But she had lately become so cold, so hard, so loaded with resentment that he could no longer picture her as a sexual being. It didn't occur to him that her calcified loathing was reserved for him alone.

Jerry checked the time again. Patson's implacable lateness bugged him. Actually, it wasn't the lateness so much as the easy dishonesty with which the guy estimated an arrival time and avoided questions of his whereabouts – *Yes, Uncle. At the clinic? I will be there now now. / Where am I? I am near. Very near. / Ten minutes, Uncle. No more than half an hour. I am on my way.*

Jerry considered his options. If he went home now, he could give Theo his bath and supper and put him to bed. Indeed, if he went home now, he could do all that and still have time to call Bessie back to babysit and be gone before his wife's return.

Trouble was, Jerry wanted a drink. He told himself it was the beer with Tangwerai that had given him the taste. But no sooner did he tell himself this than he felt obliged to concede the lie: these days, he always wanted a drink. That bothered him.

April thought he had a drinking problem. Although she never spoke about it with that level of directness, she clearly worried that she was doomed to repeat her mother's mistakes. Jerry sympathised. Of course he did. But she needed to understand that the neuroses were her own, not to be projected onto him. And he seemingly didn't sympathise enough to stop drinking.

Still, Jerry was bothered by his thirst. Why? Because it was yet another signifier of the typical expat: hapless victim of cheap childcare, boredom and burgeoning self-importance. So, he vowed to go straight home. He would put Theo to bed. He wouldn't drink tonight. Maybe he'd fuck about on Facebook for an hour or, bandwidth permitting, try to torrent some new music.

The Raum pulled up, but it was Gilbert who got out, with his bright smile and cheery 'Hello, Boss!' Patson must have knocked off for the day and Jerry's heart sank. As Bessie's husband, Gilbert provoked in Jerry an almost paternal sense of responsibility, but Gilbert was also a talker and Jerry much preferred Patson's quiet concentration. Jerry hadn't seen Gilbert since the 'incident' and knew he'd have to ask him about it. Worst of all, if Gilbert had no other fare, he'd want to visit Bessie for an hour or two. Jerry couldn't really face attempting to revoke his laissez-faire attitude, but he knew that if the taxi was in the driveway when April got home it would undoubtedly put her back up.

'Where are we going?' Gilbert asked.

'The house.'

'No drink tonight?'

Jerry found the question, the smile, grating. 'No,' he said. 'No drink.'

He asked the obligatory question about the beating and, in spite of himself, found he was intrigued and increasingly horrified by Gilbert's story. He discovered that Bessie had given him the sanitised version. He had often thought April knew nothing of what it meant to live in this country for the majority of its population, not compared to Jerry, who worked in a ghetto clinic. But as Gilbert unfurled the brutal absurdity of what had happened,

Jerry appreciated that his own limited experience only allowed him to confirm his wife knew nothing, not to pretend that he knew more.

'Did you go to the police?' Jerry asked, but he knew the answer even before the young man's snorted response. Then, 'Chipangano: they shouldn't be allowed to get away with it.' He said this only because it was true, not because it had meaningful consequence.

'You are right,' Gilbert said.

'And how are you feeling?' Jerry asked pathetically. 'Are you better?'

'I am quite OK.'

'Good,' Jerry said conclusively, but his burst of sympathy had already given the young man all the encouragement he needed to continue.

So, Gilbert told Jerry that the beating had been a watershed moment, and he now admitted the city wasn't for him. He said he'd come to Harare to be close to Bessie and further his ambitions. He'd studied at KBC – had Jerry heard of it? Jerry shook his head. 'Kadoma Business College,' Gilbert said seriously. 'It is an excellent school.' He said he'd planned to work for Patson, to save enough to find a job commensurate with his skills and interests, to set up a business of his own.

'So what happened?' Jerry asked dutifully.

'These are dreams, Boss. These are dreams.'

Gilbert then launched into an impassioned if semi-comprehensible diatribe. 'You think it is possible,' he said. 'You think anything is possible. Education opens doors – that's what they say. But what doors does it open? I have read many books – very many books. I am an educated man, but what doors are open for me? None of them. I am just a poor African, Boss.'

Jerry made a noise somewhere between demurring and sympathy – what else could he do?

But this only prompted Gilbert to outline his plans to return to Mubayira with Bessie and become a farmer. He seemed energised by the prospect: 'I will be the best poor African I can be.'

'With Bessie?' Jerry said, suddenly engaged.

'Of course.'

Gilbert said he was just hoping to raise enough money for the move. Land wasn't a problem because his father or the headman would allocate him a plot. But he needed capital for seeds, fertiliser and a few chickens to get started. 'If I have a thousand dollars ...' he said, in an open-ended, musing fashion that left Jerry in no doubt of the underlying intent. Then, 'How long has my wife been working for you, Boss?' Then, 'I have been driving you three months, isn't it? And we often talk like this. We are friends. I think of you as one of my good friends, one of my very good friends.'

In the back of the taxi, Jerry shook his head. He knew where this was going. He hated where this was going. He had lent money before – relatively small sums to Thomas, the gardener, to buy a handcart for his rural home, to Bessie for reasons unspecified (probably, in retrospect, to get her husband to Harare) – and it had felt good: the gratitude, the sense of contribution. But local problems, like his own, were a bottomless pit and, at heart, he knew that he couldn't actually afford a thousand dollars and, besides, it wouldn't solve Gilbert's problems any more than it would solve his own were he to spend it on flowers for his wife. Jerry said, 'I can't afford that kind of money, Gilbert.' And the young man lapsed into sullen silence.

Jerry's phone rang. He looked at the display. It read: 'Albert Mandiveyi'. He answered. He listened briefly. He needed no further excuse. He said, 'Sure. Why not?' He rang off. He leaned forward to talk to Gilbert. He said, 'Change of plan.'

47

*These days, I watch TV all the time and Momma not even there to dis-
aprove. When I get up in the morning, Gladys give me bathtime an then
I watch TV while I eat breakfast – Sofia the First; iss bout an ornary
little girl who become a princess. Sumtime, if he not workin, I watch wid
Daddy an he give me a big squeeze an say, 'You're my princess, little
bird.' An I don say nuthin, but I know I not a princess cos princesses
not black: thas true on TV an iss true at school too where Emma-Jade
say the same thing an she a big girl wid long red hair like Sofia. I watch
TV after school, an sumtime I even watch after supper.*

*Sasa say, 'You see? Iss good thing Momma gone, little bat, cos now
you watch TV whenever you like.' Usually Sasa talk like a screech, but
he say this real soft like a bird – chirrup-chirrup.*

*But it still make me sad an I say, 'Mom's not gone, she sick. An when
she a bit better I gonna be allowed to visit.'*

Sasa say, 'I think your daddy better already.'

An I say, 'What you mean?'

*An Sasa sing, 'Better with the white bitch! Better with the white
bitch!' Chirrup-chirrup.*

*I miss my mom real bad, only I try not to show it cos it make Daddy
sad when I cry, an sumtime it make Sasa angry. Also, the white bitch*

229

roun the house all the time these day, an why I gonna show her how I feel when I don barely know her at all? I mean, she nice enough, but she smell funny and I don wanna call her 'Aunty April' like Daddy say, specially when she all embarrassed an go, 'I don't know about "Aunty", April's fine,' in that funny voice of hers. An I don wanna call her April neither.

The night Mom have an accident I wake up real thirsty an I call out, 'Mom! I want sum water! Momma! I need water!' Like that. Only she don answer, so I get out of bed an try an find her.

Sasa waitin for me at the kitchen door. He go, 'You wanna see sumthin real funny, Rosie?'

I open the door an Mom lisnin to music, which is why she don hear me. She turn an she look at me an I swear she look so scared like I'm spooky. Sasa fly roun the room screechin, 'Funny funny funny!' But he don sound like nuthin funny.

An Mom start prayin real fast: 'Father God, Yahweh, my blessed saviour, protect us from this evil spirit made manifest! Protect us, Father God! Protect us, sweet Jesus!'

An Sasa go, 'She can see me! She see me!'

An I go in my head, 'Don be silly! No one see you but me!' An then, out loud, 'You don see Sasa, do you, Momma?'

An Sasa squeechin (I made up that word – cross between a screech an a squeal), 'Cut out her eyes! Cut out her eyes!'

I don know what happen after that. It like I blink and the clock move on without me, jus like when Momma take me to church an the pastor put his hand on my forehead an my chest. Nex, I jus standin in the kitchen an iss all quiet like a mouse. Sasa nowhere to be seen an Momma sittin on the floor wid a face all tired an tea-towels wrap roun her arms. I say, 'You OK, Momma?'

An she smile at me an go, 'Wash your hands, little bird.' So I go to the sink, stand on my step, get soap an I wash, an Mom say, 'Are you washing them really well? Scrub scrub scrub!'

I say, 'Yes, Momma.'

I get down an I show Mom my hands and she say, 'Good girl.'

I look at the tea-towels roun her arms an I see they thick an wet wid blood, so I aks her again, 'You OK, Momma?'

'Yes, my love.'

'Did you have an accident?'

'That's right,' she say. 'I'm feeling a bit weak, but I'll be OK.'

Then she tell me she want me to go to bed, but before I do I gotta pass her phone, which sittin on the counter. I do like I's told an she say, 'Thank you, little bird.' Then, 'Come here.' I lean forward an she kiss me on the forehead an she whisper sumthin an I aks what she say an she go, 'Just a little prayer.' Then she smile at me. 'Go back to bed, my love.'

'Are you gonna tuck me in?'

'I'm feeling a bit sick,' she say. 'You're a big girl, aren't you? You can go to sleep on your own.'

I pull a face and do a big sigh, but I's atchly kinda happy cos she call me a big girl. So I go back to bed on my own an I asleep jus like that.

I wake up cos I need to go pee. Iss all quiet and I can't hear nuthin, not even Sasa. I go to find Mom, but all I find is the white bitch sittin on Mom's bed. I tell her I need the bathroom, but iss dark. She turn on the light for me. I aks where Momma is an she tell me that she had an accident and had to go to the hospital. She tell me Momma gonna be OK. She tell me to go back to bed. But I go, 'I don wanna go to bed. I'm not tired any more. I wanna watch TV.' An the white bitch let me so I know that, whether Momma gonna be OK or not, evrythin not OK.

We sit on the sofa an watch my Henry Hugglemonster DVD. I think about Sasabonsam an I tell her that I worried that Momma's accident his fault. She look at me all strange an go, 'Is he pretend or is he real?' An her face tell me the answer she wanna hear, so I go, 'Pretend, I guess.'

I mean, thas what Daddy say too – that Sasa pretend – but I's

231

not sure I know the difference; at least not all the time. Like, I know Momma had an accident an now she sick an thas real; an I know when Emma-Jade play Sofia the First, thas pretend. But how you gonna tell me Sasabonsam real when nobody see or hear him but me? An how you gonna tell me he pretend when I see an hear him as clear an loud as the TV? Like, when Daddy put me to bed, he go, 'Let's say our prayers, little bird.' An we make a list of all the people we love an we pray that the Lord Jesus Christ, our risen saviour, protect them. But I don know if what Daddy say real or pretend, because if he love Momma, how come he fuckin the white bitch?

48

Mandiveyi had seen the Englishman enter the Jameson public bar ten minutes before, but he felt no inclination to move. He took out his hip flask and swigged whisky. Just now, in a moment of reflection, he had concluded that his life was falling apart. And a moment like that requires acknowledgement, does it not?

Men are liars, Mandiveyi thought, and all lies tumble like a house of cards, but my lies, my lies …

Men lie to their wives, to their bosses, to the other woman, to other women; to friends, colleagues, children, wider family. Men lie about three things – their success, their loyalty and their lies. But most men? When the cards tumble, they find solace in truth – with their wife, their boss, the other woman, whoever. Mandiveyi knew he had no truth. He was barely a man at all, but an ephemeral fabrication, a chimera of flesh and falsehood. He was not lying with purpose, only to maintain other lies. He was not lying to maintain his marriage, but the lie of it; not to maintain his job, but the lie of it; not to maintain himself, but the lie that he existed beyond a sagging sack of flesh and bone.

Two days ago, he had broken it off with Nature. It had been an easy decision. His feelings for her remained largely unchanged (though the attraction had undeniably dimmed and that was, perhaps, the extent of his feelings). However, he knew that such relationships were necessarily temporary: maintain them too long and the woman inevitably became comfortable, possessive, demanding, indiscreet. This was intolerable for someone in his position.

He knew the process well. He had been through it more times than he cared to remember. You told the woman. You accepted her anger and grief with some degree of penitence, but remained steadfast in your conviction and, importantly, authority. You allowed the storm to blow itself out and carefully made a token offer of monetary recompense for her time and trouble. And if she still resisted? You pointed out the lies she'd told – about her hopes, her expectations, that which she was prepared to accept. Finally, you told her that she'd be better off without you. And you were able to do this with complete and irresistible conviction because it was most likely the first true thing you had ever said to her.

Of course, there were always repercussions. You might have to ignore text messages and phone calls, perhaps even avoid your usual watering-holes for a month or two in case the woman was lurking to publicise her grievances. But Mandiveyi had never known a woman to react like Nature. Of course he had heard stories . . . but such things should never have happened to someone like him.

Maybe he should have expected it, considering the range and duration of her fury. She had flown at him like a harpy, raked his neck with her fingernails and spat in his face. He had been forced to slap her several times, just to make her sit down. Flustered, he'd stumbled over his prepared speech in his rush to reach the knockout blow: 'You will be better off without me.'

She didn't appear to hear it. She said, 'Fuck you, big fucking man! You think you're a big fucking man! We'll see. We'll see I don't fuck you up!'

Yesterday Mandiveyi had gone to his son's school. As he grew, Tendai was finding it ever harder to walk, even with his frame, and was increasingly forced to use the wheelchair. He was now struggling to get from lesson to lesson and, though he said the other boys were generally supportive, his studies were suffering. Mandiveyi had made an appointment with the headmaster to raise the problem.

The headmaster was sympathetic. He leaned forward and clasped his hands in front of him on the desk. He said he would assign two pupils in each class to help Tendai get around. Mandiveyi expressed his thanks. The headmaster said, 'Unfortunately, there is nothing I can do about the school's physical geography.'

Mandiveyi nodded – *Of course not*. The headmaster nodded, too, then sat back in his chair. He weighed his words carefully. He asked Mandiveyi if he and his wife had considered what they might do should Tendai's condition continue to deteriorate. In such circumstances, would there come a point when a mainstream school would no longer be appropriate?

Mandiveyi simply stared at him. He didn't know what to say. There were no lies to tell.

The headmaster made a point of stressing the admiration that he and the other staff had for Tendai. He described the boy as a fighter; he described his generous spirit and popularity, not the brightest kid but certainly one of the most hard-working. Tendai was, he said, a credit to his parents: as honest as the day was long.

Mandiveyi returned home downhearted. His son, the cripple:

it was impossible for him not to consider the boy's disability somehow his fault; not genetically so much as spiritually, as if the child were the receptacle of his father's sin. And the more he tried to shake this feeling loose – tell himself that it was just an expression of the superstition he'd dismissed long before but must be latent somewhere within him – the more the idea took grip. And he had no idea how he might tell his wife, Plaxedes, the details of his conversation with the headmaster. She already considered their son twice the man his father was.

As it transpired, he didn't get the chance to find out. He met his wife in the living room, sitting forward on the large grey leather lounge suite, holding a pair of his underpants in either shaking fist.

Nature had not ambushed Mandiveyi in a favourite bar. Instead she'd ambushed Plaxedes in the dairy aisle of Bon Marché, depositing his underwear in his wife's shopping trolley and leaving no doubt about its recent provenance. 'Your fucking big man!' she'd spat. 'Your fucking big man!'

Mandiveyi felt little option but to retreat immediately to his last line of justification. He told his wife that she knew the character of his job (which she didn't – he'd made sure of that) and that he couldn't possibly discuss the nefarious activities in which he was involved for the sake of the nation. All he could tell her was that the woman was implicated in a case he was working on, a matter of life or death, and that he had done nothing that was not in his line of duty.

At this point, Mandiveyi had twin realisations that yawned in front of him, like gaping mouths, either of which could swallow him whole. The first was that his wife hated him. More than that, she didn't care whether he was telling the truth. It wasn't the infidelity that bothered her, but the shame of public humiliation. And, while his sexual activity might be swept beneath a façade of normality, the shame could not: there was no coming back from the shame. The second was that he was indeed working on a case that was a matter of life or death, quite possibly his own, and he had lost control: he was not going to find the taxi driver, he was not going to find the gun and he would pay the price. The house of cards was already tumbling.

Mandiveyi got out of the car and entered the Jameson public bar. He affected the affectations he affected on such occasions – each designed to project a kind of earnest mateyness – and approached Jerry Jones, the English nurse.

He bought Jerry a drink. They shot the shit. He asked after Jerry's family (did he have a family? Mandiveyi couldn't remember) and Jones shrugged. 'You know.'

He laughed. He said, 'I do. Of course. What man doesn't know?'

He asked about Jerry's work, a question that elicited an elaborate and effusive response that the Englishman punctuated with expressions of incredulity and occasional bursts of bitter laughter. It concluded with a shake of the head and a heartfelt 'This fucking country!'

Mandiveyi raised his glass to toast: 'This fucking country!' Because he knew there was no stronger bond than one forged in self-righteousness.

Mandiveyi allowed the bonhomie to settle. Then he said, 'You know I saw you? The other day. That's what made me think to call you. Outside Corporate Health. You were with that guy: Appiah.'

'Shawn?' Jerry swigged his drink. 'Yeah. That's a tough one.' Then, 'You know Shawn?'

'Not really,' Mandiveyi said. 'He is Ghanaian?'

'Ghanaian? No, I don't think so. I mean, I don't know his

heritage, but he's an American. At least, that's what's on his passport. Shawn Appiah? The gold dealer?'

'Exactly.'

'American. Poor fucker. I mean, that's some fucked-up situation, I tell you.'

Jerry began to tell another elaborate story. But Mandiveyi was barely listening. His mind, trained to an unusual facility for the machinations of power, deception and the negotiation implicit therein, was double timing on one word: *American*.

He had thought he would stand or fall on his capacity to find the gun – and he would not find the gun. But what if he brought in an American for dealing gold illegally? An *American*. It would be the biggest coup for the Organisation since the arrest of Simon Mann and the whole hilarious debacle of the 'Wonga Coup'. Phiri, and more importantly *Iganyana*, would be forced to acknowledge his worth. Jones was still talking, but Mandiveyi took a second to switch off his senses and revel in his remarkable resilience. The house of cards was still standing for the moment. Mandiveyi was invigorated. Why had he ever doubted himself?

Mandiveyi allowed Jerry's story to play out. He made the appropriate noises. He glanced at his phone. He pretended he'd just got a message. He said, 'Something's come up.' He drained his drink. 'I have to go.' He shook Jerry's hand and smiled, gummy and piscine.

The Englishman showed no sign of moving. Mandiveyi said, 'You're staying?' Then, to the barman, 'One more for my friend here.' He dropped a ten on the counter. Jerry demurred. Mandiveyi insisted. He said, 'It's good to see you again, Jerry. We must do this regularly.' He clapped Jerry on the shoulder. He said, 'Remember what I told you: you need friends in a town like this. Anything you need. Anything at all.'

Jerry laughed. He said, 'I can't think.'

'You never know,' Mandiveyi said. 'You have my number, isn't it?'

'I have your number,' Jerry confirmed.

49

Kuda was released from hospital, not into Shawn's care but that of her parents.

When the consulting psychiatrist first raised the possibility of her discharge, Shawn was dismayed. He pointed out that his wife was barely speaking: she was listless and unresponsive. What if she were a danger to herself?

The psychiatrist, an ageing white guy with bad skin and extensive moustache, said, 'Do you *think* she's a danger to herself?' He paused. He said, 'Her current state is not untypical: a combination of the shock of the event and the drugs I have prescribed. It will change in time. Besides, Mr Appiah, the risk in a situation like this is that she becomes institutionalised. How can I explain it? That she comes to see these four walls as her only safe place, and the longer she stays, the harder it becomes to leave.'

Shawn thought for a moment. He said, 'My work takes me around the country. Days at a time.'

'Somewhere else, then? Other family?' The psychiatrist smiled weakly and twisted a fleck of saliva into his whisker, a habitual tic that turned Shawn's stomach. 'The other thing I am obliged to raise, Mr Appiah, is that your insurance places certain financial limits for psychiatric care. We are approaching those limits. Wouldn't it be preferable to save on her bed and so forth and allow me to continue to treat Kudakwashe as an outpatient? More bang for your buck, so to speak.'

Shawn glared at the man. 'It's not about money,' he said. 'We don't even know what happened. She has hardly said two words to me.'

The psychiatrist looked uncomfortable. 'Perhaps we will never know exactly what happened,' he said. 'But I think we know enough.'

Shawn raised an eyebrow – *And?*

'You are putting me in an invidious position, Mr Appiah. Of course there are issues of confidentiality.' Then, before Shawn could protest, 'But you are her husband. Kudakwashe has talked to me a little and I believe we're looking at a brief psychotic episode, hallucinatory in nature. The question is whether it was an isolated incident or something that may repeat.' Again, he smiled uncomfortably. 'Sadly, psychiatric diagnosis can never describe a problem, merely the manifestation thereof. But I am confident that the medication I've prescribed will ensure no further episodes for now. After that, it's a question of trial and error, of wait and see.'

When Shawn left the hospital, he drove straight round to see Kuda's mum and dad. Mr and Mrs Gorekore lived in the decaying grandeur of a large but crumbling house off Twickenham Drive. Kuda's father had been something big in the NRZ, Zimbabwe's railway, but, long since retired, he'd seen his pension and savings decimated in the meltdown of 2007. All he'd been left with was the house and he couldn't afford its upkeep.

Shawn considered it a depressing place of cracked driveway and dying lawn. Of course, Shawn's own home bore similar scars, but he was renting, wasn't he? Besides, the Newlands house was a stepping-stone on his way up to something better, not down to the grave.

The interior of the Gorekores' got no sun. It felt unnaturally cold and Shawn was always picking his way through its dim rooms, fearful of banging his shins on some piece of thirty-year-old teak furniture, as indestructible as it was threadbare. Even if you turned on a light, the bulbs seemed half-hearted, as if they were reluctant to illuminate shabby paintwork, broken skirting and cracked tiles.

Nonetheless Mr and Mrs Gorekore were a sprightly couple: he, stick-thin with flint eyes behind reading spectacles, a three-piece suit swallowed in the armchair from which he rarely moved; she, a large, cushiony woman in a state of perpetual motion, despite the crippling effect of two arthritic hips that undoubtedly needed replacing. They were engaged and enthusiastic. The mother did most of the talking, but Gorekore would occasionally interject some wry aside, which invariably reduced his wife to giggles that wouldn't have sounded out of place from a ten-year-old. They never complained. They seemed to personify the possibilities of happy marriage. Shawn had observed to Kudakwashe more than once that she had learned little from them.

The Gorekores lived alone, but their house was a teeming hub for the extended family, especially at weekends when relatives whose connection Shawn couldn't fathom descended in droves. There were uncountable kids, who tore around the garden in unstoppable high spirits and, much to Shawn's irritation, showed no particular affection for Rosie, whom they called 'American': *American – come and run! American – come and climb!*

Back in New York, before he left, Shawn had told his boys that this was something he looked forward to: 'The wider family. It's not like it is here, yo. It's more like *mi casa, su casa,* you know? Like, over here? We become so *white*, bro: you got to call before you visit, you got to plan this and plan that. And you think a black man these days ever going to take responsibility for his own blood in trouble? No way. But that's our true selves.'

'Deep shit,' Malik had said. 'Deep shit, for real.'

Deep it may have been; shit most certainly. Because Shawn now had more relatives than he'd ever wanted, with more troubles than he'd imagined possible, and he was fucked if he was going to take responsibility for any of them. *That* shit? It may have been African or Zimbabwean or whatever, but there was a reason it hadn't stuck in the development of the black man.

Shawn presented his dilemma about Kuda's discharge to the Gorekores. The conversation went better than he'd dared hope. He addressed the problem to his mother-in-law and the only awkward moment came when she said, 'A wife looks after her husband, a husband looks after his wife. In sickness and in health. That's what marriage is.'

There was a moment's silence. Shawn didn't know how to respond but, before he could try, Gorekore leaned forward and said definitively, 'Shawn has to earn a living. That *is* looking after his wife.' For once, Shawn's mother-in-law found nothing to giggle about.

Gorekore picked up Kuda from the hospital. They'd agreed that Shawn would bring Rosie over to meet them at the Mount Pleasant home. She hadn't seen her mum since 'her accident' (as they had all come to refer to it, encompassing acknowledgement of haphazard misfortune, qualified with that possessive pronoun). It hadn't seemed appropriate when Kuda was unconscious, or when she'd recovered only to a state of torpid detachment. But perhaps it would be easier in the family house where she'd grown up.

At first it had all gone well. Kuda appeared delighted to see her daughter, momentarily snapping out of lethargy to embrace her and whisper, 'My little bird! My little bird!' However, a second later, the relieved smile froze on Shawn's face as Kuda thrust out her arms and pushed Rosie away, fear written deep into her features. 'He's here! He's here!' Kuda said. Then, directly to her mother, 'He's here, Mummy! He's here!'

Mrs Gorekore led Kuda, protesting, to her bedroom. Rosie, remarkably, retained her equilibrium. She turned to Shawn: 'Is Momma sick, Daddy?'

'Yes, baby,' Shawn said. He looked at his father-in-law, whose face shone horror through its mask of habitual implacability. 'I gotta look after my daughter.'

'Yes,' the old man said. 'Of course.'

Shawn knew that his parents-in-law didn't like him. He knew that Kuda had told them sketchy details of the sketchy details she knew of his serial infidelity. But as he sat Rosie on her booster and strapped her into the cab of the Isuzu and Gorekore waved them away, he also knew that they agreed he was doing the right thing. And the fact that what was best for Rosie coincided with what he wanted? That was just his good fortune.

50

April took Shawn's call at work. In spite of herself – in fact, to her irritation – she felt a flutter of excitement. He asked her to come over. She said, 'When?'

'I don't know. Soon as you can?'

'I'm at work.'

'I know that. And I don't want to put you out, but I got a problem and I don't know where else to turn. Serious, boo.'

April hesitated. She was busy. One of the cleaners was accused of stealing petty cash. It wouldn't have been a big deal, but the cleaner in question was Henrietta Gumbo, the woman she'd reinstated at Peter Nyengedza's request. It was embarrassing. It made her look like an idiot. Perhaps it would be good to get out of the embassy for an hour or two – dodge the flak. She checked the time on the monitor in front of her. She said, 'OK.'

Driving across town to Newlands, April analysed the momentary thrill she'd experienced at the sound of Shawn's voice. It had nothing to do with him, that was for sure. Rather, it reflected her state of mind. Why had she begun the affair? She could barely remember. She had not been seeking intimacy, certainly; or, she thought, sexual fulfilment per se. Perhaps most accurately it had been an enactment of her resentment. Now, however, her motivations had morphed into something quite different as she was simultaneously enlivened and appalled by her feelings of degradation – *Is this me? Is this who I am?* Even as she pulled into Shawn's driveway, therefore, she knew she had to end it, fully intended to do so and yet suspected she wouldn't. She was on that downward spiral she intuitively understood, but couldn't face. Like a drunk, she simply had to stop before it was too late. But she couldn't stop.

She walked to the back of the house and found Shawn pacing the veranda, cigarette in one hand, coffee in the other. He was barefoot, in a Knicks T-shirt and grey sweatpants and, briefly, she remembered her initial attraction. He was undeniably good-looking, albeit in a generic TV-movie kind of way. Trouble was, he talked like a TV movie too. He stopped at the sight of her, dragged on his cigarette and smiled slowly. 'Look at you. All dressed up in your suit. I love that shit.'

April was aware that English people liked to laugh at Americans for their lack of irony, but it wasn't anything she'd particularly considered until she met Shawn. Specifically, she found his unironic behaviour in the realm of sexual interaction almost bewildering. The lines he dropped, his manoeuvres, the pillow talk: it all smacked of . . . a TV movie. Weren't the emotions, the negotiations, the very *mechanics* of sex fundamentally absurd, worthy of mutual tittering, giggled apologies and joyful but bizarre intimacy? Not for Shawn. He seemed to regard the whole game to be contract work with targets to be met and bonuses paid. She almost missed Jerry's honest fumbling, pained concern and grateful relief.

'I'm glad you called,' she said. 'I need to talk to you.'

'Yeah? I need to talk to you too.' He smiled again. 'That's why I called.'

He sat down in a heavy wicker armchair and, for all his habitual confidence, she saw for the first time that something must be wrong. Perhaps it was the wheeze as he sat, the overflowing ashtray on the table in front of him or the fact he hadn't kissed her like a matinee idol.

April said, 'Where's Rosie?'

'School. Gladys is picking her up.'

April perched on the edge of a chair opposite him. 'Aren't you supposed to be out of town?' Then, off his apparent surprise: 'That's what you said. You'd be away for a few days.'

He nodded slowly. 'Yeah. That's what I said. Away. Supposed to be.'

April stared at him. Something *was* wrong; something had happened. Her mind ticker-taped possibilities, but came to an abrupt halt at just two: either Kuda had managed to commit suicide or she had somehow discovered the affair. A small part of her hoped for the former. The rest of her hated herself for the hope. She said, 'What?'

Shawn stubbed his cigarette. He lit another. He said, 'Any chance you could take Rosie a couple of nights?' He noted her expression. 'I know it's asking a lot. But Jerry'll be there, right? And he's good with kids. And you've got the maid . . .'

April shook her head: 'It's not asking a lot. It's just . . . I mean, fuck, Shawn! What's going on?'

Shawn told her.

He'd had a visit from his mother-in-law. She'd brought her pastor. When was this? This morning, first thing.

They told him they believed Kuda had been attacked by an evil spirit that night in the kitchen, the night she'd called April. An evil spirit? Yeah, an evil fucking spirit – an evil fucking spirit *within Rosie*. Are you serious? Yeah, he was fucking serious.

His 'fuckings' were out of character, not the cursing itself, but its intonation – desperate and confused. The 'fuckings' illuminated his distress.

The pastor said he'd already tried to make the spirit manifest in church. This was the first Shawn had heard of it. In fact, the pastor thought he'd succeeded in casting it out. But the spirit had returned, angry and vengeful, and tried to kill Kuda.

What the hell?

Yeah. What the fuck, right?

His mother-in-law wanted to take Rosie; the pair of them like some kind of apostolic fucking intervention. The little girl would be better off in a Christian household, they said, among people who knew how to deal with this kind of thing.

Shawn reminded Mrs Gorekore that she was looking after Kudakwashe, and the last time his wife had seen her daughter she'd pushed her away – literally *pushed her away*. In what sense was that good for a kid?

His mother-in-law told him that Kuda hadn't been pushing Rosie away, but rejecting the bad spirit.

He looked at her. Right then, he wanted to hit her; at least pick her up and try to shake some sense into her. He asked if she actually thought this, this madness, was in the best interests of the child: 'Is it in her best fucking interests?' he asked. 'You're all fucking crazy.' He said that. He actually said that.

As if expecting this response, the pastor asked if he'd consider bringing Rosie to the church – they had to manifest the spirit again.

An exorcism?

The pastor nodded. It wasn't the language he would choose. But, yes, for all intents and purposes, an exorcism.

'You're all fucking crazy.'

Shawn was livid. What is it with this place? What is it with this country? What is it with these crazy fucking people?

What did he do?

What did he *do*? He threw these crazy fucking people out of his fucking house, that's what he did.

He leaned forward. He took April's hand. He let it go again and sat back. He blew smoke. He said, 'I got a deal out in Murehwa. It'll set me up. I was going to leave Rosie with Gladys, have her stay here at the house. But what if these fucking people come back?'

April said nothing. She was bewildered by the story. But part of her was excited to hear Shawn beg, another part thrilled to be centre stage in an African story – Jerry could bottle his endless boring tales of the ghetto clinic and take a running jump . . .

'Look,' Shawn said, 'I know it's asking a lot, especially after that whole swimming pool thing. I mean, fuck, I know. But she's a good kid. She's my daughter.'

'It's fine,' April said. 'Of course it's fine. Just tell me when.'

'Tonight?'

'Tonight? Fine. I'll pick her up.'

They parted company almost formally. April offered Shawn her hand. He pulled her in to kiss her cheek, but it was awkward.

As she got behind the wheel, he leaned through the window. 'You said you wanted to talk to me too?'

She shook her head. 'Nothing important.'

51

Fadzai was at her kitchen in Mbare. She was feeling sick, so sat on an upturned barrel and let her younger brother do most of the work. She hadn't told Gilbert about the nausea, but he seemed content to get on; eager, even, for the hectic but mundane tasks of dishing plates, taking payment and sharing habitual cheery banter with her customers.

It was Gilbert's first week back. Initially, she'd discouraged the idea that he should come back at all. She said, 'You have made your decision, Gilbert. Soon you'll be going home, isn't it? And then I will be working alone again. I may as well get used to it.'

He smiled. He said, 'And I may as well help, so long as I'm here.'

Eventually, she agreed that he work Monday to Thursday, saying he should take Fridays off so that he could sleep in preparation for his weekend at the wheel. The reasoning she gave him was untrue but, to her surprise, he didn't question it and agreed to her suggestion.

Since deciding to return home, the young man certainly seemed happier; in fact, she would have gone so far as to say reborn. He had always been optimistic, but this had been tempered by a restless ambition that gave him an argumentative nature and the tendency to regard life's drudgery as beneath him. Now the restlessness seemed to be gone, which gave his positivity an almost ecstatic quality that, if anything, struck her as more deluded still.

Of course she understood his desire to leave Harare. For all his contribution to the household, he had made no personal progress towards his stated aims, and the beating at the hands of Chipangano must only have confirmed what she'd told him at the very outset: 'There are a lot of dreamers here who would like to think otherwise, but the city is hard.' What she didn't understand was why he thought he would find anything different back home. He had run away from the inertia of rural life and its limited opportunities. What did he think had changed? She asked him point blank and he said, 'Me. I have changed.'

'In what way?'

He couldn't or wouldn't answer and offered only a lazy and, she thought, arrogant shrug.

'So when will you go?'

'I am waiting for Bessie. I need my wife to come with me.'

'She will never agree.'

Another shrug.

A brief respite at the kitchen gave Gilbert the chance to come over and hand her a fistful of filthy dollar bills. 'Can you count these?'

'Sure.'

'Business is good,' he said. 'You are resting?'

'Do you need my help?'

'No. No, I am fine.' He smiled at her brightly. 'Everything is back to normal.'

Fadzai watched him return to serve customers straggling at the end of their lunch break. She considered what he'd just said. He may have been academically bright, but she sometimes thought he was quite the stupidest person she knew. Back to normal? How could he not see that normality for people like them meant navigating the daily struggles with no propulsion but the swell and lull as they lurched from crisis to crisis.

Patson had once said to her: 'There is nothing we can do. But there is one thing we must not do: we must not panic. If we panic, we will only make more problems.' It was after his mother died and the hospital bills and funeral costs had threatened to break them. She had dismissed his comment at the time as meaningless and placatory, but now she admitted its wisdom. Family demanded a better casket, better food, a better send-off and, in a state of grief and anxiety, she'd happily have caved in. Poverty makes you panic. It is an impossible situation that fosters impossible solutions. But Patson had stood firm. She was lucky to be married to such a man. She was now reaching a point where she couldn't remember the reasons – held for so long and so vehemently – she'd imagined otherwise. This was a thought that gave her a moment to enjoy a private smile.

Lunchtime was over. Fadzai raised her eyes and found her brother beginning to pack up. Behind him, she saw Chipangano approaching. Castro led the way, striding purposefully, his delight at finding Gilbert at the kitchen unconcealed. Fadzai uneasily hauled herself to her feet. Her stomach rolled disconcertingly. She arrived at Gilbert's side at the same moment as Castro spoke. 'You are back, country boy.'

Gilbert looked up slowly. 'Yes, I am back.'

'I heard you were sick.'

'No. I was robbed. They took my shoes. They beat me.'

Gilbert was utterly calm. Castro had no choice but to respond likewise, but Fadzai could hear the sharpening edge in his voice.

'I'm sorry to hear that. It is a terrible thing when people come to the city and others take advantage. You know that is why we are here? To protect people like you. We will find them for you. Did you see anything?'

'I saw nothing. I saw they took my shoes. They were like these ones.' Gilbert pointed to his shoes, now worn by one of Castro's compadres: a tall, slim young man – probably the youngest of the gang – who was making every effort to appear menacing. 'Very similar. But I always kept them clean.'

Fadzai intervened. She could now see the fire rising in Castro. She said, 'I thought you would come Friday?'

The thug spun towards her. 'And instead we come today. Is it for you to tell us when we can come and collect what you owe?'

Gilbert had turned back to the food, which he had slowly begun to unpack again. He said, 'You guys must be hungry. You are very busy.'

Castro's eyes darted back, searching out some deceit in Gilbert. But there was none to find. Instead, Gilbert was holding out money and a full plate. He said, 'Ten dollars, isn't it?'

When the Chipangano thugs were gone, Fadzai retreated to the back of the kitchen to vomit. Gilbert found her bent double. He said, 'There's no reason to be scared.'

Fadzai wiped her mouth with a tissue. She said, 'I'm not scared.'

Patson collected them and their equipment and drove home. Gilbert told him about the Chipangano and his wife's vomiting. Fadzai said, 'It had nothing to do with Chipangano.'

At the house, Gilbert carried in the leftovers, pots and pans. Patson wanted to get straight back to work, but Fadzai insisted he stop for tea. Patson knew better than to try to contradict her.

Husband and wife sat opposite each other at the table. Patson ladled sugar into his tea until the bowl was empty. Fadzai stood up. She said, 'Do you want more? We have more.' He didn't answer, but she was already refilling the sugar bowl. She sat down again.

'What is it?' Patson said.

'I am pregnant.'

'Are you sure?'

'Of course I am sure.'

Now it was Patson's turn to stand up. He went round the table and bent forward, wrapping his arms around Fadzai, sliding his hands around her midriff, under her breasts, and pushing his face into the nape of her neck until she felt his lips, hot and wet. She eased him off. She stared into the sugar bowl. She heard him say, 'That's good news. That's very good news.'

52

Mandiveyi was fighting fires. He'd left the family home a couple of nights before, deciding he needed to give his wife time to cool down. Over dinner, in front of the kids, he said he had to go away for work. The context made it impossible for Plaxedes to argue. She looked at him contemptuously.

He was staying at a flat in Avenues owned by the Organisation, one of several for the use of travelling operatives, stashing witnesses and occasionally interrogation. The administrator who gave him the keys hadn't questioned his requirements. Nonetheless, Mandiveyi was worried that Phiri would find out. He couldn't afford his boss thinking him any more unstable; not at the moment.

It was now approaching four months since Rex Nhongo's death, but the newspapers were still full of the story. A security guard at the Alamein farm said he'd heard gunshots hours before the fire, there was talk of a second man arriving with Nhongo that night, and rumours that only the president had been present at the autopsy, which had been conducted by a Cuban pathologist who'd been in the country a matter of weeks. Most recently, Nhongo's daughter had been shooting her mouth off about inadequacies in the inquiry. And still the state made almost no comment, no effort to quell the rumour mill; at least, nothing more than that the investigation must be allowed to run its course.

On one hand, this seemed surprising, since the wildfire gossip wasn't choosy about which member of the establishment it threatened to engulf next, all the way from the president down. On the other, Mandiveyi knew it was a long-standing Party tactic, employed to great effect after the 2008 election. The Party answered the indignation of foreign powers, the media, even, to some extent, their own people, with a single sentence (albeit one generally framed within verbose anti-colonial rhetoric); whether *This is an internal matter of a sovereign democracy* or *We must allow time for due process*. And these single sentences amounted to one pertinent question – *And what are you going to do about it?* Experience proved that the answer from foreigners, media and citizens alike was *Nothing*.

The truth was that all fires burned themselves out in the end and, so long as you had no fear of the collateral damage, the trick was simply to be still standing in the ashes. It was a trick, Mandiveyi realised, that he might wisely apply to his own situation.

Mandiveyi's own connection to the death of Rex Nhongo seemed both incontrovertible and utterly circumstantial. The news had already broken when, the following afternoon, on Phiri's orders, he had met the man at a bottle store on Simon Mazorodze Road.

The man walked over to him with certainty, as if he knew who he was. Mandiveyi was sure he'd never seen him before. The man handed Mandiveyi a plastic bag with something inside wrapped in newspaper. Mandiveyi said, 'What is it?' But the man didn't answer. In fact, in the thirty seconds of their meeting, he never spoke. Mandiveyi remembered his face precisely. He thought he looked foreign, perhaps Tanzanian or Kenyan, but he couldn't be sure if he was right, or whether it was significant.

The man was gone just like that. Mandiveyi ordered a beer out of habit, but took only one gulp before curiosity got the better of him. He went out to the car. He sat in the driver's seat, the door open, and examined the contents of the bag. As soon as he saw it was a gun, he swung his legs in and shut the door.

He carefully extracted the weapon, his hand wrapped in a handkerchief. It was a SIG Sauer. He was guessing a P226, but he'd never seen one before. As far as Mandiveyi could remember, it was a model widely used by security and military worldwide, but not one issued to the Zimbabwean police, army or intelligence or, so far as he knew, in common use in the region.

He checked the barrel. There was some tell-tale fouling, which revealed it had been fired since last cleaned, but what did that prove? He snapped out the magazine: half full.

Mandiveyi's thoughts were gathering pace and his heartbeat followed suit. His mind inevitably leaped to Nhongo's death. Of course, so soon afterwards, there was as yet no meaningful talk of suspected foul play. But Mandiveyi was parked off Simon Mazorodze, the Harare end of the road that led to Beatrice and, therefore, indirectly, Nhongo's Alamein farm. He rewrapped the weapon in the newspaper, put it into his briefcase and locked the briefcase in the boot. Then he went back into the bottle store, located his beer, slugged a mouthful and ordered a double tot of brandy. He needed time to think.

He was back in his office by four p.m. His thinking time had resulted in no productive outcome, only drunkenness. He cracked open the bottle of Viceroy he kept in his desk.

He considered taking the gun straight to Phiri, his boss, and simply handing it over. That would, he thought, have been a way of passing on the problem. But passing on a problem also passed on *control* of that problem.

Trouble was, Phiri's instructions had been so vague. He'd delivered them in person. He said, 'You are to secure a package.'

'Secure?'

'Secure.'

'And what am I to do with the package?'

Phiri looked at him with the extreme condescension that can only come from self-doubt. 'You are to secure the package,' he repeated. Evidently Phiri's own orders went no further. Perhaps Phiri himself had no idea what the package contained.

Mandiveyi considered his boss an idiot, but it wasn't a thought that offered him any solace – quite the opposite. If Phiri was an idiot, then he was one who'd risen higher than Mandiveyi at a younger age. Such apparent idiocy was, therefore, a key part of a dangerous skill set.

And now, as he thought all this through in the Organisation flat, he recognised that he had been lying to Phiri (and, both directly and indirectly, *Iganyana*) for months and his stories were becoming ever more fanciful. Initially, he'd told his boss that he'd secured the gun by burying it on an empty plot near his house. This had since extended into a tale that the plot was now fenced and guarded and he was just waiting for the right moment to retrieve it. He was, he said, cultivating a relationship with security that they might let him onto the land unattended – he was sounding ever more like a child making elaborate excuses for undelivered homework.

He knew Phiri didn't believe him. His only saving grace was that Phiri would ultimately have to admit any failure to *Iganyana*, something he would want to avoid at all costs. For all Phiri's posturing, Mandiveyi suspected that, if he was going down, he'd take his boss with him.

Ultimately, Mandiveyi had no idea whether the gun he'd fired drunkenly at some off-duty army thieves and dropped in a taxi was indeed the gun that had killed Rex Nhongo or, in fact, whether the Independence hero had been murdered at all. But it didn't matter. All that mattered was the gun; not what it had done, the very fact of it.

'The right hand does not know what the left hand is doing': Mandiveyi knew this phrase was used to describe failing administration, but in the case of the Organisation it was actually systematic principle. The nature of intelligence was that an operative should see only specific details and not the big picture. But Mandiveyi increasingly wondered whether anyone saw the big picture or if there was even a big picture to see. The upper echelons had discovered that chaos profited their scheming, but it was chaos nonetheless. The upper echelons were scared they were on their way out, so they were torching anything that burned and Mandiveyi was fighting fires.

But, charred and choking, Mandiveyi still held a match. If he could arrest the American, Appiah, for illegal gold transactions, couldn't he light a firebreak, scorching the earth between him and a rampant conflagration he couldn't hope to contain? He pictured himself standing safe behind a strip of blackened, dead vegetation and celebrating the greatest victory of his career.

53

Mandiveyi had successfully extinguished one fire.

He was in Nature's bathroom, washing himself. He'd found a clean shirt in her wardrobe. It was possibly ironic, certainly sad, that she'd thrown his soiled underwear at his wife, but still laundered, pressed and hung one of his shirts.

He had spoken to her calmly. He asked her what kind of stupid bitch she was to go to his wife in a public place. He asked her if she had not considered the consequences because now she would have time to do so at her leisure. Her pride and defiance quickly gave way to tears and apology, then, dropping to her knees, holding his legs, simpering caresses. She had begged him to fuck her like he had when they first met. So he did.

Afterwards, she lay next to him, post-coitally confident of the renewed intimacy between them. He sat astride her playfully. He picked up a pillow and thrust it down on her face until her thrashing turned to a quiver. He had no intention of killing her. He removed the pillow in time for her to suck air and know what was to follow. He then beat her almost senseless. Her nose spurted blood. He should have stripped naked. He hadn't thought it through. Luckily, she'd pressed a shirt for him.

He flexed his knuckles as he inspected himself in the mirror. He hadn't broken a bone, but they were sore from where he'd caught her teeth flush. She wouldn't be fellating anyone else any time soon. He had taken no pleasure in what he'd done, but he felt no regret either. Mandiveyi didn't really believe in 'pleasure' or 'regret'. He considered them an indulgence of people who didn't lie and therefore had the option to serve other masters.

After his conversation with Jerry Jones, the British nurse, Mandiveyi had looked up Shawn Appiah at the Chamber of Mines. He found a recently formed company called NA Holdings and a list of transactions with Fidelity Printers, the central bank subsidiary charged with purchasing gold. The indigenous partner in NA Holdings was a man called Peter Nyengedza; an address in Waterfalls. Mandiveyi couldn't be sure, but he thought he recognised the name.

Mandiveyi left Nature's flat with a renewed sense of purpose. He drove out to Waterfalls and turned on Derbyshire. Nyengedza's house was an unremarkable one, no more and no less neglected than the rest on the street. However, there was a smart white Corolla parked in the driveway that suggested a recent upturn in fortune.

The door was answered by a maid, who showed him through into a sun lounge that had been converted into something like an office. Nyengedza sat behind a small desk, upright, staring meditatively out of the window. At Mandiveyi's appearance, he looked slowly round but didn't stand.

'My name is Albert Mandiveyi,' the CIO said.

'How can I help you, Mr Mandiveyi? If you are seeking representation, I am no longer in legal practice, but I will happily recommend someone.'

'May I sit?'

'Please.'

Mandiveyi sat on the wooden chair opposite Nyengedza. It wobbled slightly beneath him and the old man smiled an apology and mumbled something about the need to purchase modern office furniture.

Mandiveyi said, 'It is quite all right.' Then, 'I work for the Central Intelligence Organisation.'

It was a tactic he often used. A response to this bald statement, whether spoken or unspoken, could tell him much of what he needed to know. However, on this occasion, he learned nothing – Nyengedza was unmoved. He simply said again, 'How can I help you, Mr Mandiveyi?'

Mandiveyi said, 'I am sorry to disturb you at home. But this was the address listed for NA Holdings.'

'This is my office. We currently have no need of additional business premises – an unnecessary expense.'

Mandiveyi nodded. Then he said, 'Peter Nyengedza,' ruminatively, chewing over its every syllable. 'I thought I knew your name. You are a comrade, isn't it?'

Nyengedza regarded him steadily. His shoulders sagged, as if he found the weight of that word a burden. 'That is what they call me. I trained at Nyadzonya . . .' His visitor made a reflexive noise of surprise, but Nyengedza shook his head. 'No. Before the massacre. By that time I was already in England. I was not cut out for warfare, so I was sent to study law. I worked for Zvobgo at Lancaster House and, when we came home, redrafting local government legislation.' He smiled slowly. 'I am not a veteran of the war so much as the peace. But I believe the battles were just as hard fought.'

Nyengedza leaned forward and looked closely at his visitor, much to the latter's discomfort. The old man's eyes were curiously opaque. Most likely this suggested the beginnings of cataracts but, to Mandiveyi, his gaze had an intrusive, almost psychic quality, as if Nyengedza were sifting his character.

'And you?' Nyengedza said.

'Excuse me?'

'You fought in the war?'

'I was very young at Independence.'

'We were all very young. Many of those who were martyrs to the cause were the youngest of all.'

This conversation wasn't going at all as Mandiveyi had expected. He had the disconcerting sense that he wasn't the one controlling it; that, in fact, the lawyer had just asserted his own authority. He had no sense, therefore, of how it might play out; no idea whether Nyengedza knew about his American business partner's actions or how he would react to questioning. He wondered if the old man still had connections in the Party. He wondered if he was about to stick his nose into a hornets' nest. It didn't matter. He had to get to the point. He said, 'Let me get to the point.'

'Please do,' Nyengedza replied.

Mandiveyi came straight out with it. He said that he suspected Shawn Appiah of selling gold on the black market. He asked if the lawyer knew anything about this, whether he knew an Israeli called Feinstein, or the prison sentences the courts were likely to impose for such activities.

'Are you accusing me, Mr Mandiveyi?' Nyengedza asked.

Mandiveyi shook his head. For, at that very moment, he knew that any accusation would be ridiculous. There was no way this fellow knew about any crime. If Mandiveyi had thus far found the old man enigmatic, it was actually because he was anything but – he was the CIO's opposite: a man of integrity. It was a quality that Mandiveyi had barely recognised because of who he was, because he came across it so rarely. It was a quality that, ironically, manifested similar characteristics to his own – a kind of inscrutability derived from a lack of interest in the petty mores of human interaction, thanks to an entrenched belief in truth on one side and lies on the other.

'I am not accusing you,' Mandiveyi said. 'I am asking for your help.'

Nyengedza said, 'Shawn is a very ambitious young man.' He spoke sadly. He wasn't defending the American so much as taking a moment to express his disappointment. Mandiveyi imagined an honest man like this one must be frequently disappointed. He said nothing. He waited for more.

'It is my job to prepare our accounts for ZIMRA and the ministry,' Nyengedza said. 'Of course I noticed a certain diminution in the value of our transactions but I had no specific reason for suspicion.'

Still Mandiveyi said nothing. Still he waited.

'He is out of town,' Nyengedza said. 'Somewhere near Murehwa. We buy from *makorokoza* in the area. Maybe he will drive to Mazowe. He likes to use a mill there. I asked him why he wanted to drive so far. He said he wanted to use people he can trust. Now I know what he means – the mill must be getting its cut.'

Mandiveyi considered this. He had no desire to go on some wild goose chase around the country. He said, 'When will he be back in town?'

'Tomorrow. Maybe the next day.'

'Right. Good.'

Nyengedza showed his visitor to the door. The old man's handshake was strong and confident. Mandiveyi felt a rush of fraternal solidarity with the lawyer, some regret for the trouble he was causing him, even a certain osmotic cleansing from a straightforward conversation with an honest man. He gestured towards the Corolla. He said, 'A new car?'

Nyengedza nodded confirmation. 'A new car.'

'There will be an investigation,' Mandiveyi said. 'I'm sure accounts will be frozen and so forth. Of course it is harder to seize an asset than to freeze an account. I believe it is a good time to buy a car right now. They keep their value very well. I know you understand what I am saying.'

'I understand you quite clearly,' Nyengedza said. His face was expressionless, but he looked at his visitor through those milky eyes again and Mandiveyi was left in no doubt of his contempt.

54

Jerry took a phone call over dinner. He stood up from the table. When he returned, April said, 'Who was that?'

'Tapiwa,' Jerry said. 'My work permit's been approved.'

'Great! That's great news!' Her husband made a face. 'What? It's great. You can get a job.'

'Right. I can get a job.'

'What's that supposed to mean?'

'Nothing. I can get a job.'

April sniffed. She pursed her lips. He knew she was fuming, but she avoided confrontation by turning to Rosie, who was sitting next to her. 'Look at you!' she said. 'Eating your chips! You like chips, Rosie? Of course you do. Don't forget your broccoli. And some omelette. What good eating!'

Jerry found her sing-song tone infuriating. Rosie was eight years old, not a baby. He said, 'When's your dad coming back, Rosie?'

The girl answered, through a mouthful, 'I dunno.'

April glared at her husband. She said, 'He's back tomorrow.'

'You spoke to him?'

'Yeah, I spoke to him.'

'Oh,' Jerry said. 'You didn't tell me.'

Rosie had been with them three nights. This would be the fourth. April had said, 'A couple of nights, max.' Truth was, it was no skin off Jerry's nose either way, but he allowed himself to be annoyed. He told himself that he didn't much like Shawn Appiah 'taking the piss', but really he just wanted an excuse. Now Jerry was no longer at the clinic, he stayed home with the kids while April went to work, but it was actually easier with two than one. Theo worshipped the little girl, following her around like a puppy, and Rosie was sweet and endlessly patient, casting their son as the baby in her various games of fantasy families.

If her presence presented a difficulty, therefore, it was only because April was getting home from work at half past five – 'You know,' she said, 'it was me who said we'd take her. I really want to try to be here.' April and Jerry now shared two hours before the kids went to bed and at least two hours thereafter. And the atmosphere between the couple was one of unalloyed irritation: of sharp comments and muttered asides, sulking and skulking.

Both Jerry and April were dismayed by what was happening to them. Each approached the end of every day determined to be patient, loving and kind. Jerry, for example, was not drinking (three days – he deserved a medal). He bathed Theo in time for his mother's return and greeted his wife with a kiss. But, somehow, he'd become so sensitised to his diminished role as husband, father and man that April's smallest reaction inevitably opened some or other long-standing wound. A comment about the broken security light undermined him as husband, a change of pyjamas for Theo undermined him as father, an unreturned kiss undermined him as man. And his wounds would fester and inflame. As for April, she was riddled with guilt though she couldn't admit as much. Instead, therefore, she decided it was all

267

her fault, not because she was sleeping with another man, but because she had settled for a fundamentally kind but lumpen husband who hadn't the sophistication to match her intellectual, social, emotional and sexual ambition. She genuinely tried to use this admission as a spur to loving action, but that's not how love works. The fact is that some people choose a partner in the belief they will change, others in the belief that they themselves never will – and they are equivalent mistakes.

Jerry pushed his chair back from the table and said brightly to Rosie, 'Bath time!'

April looked up at him. 'Don't worry. I'll do it.'

'No. It's fine.'

They were both trying to be nice. The mutual antipathy built.

Rosie asked, 'Can I bring Sasa?'

'Sasha?' Jerry said. 'Who's Sasha?'

'*Sasa*,' the girl repeated.

'Sasa,' April said. 'It's Rosie's friend. In her imagination.'

'Right.' Jerry nodded. 'Why not? The more the merrier.'

While Rosie bathed, April put Theo down. The kids were sharing Theo's bedroom – there were two beds, it made sense. But it had been another source of conflict.

On the first evening Rosie stayed, Jerry had found Bessie changing the bedding in the spare room. He had asked his wife about it. She said, 'For Rosie.'

'Isn't she sleeping in Theo's room?'

April looked uncomfortable. She pointed out that Theo often stirred in the night and she went to him and sometimes climbed into bed with him too. Maybe it would disturb the little girl.

Jerry stared at her. He said, 'She won't wake up.'

April appeared more uncomfortable still. She stumbled over a further explanation. She shook her head. She shrugged. She said,

'I don't know … after the pool … I don't know … I just feel uneasy.' Then, off the laugh Jerry stifled in the back of his throat, she brought up the visit Shawn had described from his mother-in-law and her pastor – the accusations of demonic possession.

Jerry listened incredulously, but he didn't ridicule her. In fact, he suppressed a cold shiver. 'Christ,' he said. Then, 'So her father sent her to us because it's madness, right? So, now are we going to start believing it too?'

'Theo's our son!'

'What's that supposed to mean?' Jerry said. 'I mean, what do you think's going to happen?' April's jaw tightened. She looked at him resentfully, but she had nothing more to say. Jerry sniffed, creased his brow. 'And where will I sleep?' he asked.

It was an awful question. He had been in the spare room for more than a month, but this was the first time the arrangement had been spoken about and it marked some kind of codification. April continued to look at him and, behind the anger, he recognised the desperate sadness in her eyes. In times past, that look would have broken his heart, but he was already heartbroken.

'Fine,' his wife said quickly. 'Really. Whatever you want.'

55

Jerry was woken by screaming. Or, more accurately, it invaded his dreams and painted them electric until he had no choice but to open his eyes. Even then, like a diver surfacing too quickly, he was disoriented and unsteady. He scrambled for his phone: two a.m. Momentarily, he thought he was imagining the cacophony, but there it was again. He said, 'Fuck!' and stumbled into the passage.

Now he distinguished two voices. One was certainly his wife's. He slid his hand along the wall for the light switch. It was pitch black and he couldn't find it. He said, 'April!'

By return, he heard, 'Jerry!' Short and sharp, breathless, terrified.

His eyes were gradually adjusting to the dark and he made out his wife's shape at the far end of the corridor, where she'd just emerged from Theo's room.

He said, 'Jesus!'

'There's something in there!'

'What?'

'There's something in there!'

Suddenly they were close enough to touch. He could still hear the screaming. He didn't know who was screaming. He couldn't quite accept it as real. He didn't know what was going on. He was confused. He said, 'Where's Theo?'

April said, 'I've got him.' And Jerry grasped that the thick outline over her shoulder was in fact his sleeping son.

'Rosie?'

'She's in the room!' April sobbed. 'She's still in there!'

'Jesus,' Jerry said. 'Calm down.'

He went into his son's bedroom. He could hear the little girl wailing, panic-stricken. In the split-second it took to reach the light switch, he heard beating wings and, more poignantly, felt the presence of another creature. His blood chilled, his skin creeping. He flicked the overhead light. It blinded him almost as much as the darkness. He squinted at Rosie sitting up in bed, knees to her chest. Her hands were covering her ears. Her eyes were wide and her mouth wider still, the sound coming from it almost inhuman. He said, 'Rosie!' Then, 'Sweetheart! What's the matter?'

He went towards her and her arm thrust out, finger pointing to the far wall. He turned and found himself looking at a distinct black shape: a small bat, resting with its wings wide. The anxiety washed out of him. He said, 'Bloody hell!'

He moved towards the bat, but Rosie turned her screams up a notch. He returned to her and sat on the bed. He looked back at the bat. It remained motionless. He put his arm around Rosie and she recoiled automatically, but he pulled her into his chest and eventually she acquiesced. He said, 'It's nothing. It's nothing.' Gradually she sank into him. Her screaming had stopped. He began to laugh. He said, 'It's fine.' He stood up. She clung to his T-shirt. He peeled off her fingers. He said, 'It's fine. Let me get rid of it.'

He considered the bat. How the hell was he going to get rid of it? He knew nothing about bats. Was there a method? He considered calling Joseph, the gardener – a local would know how to deal with this. But the bat twitched its wings and Rosie started screaming again, and that made up Jerry's mind. He opened the window. He approached the animal cautiously before lurching the last distance to secure it in his hand. He didn't particularly want to hurt the thing any more than he particularly cared whether it lived or died. He took two steps to the window. He felt a brief, sharp pain in his index finger. He hurled the bat outside. Heaven knows whether it landed on the veranda or flew off into the sky. He shut the window. He said, 'It's nothing. It's fine.'

Jerry emerged from the bedroom with Rosie clutched to his chest. He found April cowering in the passage, their son still asleep on her shoulder. He said, 'Just a bat.' The relief, the gratitude in his wife's face – he felt like a superhero. He put a hand on her arm and she leaned into him in an awkward kind of embrace, separated by the two kids. Rosie was still snivelling. 'That was a shock,' he said quietly. Then, 'Let's get them to sleep.'

April pulled back. Her eyes were haunted, her complexion filmy. She looked older than he remembered. This wasn't a pejorative observation so much as a surprising one: it was as if he hadn't seen her for a long time. She said, 'I want to keep Theo with me.'

'OK,' he said.

He returned Rosie to her bed. Her terror had dissipated and her eyes were drowsy. He turned off the light, she slipped under the covers and he sat next to her, resting a hand gently on her shoulder. 'You sure he gone?' she murmured.

'The bat?' he said. 'Positive. He's gone. What a fuss over nothing.'

'His name Sasabonsam.'

'Who?'

'His name Sasabonsam. I call him Sasa.'

Jerry was feeling sleep steal up on him too. He said, 'Your friend?'

'The bat. He want me to fly away with him again, only I don wanna go. I don have to go if I don wanna, do I? He can't make me.'

Jerry chuckled softly. He said, 'No, he can't make you, Rosie. I won't let him.'

'And what if you not there?'

'I'm not going anywhere. I'm going to sit right here. And, tomorrow, when you go home, your daddy's going to look after you and he won't let anything happen. That's what daddies are for.'

Jerry sat for a minute or two longer until he heard her breathing even, lengthen, deepen. Then he padded out of the room and pulled the door behind him, leaving it open a crack. He was about to go back to bed, when he heard April call his name. 'Yes?' he whispered. He stood in her doorway. 'You OK?'

'I'm sorry,' she said.

Jerry couldn't see anything. He couldn't tell if his wife was sitting up or lying down, but her voice sounded sleepy. He was feeling a little cold. He shivered. His finger was throbbing. He didn't know what she meant. What was she apologising for? Perhaps she was simply expressing a generalised regret for the way things were. He had no idea. And when he said, 'I'm sorry too,' he didn't know what that meant either. However, when he chose not to go to her, not to climb into bed and hold her, but instead to return to the spare bedroom and its cold sheets, he assigned both their apologies their meaning.

Jerry examined his finger. He had two small puncture marks above the knuckle. He'd been bitten by a fucking bat. He went to the bathroom and bathed the small wounds in antiseptic. He'd need to get a shot in the morning but, for now, that would prevent any imminent infection.

56

It was quiet over breakfast. April seemed preoccupied. Jerry said, 'You OK?'

'Just tired.'

'You have trouble getting back to sleep?'

She shook her head. 'No, but I had . . . I don't know . . . terrible nightmares.'

'About what?'

She shook her head again. She changed the subject by addressing their son. She said, 'And what are you two going to do today?'

Jerry answered for him. He said, 'I don't know. Maybe we'll do something fun.'

April dropped Rosie at school on her way into the embassy. Jerry spent an idle twenty minutes fitting square blocks into square holes with Theo. Then he asked Bessie if she could bring her ironing board into the living room to keep an eye on him. He put the TV on: a *Teletubbies* DVD. He said, 'I've got some work to do.'

He spent an idle morning reorganising his Spotify playlists and browsing iTunes until he saw Ant sign in to Skype. He called him.

The record shop where Ant worked was quiet, so they chatted for more than an hour. His brother told him about a gig he'd been to in London: a band he'd first seen two years ago in a Camden pub had been playing the Shepherd's Bush Empire. It hadn't been all that. It had lacked intimacy and the band's new material reflected their success; not in a good way. 'Second-album syndrome,' his brother said.

'That's what happens.'

'That's what happens.'

Ant had been to the gig with his new girlfriend. She was Swiss. She lived in a basement flat in Balham, so they only saw each other at weekends. She worked as a PA in an ad agency, but she was really a graphic novelist. 'Dark shit,' he said.

'Dark shit.' Jerry nodded.

The conversation meandered, but neither of them had a reason to end it. His brother asked about Theo, and Jerry briefly precised all his son's latest developments. Ant said, 'That's so cool!' Then, 'Where is he now?'

'With the maid.'

'The maid? How the other half live.'

'How the other half live.'

Jerry and his brother had always been close. They didn't finish each other's sentences, but repeated them in that curiously male style of lazy affirmation. But today Jerry felt the distance between them. He could no longer imagine what it would be like to work in a record shop and have a Swiss graphic-novelist girlfriend – it sounded impossibly, intoxicatingly exotic.

'What else is new?' Ant asked.

'Nothing,' Jerry said. Then he remembered the dull ache in his finger and looked down at the small twin wounds. 'I got bitten by a bat.'

Ant thought this was the funniest thing he'd ever heard and laughed for a solid minute until Jerry started to laugh too. 'Actually, I should go,' Jerry said. 'I need to get a shot.'

He rang off. He called the GP. He made an appointment for two p.m. He checked the time. He had to pick up Rosie at twelve thirty. He was running late. He rang Patson. The driver arrived promptly for a change. He brought Rosie back for lunch. He asked Patson to wait. He ate with the kids before heading to the doctor.

For once, Jerry felt like small-talking, but Patson was even more taciturn than usual. Jerry said, 'I'm going to the doctor. Last night I was bitten by a bat.' He started to laugh.

'I'm sorry, Uncle,' the driver said noncommittally.

'No!' Jerry said, still laughing. 'It's funny if you think about it.'

But Patson didn't appear to find it funny, or simply didn't think about it.

Jerry was home within the hour. The kids were at the washing-line playing while Bessie beat the rugs. He watched Theo duck carefully between the swinging runners. He thought that if April were there she'd have been complaining about the potentially dangerous dust he might be inhaling and an article she'd read about infant asthma. He saw his son laugh delightedly at something Bessie said. He recognised how attached Theo was to her. He felt no jealousy, but he wondered at the ease with which Bessie entertained him, even as she worked. He compared it favourably to his and April's parenting, which seemed to require research, planning and endless accessories. Was this a failing in them or the whole modern Western culture of childcare?

Back in the house, Jerry bought the second album by the band his brother had watched at Shepherd's Bush Empire. He would listen for himself. The internet connection was even lousier than usual and the album took an age to download. He checked the time. He hoped it would finish before April got home and gave him grief for buying more music.

While Bessie bathed Theo, Jerry took Rosie to the bedroom to pack her bag. April was due to pick her up and take her home. Jerry folded the little girl's clothes carefully. He tried to cajole her to help, but with little enthusiasm and no success. She preferred to sit on the bed, watching him, curious. She was so strangely still and silent that Jerry felt almost unnerved. He asked her questions – what games had she been playing? Was she looking forward to seeing her daddy? That kind of thing. Rosie didn't answer one of them. Eventually Jerry zipped the bag and looked up at her. He said, 'You're very quiet.'

For a moment, Rosie seemed to consider this. Then she said, 'Just thinkin.' Then, 'You don sleep in bed with Theo's momma.'

Jerry laughed. He said, 'Not always.'

'You fuck the white bitch tho?' Rosie said. 'Like Daddy? He fuck the white bitch all the time.'

Jerry stared. 'Those are bad words,' he murmured.

April collected Rosie as arranged. She found her packed and ready to go. She said, 'Give Jerry a hug.' The little girl briefly wrapped herself around Jerry's thighs, but he barely responded and he said nothing. April ignored his behaviour. He was presumably harbouring some or other bitterness. What was new about that?

She planned to talk to Shawn as soon as she got to the house. This time, she fully intended to tell him it was over between them. It felt right – she'd done him a favour; they'd had a few days without seeing each other; it was time to move on. Besides, she'd been haunted all day by her nightmares. She couldn't remember anything specific, but they'd left her with a general feeling of unease that seemed to her an unconscious spur to action. However, at Shawn's house, she found only Gladys and the gardener, whose name she'd never known.

April got out of the car and unclipped Rosie from the back. Gladys met them at the door. She appeared flustered. She said, 'Madam, the geyser: it is leaking.'

April followed her inside. The house smelt thickly damp and, sure enough, the ceiling and walls of the central passageway showed a spreading brown stain. 'Where's Shawn?' April asked.

'The boss is away, madam,' Gladys said. 'I have not come into the house for three days. He told me not to come in. And now this has happened.'

'I know he's away. When's he back?'

'He called. He said he will be back just now.'

April looked at the maid. Her expression was panicked on account of the leak and she was looking to the white, the *madam*, for some kind of solution. April felt a momentary surge of irritation.

Behind her, the gardener said, 'Excuse me.' He was carrying a stepladder, which he positioned under the hatch to the roof. He said, 'I can turn it off.'

'There you are,' April said. Then, 'Where did Rosie go?'

She found the little girl in her bedroom, playing quietly among her stuffed toys. She gave her a hug. She said, 'Your daddy will be home soon.'

'Don worry,' Rosie said. 'Sasa here an he in a good mood for once.'

April picked up a lion. She said, 'This one Sasa?' Then, 'Which one's Sasa?'

The little girl laughed. 'None of these Sasabonsam, silly!'

'Oh, of course! Your friend.'

'He jus pretend,' Rosie said.

April was home by seven. Theo was already asleep and Bessie finished for the night. She found Jerry in the living room. He was swigging from a beer. There was an empty on the table in front of him. 'Didn't take you long,' she said.

Her husband didn't look at her. He said, 'I know you've been fucking Shawn.' April froze. She made an involuntary noise that might or might not have been an effort at speech. Now he looked at her. 'Don't bother,' he said. 'Rosie told me. *Rosie*. Jesus.'

The doorbell rang. Jerry stood up to answer the intercom. He pressed the button to open the gate. He said, 'That's Patson. I'm going out. I'm going to get shitfaced.'

'We should talk,' April said feebly.

'About what?' Jerry asked. He shook his head. 'Don't worry about it. I'm not even angry. That's you. That's what you do.'

April stared at him. He was telling the truth: he wasn't angry. She found him terrifying. She said, 'So you're just going to get drunk?'

'Sure,' he said. 'That's what I do.' He picked up his keys and left.

57

Patson shouldn't have been driving. Generally, he returned home between five and six and Gilbert took the taxi out after they'd eaten. That night, however, Patson got back to Sunningdale to find his house in a state of some chaos.

Gilbert had taken a phone call from his father late in the afternoon telling him that he'd spoken to the headman, who owed him a favour, and there was a plot of land waiting for him, should he want it. 'It is nothing much,' Gilbert said excitedly. 'Barely four acres. But it is close to the river and the drainage is good. It will be a start.' He was in the middle of packing his small suitcase, a process that for no apparent reason seemed to involve the eager assistance of both Anashe and Chabarwa, and turned the whole Chisinga household upside down. 'The bus is at half past six,' Gilbert said. 'I must hurry.'

Patson turned to his wife. He said, 'And why must he go tonight?'

Fadzai shrugged. She didn't know the answer and she clearly wasn't feeling well enough to ask. She was struggling terribly with nausea and the effort to appear otherwise was taking its toll. She hadn't yet told anyone but Patson about the baby. She felt that at her age, after so long, it would be asking for trouble – especially considering her own mother's history of miscarrying.

Patson sat at the table. There was no point involving himself in his brother-in-law's manic activity. He watched his wife putting water on the hot plate. Her movements around the pan were slow and forbearing. Patson stood up again and whispered in Fadzai's ear, 'Please, go and sit.' He made himself tea and then perched next to her. He squeezed her hand companionably. In that moment, he knew that the revival of their sex life was now over for the time being and the most he had to look forward to was companionship. But he looked forward to that too. He said to Gilbert, 'When you are ready, I will take you to the bus station.'

Gilbert laughed. 'I'm sure you can't wait to be rid of me, my brother.' Then, 'No, but you have been so kind, all of you. I would never have reached this decision if you had not allowed me to come here and see the city and find out for myself.'

Patson considered the young man. Gilbert had an extraordinary capacity for emotive straight-talking that he found simultaneously bewildering, touching and somewhat implausible – after all, if you are always declaring your feelings, what value have such declarations when feelings change?

Fadzai mustered a question. She said, 'And what have you told Bessie?'

'I have told her that I am going home, that *we* are going home. She will meet me at the bus station.'

'She is going with you?'

'No, of course not. But she will follow. She is my wife.'

The kids wanted to come to Mbare Musika. But Patson wouldn't allow it. He said, 'I will rank afterwards. I don't want to be driving all the way back here.' Fadzai hugged her brother, then she hugged Patson too. This was unusual. She had tears in her eyes. Patson said, 'What's the matter?'

'I'm not sure,' she said. 'It's probably just ...' She didn't need to say any more. She rested a palm on her stomach.

Patson and Gilbert drove to the bus station with little conversation. Gilbert's high spirits seemed to have given way to a taut, nervous silence, while Patson felt the time was right for wise, avuncular advice and couldn't think of any. Eventually he said, 'You have shown you are a worker. That is the main thing.'

It was a feeble attempt and the words dropped between them without resonating, but at least they seemed to shake Gilbert from his reverie, as he now asked Patson about the day's takings. Patson shook his head. 'You know, it is slow.'

He'd had only two customers the whole day – Salim, the Indian, who seemed to have fallen on hard times (in the casino, no doubt) and haggled over a five-dollar fare, and Mr Jones, twice. 'I took him to the doctor,' Patson said. 'He said he was bitten by a bat.'

They were stopped at a junction. Gilbert looked at him, the light back in his eyes. Gilbert said, ' "Ask a passenger to tell you his story, and if there is one who says he is not the most miserable fellow, I give you permission to throw me head first into the sea." '

'What are you talking about?' Patson said. 'What sea?'

Gilbert produced from his jacket the battered paperback that he now seemed to carry everywhere. He said, 'It is a quotation. From my book.'

'The *murungu* was not miserable. He said it was funny if you think about it.'

Gilbert laughed. He said, '*Everything* is funny if you think about it.'

For some reason this exchange appeared to have reignited

Gilbert's high spirits. Patson considered that there were many things that were not funny, no matter how much you thought about them, but he said nothing.

Mbare Musika was hectic as ever. They found the Mubayira bus. It was still being loaded and wouldn't leave for at least fifteen minutes. There was no sign of Bessie, but Gilbert sent her a text and she appeared moments later. At the sight of her, he leaped from the taxi and Patson watched from the driver's seat as they embraced and engaged in urgent, earnest conversation. Bessie appeared concerned. Patson wasn't surprised. How must it be to be married to his brother-in-law? Like attempting to carry enough water to drink in the palm of a single hand. Nonetheless, as Gilbert talked, she was evidently mollified, as was always the case.

Patson's phone rang. It was the *murungu*. He answered. He said, 'Yes, Uncle.' Then, 'No, I am still working.' Then, 'No, it is me, Uncle. Gilbert is not working today.' Then, 'Twenty minutes. Is it too long? I will be there just now.'

He got out of the Raum. He took Gilbert's suitcase from the boot and approached the couple. He said, 'I must go. It is Mr Jones. At least I can take your wife, isn't it?'

'You see?' Gilbert exclaimed. 'Today everything is serendipitous.'

Bessie said, 'You must tell Stella that I love her and I think about her and pray for her every day.'

'Of course I will,' Gilbert said. He kissed his wife on the mouth. Some people stared. Patson was embarrassed by such a show and suspected Bessie was too. He stood next to her as Gilbert boarded the bus. She lifted a hand to wave, her face impassive. A woman must be very patient, Patson thought. It was not the first time he'd concluded as much in recent months. Perhaps it signified a change in him.

Bessie sat in the back as Patson drove to Greendale. Each lost in their own unformulated but all too real concerns, they didn't exchange a word until they reached the house. Then, at the gate, Bessie asked to be let out. She said it would be wrong to be seen arriving in the taxi. Patson pressed the buzzer.

Mr Jones emerged immediately, even before Patson had turned the car round. He got into the back without a word. Patson drove out. He said, 'Where to, Uncle?'

The man took a moment to answer. 'The Maiden,' he said.

Patson pulled in outside the bar at Harare Sports Club. Mr Jones showed no sign of moving. Patson looked at his customer in the rear-view mirror. He was staring out of the window, his eyes narrow. Patson remembered Gilbert's words – *the most miserable fellow*. He said, 'Do you want me to wait, Uncle?'

The *murungu* slowly turned his head. He said, 'Will you have a drink with me?'

PART THREE

58

Mandiveyi has two profound realisations. The first comes while kneeling over Nature, breathing heavily, pummelling her face. Nature has sought to exploit his infidelity to assert her authority over him. But she has no authority over him. It's a lie that he explodes as easily as his fist explodes her nose.

In doing so, he sees that his wife has no authority over him either. And he doesn't even need to beat her to prove it. Instead, he simply returns home and joins the family for their evening meal as if nothing has happened and, later, he climbs into the marital bed where Plaxedes is sitting up, waiting, her face taut with emotion.

'What are you doing?' she asks. 'I want you out of the house. I want you gone. I want a divorce.'

He lies on his side, propping himself on an elbow. He says, 'This is my house and you don't want a divorce. If you want a divorce, I will take you to your brother and you will have nothing, just the shame.' He then rolls over and turns off the bedside light.

For a moment his wife is silent. Then, in the darkness, she spits through her tears, 'You! You and your girlfriends! You don't think that is shame?'

'No' he says. 'Because I have no girlfriends. I have told you a hundred times, my work is complicated and private. You don't want to know about my work. You *cannot* know about my work. That is it. Finished.'

Mandiveyi doesn't even bother to make this sound true. It doesn't matter whether Plaxedes finds it plausible or not, because she has no choice but to believe it.

The second realisation occurs to Mandiveyi when Phiri calls him into his office and once again demands the gun. His boss's intimidation is so explicit, his manner so aggressive, that Mandiveyi easily sees the underpinning desperation. Phiri needs the gun to save his own skin and to get the gun he needs Mandiveyi. For the moment, therefore, any threats are only so much bluster.

Mandiveyi apologises. He says he's very busy working on a significant issue: a case so important, so valuable, so politically imperative that it might make everyone – maybe even *Iganyana* himself – forget the other matter. Phiri stares at him, as bewildered as he is furious. But he, too, has little choice but to take Mandiveyi at his word, even as he knows it's worth nothing.

Mandiveyi is sitting in his car thirty metres down from Shawn Appiah's house. He is waiting. He has been waiting all afternoon. Appiah will come. He will return from Murehwa with his illicit gold. Mandiveyi will make a single phone call and have a team there in minutes to search the house. Of course Appiah will deny the charge and brandish his buyer's licence. But Mandiveyi will tell him they are after those further up the food chain.

Appiah is an American: all arrogant defiance, no doubt. He will demand to speak to his embassy, but Mandiveyi can stall. He can produce the company records he's obtained from Nyengedza. He is confident he will make Appiah crack, confess all and give up the names of the Untouchables he met at the Rainbow Towers

Hotel. Naturally, the Untouchables will remain untouchable. But that is not the important thing. The important thing is Appiah will confess all.

Embassy officials will then arrive and reassure him. They will bleat about 'due process'. But Mandiveyi will enjoy reminding them they are in Zimbabwe, enjoy their gradual comprehension of Appiah's guilt and, especially, the look on his prisoner's face when he comprehends that his nationality cannot save him.

The light is just beginning to fade as a Land Cruiser pulls up to the gate. Mandiveyi is briefly excited, even though it is not the American's vehicle. The Land Cruiser emerges again ten minutes later. It is driven by a white woman he doesn't recognise.

Mandiveyi turns his mind to his son, Tendai, whose mobility seems to deteriorate almost daily. Tendai's condition is not a lie; neither is it founded upon a lie. But perhaps lies will provide something approaching a solution. If Mandiveyi can rise through the hierarchy, earn more money or, preferably, favours, perhaps he will be able to afford better treatment or a better school. Mandiveyi tells himself that he does what he does for his family. Like all the best lies, this contains some truth.

Mandiveyi continues to wait. It is half past nine before the headlights of Appiah's Isuzu reflect in his mirror. He catches a glimpse of the American's face as he swings the *bakkie* through his gate. Everything is coming together perfectly. Mandiveyi takes out his phone to call for back-up, but before he can dial it rings in his hand.

He looks at the name on the display. Briefly, he considers ignoring the call. But he doesn't. He answers it. The voice at the other end comes fast and barely intelligible, racing with horror.

Mandiveyi says, 'Right now? I cannot come right now. I am working.' Then, 'I know what I said, but—'

The man at the other end cuts him off and resumes his distressed entreaty.

Mandiveyi listens. He thinks. He checks the time. It is late and he sees little likelihood of Appiah attempting to move the gold this evening – the American knows no reason to be worried. Mandiveyi's operation can wait an hour or more. Perhaps there will even be some advantage in waking Appiah from sleep, catching him off guard. Besides, the opportunity to watch two stupid foreigners thrash in the Zimbabwean swell is undeniably appealing – he might save one and drown the other all in a single night, and who knew what favours and kudos might accrue?

The man is still talking. His words are garbled. Mandiveyi thinks he's misheard. He says, 'Can you say that again?' The *murungu* repeats himself and Mandiveyi almost bursts out laughing. Is it possibly the same one? Can it be true? If so, he has no need to control his destiny, because the god of lies is on his side. He says, 'OK. I am on my way.'

59

I wake up on my own. Least I think I wake up. Least I feel like I's on my own. I call, 'Daddy! Daddy!' But he don answer. I go out in the corridor an I look up at the walls an they look like they meltin ice-cream. Mebbe I sleepin after all. I go to the TV room an open the door. Gladys there, wrapped up in a blanket like a baby. I gonna wake her up, but then I hear a voice behind me go, 'Sssh.'

Even tho it sound real sweet, I know that voice anywhere.

I say, 'Where are you?'

An Sasa go, 'Up here. Come on up, little bat.'

Sasabonsam somewhere real dark. I never been here before an I can't see nuthin but his red eyes that shine like the light on the remote control.

I go, 'I can't see.'

He go, 'Come with me.' An I follow him to a window, only it not a window, more like a hole to the sky, cos through it there's the moon shinin bright. He says, 'Come.'

The air is warm an still. From here I can see evrythin. Daddy once aks me why I wanna play with Sasa when he sumtime mean to me. I go, 'I dunno.' But when you a little girl there so much things thas not for kids. Sasa never say sumthin not for kids.

From here, I see all the way to Amerika, only there iss bright blue skies. I can see my old school, Pine Hill, an thas my friend Angel Perez bein collected by his mom. Sumtime I still miss my old school an my friends an I wonder if Angel miss me too.

I look the other direction an you never believe it but I see into the United Family International Church. Even tho iss night, there still a whole lotta people. I see Momma an Gogo, an Momma on her knees with her eyes tight shut an she cry an cry, her whole body shakin like jelly on a spoon. I know she cryin bout me. I know it. I jus dunno how I know it. The night Momma got sick, I dun a real bad thing. Mebbe she cryin bout that. Sasa tell me I dun nuthin wrong and Momma tell me I dun nuthin wrong an I gotta go back to bed. But I know when I dun a bad thing, even tho it Sasa's fault, shoutin at me so loud I go blind. Sasa tell me, 'Don think on it. When you think on it, it only make you crazy.' I tell Sasa to shut up cos iss all his fault anyway. But Sasa right because now I thinkin on it and I's shiverin, no matter how warm the night.

I shake my head and blink my eyes. I look outside our gate an spot Daddy's truck on the road. Daddy hate that truck. I know that cos he say so, but also cos of the way he drive it, like he wants to make it sore. He flyin down the big road an turn off at our little road without slowin down. The beam light up a car parked near our gate an I see a face inside an I give a little shriek.

Sasabonsam say, 'What's the matter with you?' All impatient.

I go, 'I think I seen the devil.'

He laugh. He go, 'Thas no devil. He not even halfway there. Truss me.'

Daddy park up outside the house an get out of the truck real slow. He look tired. He light a cigarette even tho I told him Mrs Kloof say they kill people.

When I tell Daddy this, he go, 'That's what she said?'

'Thas what she said.'

An he laugh like sumthin the opposite of funny an go, 'A lot of things kill people, little bird. Even getting in some other folk's business.'

He say this like I sposed to unnerstan. I don unnerstan but I go, 'OK.'

Daddy walk to the house. His feet go crunch-crunch on the path. I call out, 'Daddy! Daddy!' But he don hear me. I mean, he stop a second an he look my way, but then he shake his head an go inside. Thas when I figure I sleepin for sure.

Sasa go, 'You wanna fly, little bat?'

I look at him. Sumtime he look like a toy, but sumtime he look like the realest thing you ever see. Right now he look like a toy. I make a face. I go, 'I don like it when you call me little bat. I'm a little bird.'

'I'm sorry, little bird. You wanna fly?'

Thas when I hear my dad callin from in the house. He callin, 'Rosie? Rosie?' An I hear Gladys too, her voice tight like a washing-line, 'Rosie?'

'Daddy?' I call back. 'Up here. Come an see.'

He go, 'Rosie?'

An I go, 'Up here!'

I gonna remember this place. Next time I play hide and seek, this is where I gonna hide and iss gonna be real hard to find me. Real hard. Only trouble is, Daddy now come back out on the path an I go, 'Here I am!' an he look up, so now there one person who know my hidin place. His face look like he seen a ghost an he say a bad word.

Daddy use to say bad words all the time, but he stop when Momma got sick. Mebbe iss cos Mom not here any more an stayin with Gogo and Kulu. One time, while Daddy makin eggs the way I like em, I go, 'How come you cookin?'

An he go, 'While your mom's not here, I'm going to be, like, both Mom and Dad.'

So mebbe thas why he don hardly curse no more.

While he stand over the pan, he look at me and go, 'When Mom gets better, how would it be if we had two homes, like Dad's house and Mom's house? And sometimes you stay with me and sometimes you stay with Mom. That'd be fun, right?'

An I shake my head an I say, 'No.' Then I go, 'Don you love Momma no more?'

He stare at those eggs like they givin him a problem an his face say a whole lotta things I don unnerstan. Then he say, 'Of course I do. But just because you love someone, you don't have to live together. Like, you love Gogo, right? But you don't live with her.'

I don say nuthin, but I still don unnerstan an I feel like I might start cryin. Daddy go, 'Your mom and I still love each other. We just don't love each other like that.'

'Like what?'

Daddy sigh like he don wanna converate no more. He go, 'Like we want to live in the same house.' Then, 'Don't cry, little bird. It's OK.'

I try to stop cryin, but iss hard cos I feel real sad. Daddy leave the eggs an he give me a big hug. He go, 'Your mom an I both love you, little bird. We will both always love you.' But I still feel real sad, cos he don say they always gonna love me like that. An I don wanna live in a house on my own cos I jus a little girl.

60

Jerry drinks four or five beers before moving on to Scotch. He doesn't even like Scotch. He has bought a packet of cigarettes and smoked one. He doesn't like smoking.

He is feeling numb and curiously detached and it isn't just the alcohol. Rather, he has the sense that his life has always been moving towards this point and, now that he can chart the inevitability, there seems little reason to be surprised, angry or upset. He can picture April fucking the American and those images certainly cause a pang of distress. But he also seems quite able to choose not to think about it.

Surely, he thinks, it is the cuckold's lot to consider his wife having better sex with a better man and to feel the hot knife of emasculation. But Jerry feels too old or just too jaded for such livid sensitivity.

Jerry knows himself as a simple, emotionally clumsy person, but he is empathetic and he understands April's behaviour at least as well as his own. He thinks without judgement that people do what they do in response to stimuli. When Theo is hungry, he screams. As you get older, the deterministic equation becomes longer, but no more complex. April was hungry, so she screamed too.

Jerry understands his wife's infidelity, but he can't live with it. He has to leave. But where will he go? He wants to go home, but he has no home, neither in Zimbabwe nor the UK.

He considers divorce. Presumably, as the primary breadwinner, April will have to provide him with some kind of stipend. His humiliation will be financially compensated. He considers leaving this country, leaving his son. He considers a small flat and a job at a UK hospital. He considers watching a band with Ant, the Swiss PA/graphic novelist and, perhaps, one of her girlfriends. His imagination twists with horror. He pictures the noise, the excitement, the *youth*. How strange, how human, that what looked so enticing just this morning now appears like some kind of nightmare. Worst of all, he pictures a young woman regarding him with an approximation of hope. He cannot deal with hope. He believes he is hard-wired to disappoint.

Opposite him, Patson is sipping a second beer. They have barely exchanged a word. Jerry has tried to initiate a conversation about football, the global language. But it turns out neither of them has much interest in football. They are two different species contemplating one another uncomfortably across a dirty watering-hole – a hippo and an antelope, a crocodile and a painted dog, a mosquito and an elephant. If he were with a fellow Brit – any Brit, of any proximity – they would each know what to do: *How are you doing?/Tough day./Tough day?/My wife's fucking around./Fuck!/Fuck is right./Sorry, mate, man, dude, bruv./No, I'm sorry./You want a drink?/Sure./You want to talk about it?/No, I don't want to talk about it.* And then he'd talk about it. But Patson? What would he think? What would he say?

Actually, what *would* he say?

Jerry sips his Scotch. 'Tough day,' he says, and Patson looks up. 'My wife: she's been fucking around.'

'I'm sorry, Uncle?'

'My wife. She's been seeing another man. Unfaithful.'

Patson regards him steadily. Jerry assumes he's made him feel uncomfortable, but he doesn't look uncomfortable. He says, 'I'm sorry, Uncle.'

' "I'm sorry, Uncle" – is that all you can say? Is that all you've got to say?'

Patson sits back in his chair. 'Have you spoken to the father? Someone must talk to her. You need to speak to the family.'

'Right,' Jerry says, and he starts laughing. His laughter is cut short when he belches up a mouthful of bile. He collars a passing waitress. He says, 'Two more.' He lights another cigarette and immediately stubs it. He is beginning to feel a little nauseous.

A woman approaches the table. She says, 'Buy a beer for me and my friend?' She gestures airily behind her.

Jerry looks at her. She is wearing a short skirt and implausible heels that take her all the way to five foot four. She is somewhere between the ages of eighteen and forty-five. She looks a bit like a model and a bit like a boxer. Jerry shrugs. He says, 'Sure.'

The woman goes to round up her friend. The drinks arrive. Jerry sips more Scotch. He is now definitely feeling sick. Patson is watching him. Jerry says, 'What?'

Patson nods across the room. He says, 'You don't want this woman. There are plenty of nice women. This one? She is a prostitute.'

'I know she's a prostitute,' Jerry says. 'So?'

'Let me take you home, Uncle.'

Jerry stares at the taxi driver. His defiance quickly melts and he blinks his gratitude. He says, 'OK.'

He leaves a fifty on the table. The prostitute returns with her prostitute friend. She says, 'Where are you going?'

'Home.'

The prostitute addresses Patson in Shona – a stream of incomprehensible invective. Clearly she holds him responsible for the *murungu*'s departure. Patson responds in kind and ushers Jerry towards the door. The prostitute tries to grab Jerry's arm, but the taxi driver pushes her away. So this is what it looks like to desire me, Jerry thinks.

In the car, Jerry takes the front seat for the first time in some peculiar nod to a new-found camaraderie. But they don't speak. Jerry is drunker than he'd realised – you don't get this drunk unless you're drunker than you'd realised. His stomach is churning and he begins to lurch in and out of consciousness. He wishes Patson would drive a bit slower. The nausea opens his eyes. The cab is climbing the hill to the junction of Enterprise Road and Glenara Avenue. He says, 'Stop the car!'

'I'm sorry, Uncle?'

'Stop the car!'

Patson pulls in on Enterprise Road, two wheels on the grass verge. Jerry falls out of the passenger door. Cars are streaming past. He feels a drunken need for dignity, so stumbles a few steps into the undergrowth. He hears Patson's voice behind him, but he doesn't hear the words. He is extensively sick. Even as he vomits, he thinks this is probably for the best: the alcohol has barely rested inside him, he'll be OK in a minute. He is bent double, hands resting on his knees. His eyes are streaming and he's spitting bile.

Suddenly, he is aware of a man next to him. He assumes it's Patson. It isn't Patson. He is cracked over the head by what later turns out to be a Coke bottle. He crumples face first into his own vomit. He is still conscious. He feels several hands going through his pockets.

In the taxi, Patson sees the shadowy figures approach. He shouts out of the open door at the *murungu*, but he's in no state to listen. He slides out of the car and from the roadside screams abuse at the men. One of them turns to look at him. Patson can't see his face, but he sees the smile. And he sees the bottle brought up and brought down and the *murungu* collapse.

He has no time to think. He dives back into the taxi and reaches under the passenger seat for the small drawer where he keeps the wheel spanner. His hand settles instead on the gun in the place where, unknown to him, Gilbert has left it. He has no time to think. He emerges from the car with the gun raised. He shouts a warning. Only one of the robbers looks up. Patson pulls the trigger and hits the man clean in the chest. He falls dead. The noise is surprising, both deafening and curiously contained. The dead man's partners flee.

Jerry gets to his knees. He's spitting blood. He rests a hand on something and checks for his wallet and his phone. They are both there. The robbers got nothing. He comprehends that he is levering himself up on a corpse. He looks back to where Patson is still holding the gun, raised and shaking. Where the hell did the taxi driver get a gun? He says, 'Fuck.'

The first person to stop is a white Zimbabwean in a HiLux. Jerry watches him usher Patson to sit in the back seat of the taxi. He then talks to Jerry. Presumably, he's speaking English, but Jerry can't understand a word of it. Others stop too: two young men in a brand new Mercedes, an older man in an older Mercedes, an ET spewing fascinated onlookers. All these people appear to be arguing with each other. About what, Jerry has no idea.

The police are on the scene remarkably quickly. How quickly,

Jerry couldn't say. It might be three minutes, it might be twenty, but it strikes him as remarkable. There are so many police. Did they all come in one car? It doesn't seem possible. They are solicitous towards Jerry, three of them, standing around him, the most senior repeating, 'Don't say anything. We must get you to a doctor. Don't say anything.'

Four more have dragged Patson from the taxi. They have him in cuffs. One slaps him violently and for no apparent reason across the face. 'Fuck!' Jerry says. 'Hold on.' He stumbles over. He is aware for the first time that he is covered in puke. He stands face to face with Patson. He says, 'Don't worry. I know what to do,' before Patson is bundled into the back of the police car.

Jerry takes out his phone. He frantically scrolls his address book. He finds the number and makes the call. He doesn't know whether he is drunk or concussed, but he struggles to be under-stood. He is finally understood and feels a surge of relief. He turns to Patson, looking at him through the window of the police car. He gives him a reassuring nod – *Don't worry*.

In the back of the police car, Patson's racing heart gradually slows and he has time to think. He thinks about killing a man, about whether he regrets it. He doesn't. He thinks about Fadzai, the kids, his unborn child, and finds himself considering hopes he never knew he had. Now he regrets what he has done. In the wing mirror, he sees another car pull in. He watches the *murungu* talking to the driver through the window. Mr Jones told him not to worry. He wants to believe him. The driver gets out and Patson immediately recognises the CIO, Mandiveyi. He thinks that he may die tonight.

61

Shawn is driving too fast. He is tired and on edge. He needs a shower. The last few days have been tough: sleeping in the pick-up, dealing with the panners, scrambling to find the last two hundred grams he needs to make his first kilo for the Israelis.

The *makorokoza* in Murehwa have wised up and, without Nyengedza at his side, they drove a hard bargain. He paid way over what he expected and again at the mill where the Rhodie owner sensed his desperation and demanded a bigger kick-back. Shawn knows he needs to develop some new areas, some new relationships, perhaps even take on someone else to share the burden and maximise profits. It would have to be another foreigner. He considers Jerry Jones – April's husband seems competent and unambitious. Shawn is so wrapped up in his scheming that he sees nothing untoward in approaching the husband of the woman he's fucking. Neither does he consider for one moment that anybody could be put off by the illegitimacy and immorality of his actions (or, in fact, that his actions are illegitimate and immoral). Surely they will, like him, just think of the money. *Think of the money!*

Shawn knows his feelings of urgency have no real grounds. It's not as if the Israelis gave him a deadline for an initial sale. But he believes he needs to hook it up quickly to show that he's for real. And, besides, the sooner he starts to make serious paper, the sooner he can get out of this shithole.

Shawn is running math in his head – income and timeframes. He's thinking one year, eighteen months max. He will not skulk back to New York with his tail between his legs. He plans to return a man of means. He will buy a place uptown. He will start some kind of consultancy, drawing on his African experience. He will send Rosie to the best private school. Without even thinking about it, Shawn has already written his wife out of his and his daughter's future. He will do as he pleases. Kuda has fucked up. Kuda *is* fucked up. She has his sympathy, but his sympathy is cursory.

He is stopped at a police roadblock on the Mazowe road just outside town. He has five rough taels of gold bullion in the backpack behind the passenger seat. He has his buyer's licence and can justify his cargo if not its destination, but he would rather not have the conversation.

The cop inspects the truck before leering goofily at the window. He speaks in rapid Shona. Shawn slowly turns his head. He says, 'I don't speak Shona, bruh.'

The cop considers him warily. He says, 'Where are you from?'

'The States.'

'You are an American?'

'Yeah. I'm an American.'

The cop considers this worthy of a handshake, then tells Shawn that the dates on his insurance sticker, written in ballpoint pen, are unreadable and he is to pay a twenty-dollar fine.

Shawn struggles to keep his temper. He says, 'You going to write me a ticket for that shit?'

The cop smiles, toothy and obsequious. He shrugs, as if to say, 'We don't have to go there.' Shawn slips him a five and says, 'So go buy yourself a Coke or something.'

Shawn pulls away. It's the toadying he can't handle, the Uncle Tom shit. This fucking place. These fucking people.

He's back at the house by nine thirty. As he walks inside, he thinks he hears his daughter's voice – 'Daddy!' His mind is playing tricks on him.

He heads straight for the study. Turning on a corridor light, he's confronted by the damp stain on the ceiling and walls, and the stepladder set up beneath the hatch to the roof. He says, 'What the fuck?' He ducks into the study and locks the gold in the small safe.

He finds Gladys in the living room, rising groggily from beneath a thick blanket. She says, 'Good evening, sir.'

He says, 'What the fuck, Gladys? The corridor?'

'It is a leak from the geyser, sir. We turned it off. We left the ladder in case you want to see for yourself.'

He stares at the maid. What the hell's he going to see for himself at this time of night? How the fuck's he going to take a shower? Gladys averts her eyes. He knows that she's scared of him, tentative around his flashing temper, which she doesn't understand. He shakes his head. He's too tired for this shit. He says, 'Rosie? Mrs Jones drop her off?'

'She is sleeping, sir.'

He nods. He tells Gladys she can go. She gathers her blanket. He pokes his head into his daughter's room. He is thinking about tomorrow. He will call Feinstein first thing. He doesn't want the gold in the house longer than absolutely necessary. He is looking at Rosie's bed. He is momentarily confused. He turns on the light. His heart freezes, crashes, reboots. He catches Gladys at the back door. He says, 'Where's Rosie?' The confusion and terror in her face only amplifies his own.

They stalk through the house, room to room, shouting his daughter's name, until they are halted by her voice from somewhere distant and above them – 'Daddy! Up here! Come an see!' Shawn's eyes climb the stepladder to the dark open hatch, but the voice comes from further away than that. He runs into the garden.

Shawn sees her standing on the sloping roof above the front door. She has climbed out through a small gap where the gardener has removed three tiles, presumably to let in some light while he switched off the geyser. Shawn says, 'Jesus fuck!'

Rosie hears the horror in his voice and sees it in his face and her smile evaporates. She says, 'Wossa matter?'

Shawn is running math in his head – the height of the roof, the time it will take him to get to her. Gladys is standing next to him. She screams and cries. It doesn't help. He says, 'Shut up.' Then, to Rosie, 'Stay there, little bird. Don't move.'

But his daughter is now terrified and her eyes are wide. She turns and attempts to climb back inside. She loses her footing and slips down across the tiles. She makes a small sound of surprise: 'Oh!'

Shawn jumps forward as she falls. He hasn't time to position himself. One foot catches him in the chin, but he somehow manages to extend an arm across Rosie's midriff and take her full weight on his chest. He collapses into a jarring sitting position and lets out a horrible sound of pained exhalation as his lung collapses beneath his ribcage. He can't stop his backwards momentum and his head cracks the ground with enough force to snap his neck. Rosie says, 'Daddy? Daddy?' Gladys screams. The gardener comes running.

62

London never looks its best on a chilly rush-hour evening at the back end of winter. In theory, Jerry's heading against the tide, from the clinic in Tooting to the small Lambeth flat, but the Northern Line's packed full of people with creeping colds, pinched expressions and haunted eyes. He tries to lose himself in the music on his iPhone, a song of lost love on a lake in Louisiana, but to no avail. He thinks it might have been easier to reintegrate if he'd come back in, say, July or August. He could have sat outside a pub until ten o'clock and enjoyed the novelty of twilight and the strange, anarchic ambience of a British summer, if not a drink. He glances round the carriage. He considers, wryly, that if this scene were played out in the developing world, someone could easily spin it into a story of desperate and dehumanising circumstance – *They don't speak. They can barely look at one another. It's just too awful.*

The Tube spits Jerry out at Kennington. He shivers as he walks home. He needs a winter coat. He stops at a corner shop and buys a South African chenin blanc for £5.99. He's counting the pennies.

At least the flat is warm, albeit with a constant smell of damp towels. Jerry reminds himself that it isn't actually a 'flat' but, in estate-agent parlance, a 'maisonette' – the first two floors of a dilapidated Georgian house, two bedrooms and a bathroom over an open-plan kitchen and living area that looks out on a small patio garden. Rent is the best part of two thousand pounds per month. Imagine where he'd have been living had he and April actually split up.

He calls out to her from the front door, 'Days!' She has recently told him that this was her nickname as a kid – Days or Daisy. 'It's what my dad called me,' she said. 'But I kind of miss it.' Jerry is doing his best to try it out, but it doesn't sit naturally and he doesn't think it suits her – or, rather, it doesn't seem to describe the person he knows.

He finds his wife standing over the stove, stirring a small saucepan. She's listening to one of his current favourite albums on the small dock on the windowsill. He knows she doesn't like the music – in fact, she doesn't much like music. But she's trying.

He kisses her on the cheek. He gestures to the saucepan. He says, 'What is it?'

'Jus.'

'What are you making?'

'Sausages, mash and tenderstem broccoli.' She studies his face. She says, 'What?' Then, 'I know it's lame, but I didn't have time.'

'It's fine,' he says. He laughs. 'We're the returning Brits. We want some good British food. Make it a feature not a flaw.'

'Did you buy wine?'

He shows her the bottle. Her expression asks, Is that it? He says, 'They'll bring something. Definitely. And I'm not drinking. We're broke, remember?'

Theo is already in bed. Jerry looks at his watch. He was supposed to do bath and bedtime. April bounces off his unspoken reproach. She says, 'He was exhausted. That nursery's a problem, Jerry. Some of the kids are feral. He's finding it hard.'

'He's only three.'

April misunderstands his meaning. She says, 'Exactly!'

They are having a dinner party, entertaining two of her new colleagues at the Foreign Office – Tim and Sam or Ben and Tom or Dan and John or something, and their respective spouses (Isabelle, Annabelle, Arabella, fuck knows). The guests arrive as a foursome, brandishing bottles and bonhomie.

They sit down to eat and April serves the food. Jerry rubs his hands together and says, 'Good British grub! That's what we've missed!'

It's not long before he's telling the story of the incident that propelled them home just six months into a three-year posting. He is doing so for the umpteenth time. He knows his story is the talk of the Foreign Office. He tells it in minute detail. He no longer knows if the minute details are true, but it doesn't matter. His audience punctuate his story with 'Oh, God!' and 'Christ!' and 'Jesus Christ!' Blasphemy somehow seems the appropriate response in this godless world.

When he has finished, one of the women says, 'So what happened next?'

Jerry says, 'Nothing. I told them I was prepared to testify, but the people at the embassy said my statement would be enough. Then, of course, the police lost the gun.'

'Oh, God!'

'And they were holding Patson, the taxi driver, on remand,' Jerry says. 'And then ... When was it?' He looks to April. 'A month ago? They were holding him in Chikurubi, a prison. I mean, that's a fucking horrible place. He was murdered by another inmate.'

'Christ!'

'I know,' Jerry says. 'I've been trying to find out some details, but . . .' He shakes his head and drops his chin. He feels a pang of shame and the pinprick of a tear, but he blinks it away because he doesn't want to embarrass his guests. He has told himself a hundred times that it wasn't his fault, but he wouldn't have to tell himself a hundred times if he really believed it. Secretly, part of him wonders if shame is the very source of all English restraint. Because if you open the floodgates of responsibility, how will you ever host another dinner party?

'Jesus Christ!' This is Tim or Sam or Ben or whatever. He is an analyst on the Africa desk and he tells them about the inquest into the death of Rex Nhongo – you know, the army guy, the vice president's husband – which has just completed. He concludes by exclaiming, 'Smoke inhalation! It's all a cover-up!' And the rest of them nod sagely because they don't really know who Rex Nhongo is or was, and Tim or Sam or Ben or whatever is an expert and he's in danger of boring them.

Jerry interrupts the heavy silence that follows to say, 'I sent some money to the family. Patson's family, I mean.'

Tim or Sam or Ben nods sagely. 'All you could do,' he says.

The conversation moves on. April talks about childcare in London. She talks about Theo's situation. One of the women, who has two kids, nods empathetically, but says she's lucky that her father, something big in City accounting, can afford to pay a nanny.

'A nanny? Exactly!' April exclaims, and she looks to Jerry, her new-found bulwark. 'Maybe that's something we'll be able to sort out.'

Later, in bed, Jerry watches April sleep. Though he no longer drinks alcohol, she has told him he still snores, and waking her up provokes those sparks of anger that threaten their equilibrium. So he tends to sit up, killing time on the laptop, browsing his favourite websites, until she is in deep slumber.

His phone, muted, buzzes at the bedside. It's a text message from Dr Tangwerai, now based in Brighton, suggesting they catch up. It's the third such message Jerry's received and he has yet to reply. He would like to see Tangwerai. He wants to be a welcoming host to an acquaintance a long way from home. But he can't imagine meeting in this context, or what they would catch up about. Jerry knows the doctor as a man of clear-sighted integrity who would see through his stories. Theoretically, they could talk about something else. Practically, Jerry has nothing else. He stares at the screen. He considers some kind of holding reply, but he is blunted by despair. He returns the phone to the table. It will have to wait.

Jerry rather misses sleeping separately. He finds sharing a bed with April, with no prospect of any intimacy, a consistently painful reminder of how far they have fallen. He cannot remember the last time they had sex. But it's not just sex, it's the profound if rather absurd sense of shared space where two people meld without reproach. Of course, now that he is back in the marital bed, to leave it again would be an act of grand and possibly fatal significance, on which the committee of his character can't yet sign off. Besides, in the flat, there's nowhere else for him to sleep.

Jerry and April's relationship is not reconciled. Active reconciliation requires an honesty of communication of which neither of them is currently capable. However, they have found some new bonds to stick them together: their practical terror of splitting up, for example, and, especially, the silent, separate acknowledgement that there are certain things about which they cannot talk.

They don't talk about their time in Zimbabwe at all, at least not in private. Instead, Zimbabwe has become a source of public anecdotes, told mostly by Jerry, warily at first, but now with increasing flourish and fiction, that position them both in some kind of semi-heroic role in personal and national tragedies that were never in their control. Of course, April has her stories too. But even those that are safe to tell – about a thieving office cleaner, say – risk running squarely into the one that isn't safe at all.

She doesn't miss Shawn. He died the same night Jerry confronted her about the affair, the night Jerry was attacked on Enterprise Road and saved by Patson's terrible quick thinking. But April didn't find out about Shawn's fatal accident until a couple of days later when she got a call from Terri Sedelski – 'Jeez, April! Where've you been? I figured you must've heard already.' April's initial thought ... no, her initial *feeling* ... was one of relief. Her initial thought was to be appalled by her initial feeling. Then, when she heard how Shawn had died, she felt a wound of self-hatred so deep that she believes it can never heal.

She attended one of the first days of the funeral. She went to Kudakwashe's parents' house where the widow was receiving mourners. Jerry accompanied her – despite her infidelity, despite his own recent traumatic experience. She was grateful, and recognised in her husband a rare compassion she hadn't acknowledged in too long. Broken marriages, like broken clocks, are right twice a day, perhaps even more frequently. April has begun to think that the trick is to live in the moment. The difficulty is in choosing the correct moment.

After briefly expressing his condolences, Jerry was funnelled outside with the other men, while April was left in the murky living room with the women wailing. She was extraordinarily uncomfortable, partly, of course, because of what she'd done, but partly, too, because the process of the funeral was just so alien. Kudakwashe was at its heart, sitting with dignified stillness, but around her dozens of women busied themselves with tears and cooking and chatting and sometimes even laughter. April hovered, awkward and English, and wondered when it might be appropriate to leave.

At one point, Rosie approached her and held her hand. She said, 'You know my daddy gone, right?'

'I know.'

The little girl looked at her seriously. She said, 'Iss all Sasa-bonsam an he gone too.'

April looked at the little girl who would one day have to understand exactly how her father had died and she started to cry. Rosie patted her hand and said, 'Don worry.'

April found Jerry outside. She repeated what Rosie had told her. At first, Jerry didn't respond, but when they got into the car, he said, 'I swear there's something funny about that poor girl. The thing at the pool, the imaginary friend, the way she told me about ...' Jerry paused. He shook his head. He said, 'And then climbing on the fucking roof? All that shit about evil spirits, it fucks with people's heads.'

April and Jerry didn't attend the funeral service. By then, they'd left the country. Shawn was buried in Zimbabwe.

Sitting up in bed, Jerry tires of the blog he's reading about 'nu folk versus new folk'. His mind drifts to Rosie and, for no reason he can later articulate, he Googles the name of her imaginary friend, Sasabonsam. He finds himself reading about a mythical vampiric creature, half man and half bat, who is purported to live in the forests of Ghana and Togo. Jerry makes an involuntary noise, something like a laugh, and, briefly, he feels a chill in his spine. But then he says aloud, 'Fuck me!' and the feeling is gone.

He considers waking April, but that wouldn't go down well. And, besides, with every passing second, his mind reorders the inexplicable into a Western equation of coincidence, autosuggestion and psychological trauma. It all makes sense, as everything makes sense if thought about in the right way. Maybe he will tell April in the morning. More likely he won't. Most likely, if this information resurfaces at all, it will be as another anecdote, spun out with practice into an eloquent and meaningful narrative, and told at future dinner parties alongside the one about Patson, the taxi driver, and, perhaps, the one told by Tom or Dan or John or whatever about the ruling-party bigwig who died on his appropriated farm. This latter story is not Jerry's own, but it can also be appropriated. It doesn't matter who owns what any more: small but elaborate lies are necessary to underpin the megalithic icebergs, which necessarily remain mostly below the surface.

Jerry closes his laptop and turns off the bedside light. He sleeps the sleep of the centrally heated. He snores, but April doesn't wake up.

63

Fadzai has learned a new English word from her younger brother, Gilbert, who is an educated smartarse and therefore typically the source of such titbits. The word is 'stoicism', and it is a quality that she possesses, he says. He has told her that it means 'patient durability', although it also suggests a degree of 'admirable forti-tude'. He uses the word gently when describing her conduct in the six months since Patson's death.

Stoicism: Fadzai is fascinated by this word. She can think of no direct equivalent in her own tongue. The closest sentiment she can come up with is expressed in '*Uyu ndiye mukadzi chaiye*' ('That one's a real woman'). The implications of this comparison seem significant to her, but she can't quite articulate why.

Fadzai knows that Shona has several expressions to describe an absence of stoicism, if someone behaves inappropriately, say, or without dignity. And this leads her to two conclusions: first, that the idea of stoicism must originate in a culture where it is not the norm and therefore worthy of comment – for Zimbab-weans, patient durability is standard; second, that Gilbert must see in her the desperate need to weep and scream and rage against the injustice of her loss, because otherwise he would not have said anything. While Fadzai has little experience of justice, she understands its meaning.

Fadzai knows that her mourning is now supposed to be quiet and interior and she has adopted the façade so successfully it has become second nature. However, as with all those shoehorned into an uncomfortable role, she pays for her admirable fortitude with a disquieting sense of alienation, both from those around her and her true self.

Fadzai is not so deluded as now to think that Patson was a perfect husband; far from it. She acknowledges that she frequently hated him, latterly for several years. But she believes that, even when she hated him, she was loving him too, in raising their children, in preparing his food, in washing his clothes, in giving herself to him even when he disgusted her. She has come to understand that, when you love someone like that, it doesn't define you; it isn't the boundaries of your person, but its very substance. And now that Patson is gone, there is nothing: nothing to do and nothing to be done. Fadzai is not absent, but absence itself.

Two weeks ago, she gave birth to a baby girl. Her father named her Chandagwinyira, but Gilbert called her Hope. She has yet to refer to the baby by name, but she thinks of her as Hope. She is sitting on a stool outside her father's house, nursing.

Of course the baby keeps her busy, but inevitably she feels like she's going through the motions. She has heard of a condition called post-natal depression where you resent your new child. Fadzai is not depressed and feels no resentment; she feels nothing for Hope at all. Her mother noticed this. She took her aside and said, 'You need to concentrate on your baby. That is all you can do for now. You care for her. You love her. It's all you can do.'

The implicit judgement in this reduced Fadzai to tears, which only exacerbated her mother's evident irritation and unspoken belief that her daughter was overwhelmed by inappropriate and undignified self-pity. But Fadzai was not crying for herself. She was crying because she is doing her best. As with Patson, if she can nurture, show care and compassion in the absence of those feelings, isn't that the apotheosis of love?

It is late afternoon. She sees Gilbert and Bessie approaching with their daughter, Stella, each holding one of the little girl's hands; a bank of three silhouetted against the orange ball of the setting sun. It is a picture of such beauty that it momentarily makes Fadzai forget her troubles, even the exasperation she currently feels towards her brother.

The Englishman paid Bessie fifteen hundred dollars in severance and bonus and Gilbert spent it all on chicks, fertiliser and seed, but he bought unwisely. Gilbert is no farmer. He reads books and they make him overconfident. He took no notice of the roadrunners kept by his neighbours, or their planting patterns and crop choices. He bought Buff Brahmas and soya-bean seed. He planted little maize and almost no greens. His books told him to do otherwise and his books knew best. He said, 'This is not a subsistence project, but a commercial business. This is a new beginning!' Now, his beans have failed and his chickens are plagued with coccidiosis and he cannot afford medicated feed. Such arrogance! The local farmers have read no books, but they are not foolish and they raise what thrives and plant what grows. *This is a new beginning!* Fadzai believes that Zimbabwe has become a country of many new beginnings and few happy outcomes.

The Englishman also sent a thousand dollars to Fadzai. It was brought to Sunningdale while she was packing up the house with

Gilbert and the children. Gilbert was to drive them to Mubayira in the Raum before returning it to Dr Gapu.

The money arrived with a Mr Givens from the British Embassy. Gilbert remembered him from his first visit to the Englishman's house. Givens was the *murungu* he'd seen with a Shona girlfriend, but he had clearly never been into a Shona household before. He was uncomfortable and he couldn't leave quickly enough.

A typewritten note from the Englishman accompanied the money. It included the sentence, 'I cannot help but feel partially responsible for your tragic loss.' Fadzai pored over that line. In what way was he responsible and how had he calculated the price of this responsibility?

Fadzai showed Gilbert the ten hundred-dollar bills, clean and crisp. He shook his head and made a noise of contempt, which she didn't fully understand. He said, 'You must keep that to yourself. You know how it is when you have money. There is always someone in need. That money is for you.'

Indeed, she knows how it is and she was grateful for the advice. But now Gilbert has needs of his own and the previous evening, when he was bemoaning his situation to their father, she had felt the burden of his every complaint weigh upon her shoulders. He has not asked her directly. He doesn't have to.

Fadzai doesn't know what she will use the money for. There is the baby, of course, school fees for Chabarwa and Anashe, even music lessons (for hadn't Patson delighted in his son playing the cornet?) . . . There are countless incalculable expenses stretching over the horizon of an uncertain future, and a thousand dollars will ultimately be nothing more than a coin tossed down a well. Perhaps to allocate the money to chicken feed for a novice farmer is no less productive a way to spend it than any other. However, Fadzai remembers Patson's advice that poverty makes you panic, which causes problems of its own. She is determined not to panic.

Today, fortunately, Gilbert seems to have put his worries to one side in that unique, admirable, infuriating way of his; when Hope finishes feeding, he sweeps her up and holds her in front of his face, cooing delightedly. 'Little one! Little one!' He sits on the ground with Stella and puts the baby on his daughter's knee. He looks up at Bessie and says, 'It is our turn next! A son is overdue.'

Fadzai considers her brother's joyful expression and wonders yet again at his optimism, even if its ecstatic quality has gone and the restlessness returned. She turns to her sister-in-law. Bessie is watching her husband and the two small children with uncon-cealed pleasure. But behind it Fadzai can see the worry, and she has a sudden, disquieting terror of the future: surely, Bessie will leave her brother; surely she will leave him and nobody will blame her, because the sum of books, ideas and hope has never fed a family.

Bessie is indeed worried. However, the source of this worry is not as Fadzai assumes. Rather, Bessie has a secret that she has so far kept to herself – a letter she received from Mr and Mrs Jones a month ago; a letter that's been followed by two calls in the past fortnight. The English couple have offered her a job as Theo's nanny. They believe they can secure an appropriate visa and they will fly her to London. They say that they live in a small flat and she will have to share a room with the child in the first instance, but they hope to move somewhere more spacious. On the phone, Mrs Jones explained that she won't have a work permit, but she can stay for two years. They will pay her in cash to save her owing any tax. Bessie doesn't understand the details as the woman explained them, partly because her brain stalled on the mention of the proposed salary: more than twice the two hundred dollars she earned as their maid and all her meals included. 'Think about it,' Mrs Jones said.

Bessie has thought about nothing else. She is a person without material ambition, but such characterisation is meaningless in a monetised, globalised world. If she goes, she thinks, she will save enough to secure her family's future. She could support Gilbert's efforts; or buy a plot of land, build a house, make efforts of her own; or both.

Bessie believes she should accept the job. However, she believes this in much the same way Fadzai believes she should save her small nest egg. And both women, for all their apparent practicality, are ruled by their generous hearts – often stoicism's secret ingredient. Bessie will never leave Gilbert because, as much as love is action, it's also an article of faith and, even when she can't believe in him, she believes in God enough for them both.

Gilbert will use Fadzai's thousand dollars to vaccinate his chickens and buy more seed. He will promise to repay his sister five-fold for her generosity and Bessie will work tirelessly to ensure he keeps his word. Gilbert will watch his wife in the field, bent double, pulling weeds and picking stones, and he will know that he is blessed – *uyu ndiye mukadzi chaiye*. This isn't a happy ending, but it is a new beginning and the outcome is as yet uncertain.

CODA

Mandiveyi first met the Irish journalist in the Brontë Hotel on the August night in 2013 that the Zimbabwean election results were announced. ZANU (PF) had won a resounding victory and Robert Mugabe was elected president for a fifth full term. The city was quiet and the hotel almost deserted. Mandiveyi took a table on the veranda, adjacent to a group of white foreigners who were conducting a post-mortem with a mixture of confusion and horror – *What just happened?*

Mandiveyi listened as the whites, an assortment of media and diplomats, took turns to tell stories of the stories they'd heard of falsified ballot papers, the manipulated electoral roll and assisted voting. None of them had actually witnessed any corrupt practice, but they were all convinced it had taken place. And now they were bewildered that they should have had the wool pulled over their eyes by the very black politicians they liked to characterise as almost imbecilic. Mandiveyi was amused: it wasn't just in the Central Intelligence Organisation that smart men learned to play stupid; it was also true at the heart of government.

One of the men went to the bar and Mandiveyi followed. The man was small and balding with wisps of hair flying in all directions. He was probably no more than thirty-five, but looked older.

Mandiveyi had little trouble engaging him in conversation. He told him that he was a ZANU (PF) activist and the man – Chris, from Dublin – was immediately hooked, thrilled to be drinking with the enemy and looking over his shoulder to make sure that none of his fellow hacks might usurp his good fortune.

'You know, Chris,' Mandiveyi said, with a happy sigh, 'we won the argument, the ballot and the rigging. If we had known we were so far ahead in the first two parts of this equation, we wouldn't have put so much energy into the third.'

Chris lapped this up and three days later Mandiveyi found himself quoted in the Irish press as 'a ZANU (PF) source'.

Now it is December 2014 and the CIO has been feeding the Irishman occasional stories for almost eighteen months. Loosely, it is instructive to see which make it into the foreign media: a way of taking the temperature of international opinion. Mandiveyi knows that the West loves to report every radical anti-imperialist statement emanating from the Zimbabwean government almost as much as the Zimbabwean government loves to see them reported – a mutually beneficial exercise that allows each side to retain a moral high ground above local political slurry. Mandiveyi has no specific agenda passed down from on high. He is, as he always has been, playing his own small game within the game within a game.

For the last three years, since he finally returned the gun to Phiri, his boss, and his investigation into the American died almost under his very nose, Mandiveyi has been passed over for all important work. He has not found it hard to accept this fate. He knows that he was both too stupid and too smart to climb the ranks of the Organisation and he is happy to be free of the associated risks. Besides, it has allowed him to spend more time with his family.

Mandiveyi's son Tendai's condition has deteriorated significantly as he has reached adolescence. The weakness in his legs has now referred upwards in a progressive kyphoscoliosis of the spine and Tendai is permanently confined to a wheelchair, his lungs constricted, looking at his feet.

The boy remains hardy, however, and insists on attending school. It is his neck that causes the most pain as he is forced into a terrible contortion simply to lift his head and look his peers, teachers and parents in the eye.

Mandiveyi and his wife find connection in the care of their son. When they drive to church, ease Tendai into his wheelchair, register the sympathy, fear or plain curiosity of onlookers, they are almost a normal family.

Mandiveyi has a new girlfriend. Her name is Celia. She stays in a small flat in Highfields, which costs him only a hundred and fifty dollars a month. She is very young. They rarely have sex. When he visits her, she pours him a drink and sits at his feet, massaging his hands.

Mandiveyi is coming from Celia's flat when he meets the Irishman at the Brontë again. He finds him at an outside table. He orders a drink from a passing waiter. It was the Irishman who requested this meeting, but Mandiveyi suspects he knows the reason why.

The ZANU (PF) congress has just ended amid high scandal. Vice President Joice Mujuru (Rex Nhongo's widow) has been controversially ousted from office to be replaced by former head of the Organisation, Emmerson Mnangagwa.

Chris wastes no time in getting down to business. He says, 'Have you heard?' Mandiveyi doesn't reply. 'There has been a cyanide attack on Mnangagwa's office,' the Irishman continues. 'His secretary has been taken to hospital.'

This is news to Mandiveyi, but he doesn't show as much. Instead, he just inclines his head a little – *So?* Then, when the Irishman offers nothing further, he says, 'It is a combustible time, as you can imagine. We know that many of our enemies would like to exploit a perceived instability. Even within our own body there are historical rivalries and resentments.'

'You're saying it was the Mujuru faction?' Chris says this with a tone close to scoffing.

Mandiveyi is taken aback. Frankly, he has no idea what he is saying since, until thirty seconds ago, he knew nothing of any cyanide attack. But he is irritated by the Irishman's attitude – as if a foreign journalist could possibly know any better than he. Mandiveyi says, 'It was difficult for Comrade Mujuru. Her supporters were much weakened by her husband's passing.'

The Irishman considers Mandiveyi closely. The waiter brings a drink. Mandiveyi sips it. The Irishman thinks while his companion cracks ice in his teeth revealing a large expanse of pale pink gum that is peculiar and grotesque. The Irishman does not like these meetings, but he finds them useful; even as he recognises that he must take everything Mandiveyi says with a pinch of salt. This thought leads him to imagine that pinch of salt applied to the gum and the idea it might contract like a slug.

The Irishman is aware that he has riled Mandiveyi and he is intrigued by the possibility this offers. He decides to push a little harder. 'What are you implying?' Mandiveyi doesn't answer. The Irishman says, 'I have good sources who tell me Rex Nhongo was killed by Lebanese diamond dealers. They say a deal went bad and a woman was sent to seduce him who put a small incendiary device under the bed.'

Mandiveyi makes a contemptuous snorting noise. 'Who are they, these sources?'

The Irishman smiles. 'Come on, Albert. I can't tell you that. Are you saying it's not true?'

'It's not true.'

'What happened, then? What is the truth?'

Mandiveyi stares at the Irishman. He reveals his teeth, less a smile than a simple retraction of the lips. *What is the truth?* He does not know the answer to this question, neither conceptually nor in fact. Truth is not one of Mandiveyi's tools. It is a blunt instrument in comparison to his more refined apparatus. 'One day, Chris,' Mandiveyi says, wagging a finger at the Irishman, 'one day, I will tell you a story of the death of Rex Nhongo.'